# Candy Canes and Buckets of Blood

by Heide Goody and Iain Grant

Pigeon Park Press

Published by Pigeon Park Press
www.pigeonparkpress.com

# 1

When they announced the next station stop would be Great Eccles, Esther Woollby instinctively put her hands on her homemade tote bag, even though it had been sitting safely on her lap the entire journey.

"You'll like Guin," she said to Newton, sitting opposite her.

Despite his perpetually worried expression, Esther had always thought, with his untamed black hair and proud nose, Newton would grow to be a handsome man. With a wild Byronic air about him. Right now, he just looked like a worried teenager with unruly hair and a big nose. She worried how worried he looked. She made sure she didn't look worried. It would only worry him.

"You *will* like her," she insisted.

"I'm sure I will," he said and caught her gaze. "Don't worry, mum."

"I'm not worried," she said. "I just don't want you to worry."

"I'm not worried."

"You look worried."

"I'm thoughtful."

"What are you worri— Thoughtful about?"

"Lily," he said.

Esther should have suspected. He was a teenager. They were obsessive creatures. "You'll be fine without her for a day or two," she said.

"Of course I will," he said. "But will *she* be fine?"

"You gave her a Christmas present before we left?"

He nodded.

"Then she knows you care. And you'll be back before she knows you've gone."

"She already knows I'm gone."

"How do you know? Did she text you?" She gave him her best goofy grin to reinforce the joke. Newton smiled politely, but that was all. The boy was always cracking jokes, awful jokes, but one of the unwritten rules of Newton World was mums weren't allowed to be funny.

"Listen." She leaned forward and put her fingerless gloved hands on his knees. "You miss her. I get that. But, no offence, she's not like you."

"Not like me?"

"Apart from the obvious." She bit her lip, wanting to tread carefully. "I'm just saying that she'll be delighted to see you when you get back, but in the meantime, she'll just ... cope."

"Cope, huh?" said Newton. He held up his phone and showed her a picture. "That's from her Instagram page."

"Lily has an Instagram page?"

"Yolanda at the farm helps manage it."

"Is Yolanda the cute one into all that anime manga stuff?"

"Mum! Look!" He flicked to another picture. "Yesterday." He flicked back. "This morning. Yesterday. This morning. Tell me Lily doesn't look despondent in that one."

Esther was wondering how to politely suggest that *despondent* was a strong word, particularly since she couldn't see any difference in the pictures. She was saved by the announcement they were arriving at Great Eccles.

***

# 2

Dave Roberts kept his eyes on the road.

Friday the twenty-third of December should have been one of the busiest days, but there was only moderate traffic on the hilly A roads. There'd also been a forecast of heavy snow, particularly in high places, yet although the midday sky was as cloudy and white as Christmas cake icing, there wasn't a flake of snow to be seen.

Still, he kept alert. In his time he'd been called to enough traffic accidents to know what became of incautious and inattentive drivers.

"Anyway, you'll like him," he said.

"Who?" asked Guin from the back seat.

Maybe there were only the two of them in the car but he still made Guin sit in the back, and on a booster seat. Yes, she was eleven, but she was short for her age and the booster seat was entirely necessary. No matter what she said.

"Newton. I was just saying."

Guin grunted.

Dave kept his eyes on the roads. He knew if he looked in the rear view mirror he'd see his daughter fiddling with pipe cleaners or tin foil or copper wire or something. She'd be fashioning some sort of creature or abstract shape to add to her collection. She only grunted to demonstrate she had heard but she wasn't participating in the conversation.

"You'll like him," Dave persevered. "You know Esther well enough and it's time you met her son. And he meets you. We can all spend Christmas together at our place."

There was no response for some time. They passed a sign: half a mile to Great Eccles and the train station, another four beyond that to Alvestowe.

"He's not staying in my room," said Guin eventually.

"He's not," said Dave. "We discussed it."

"I don't remember that."

"We did."

"I banged my head in year five. I still have the dent."

"You can't blame your poor listening skills on a minor bump."

"I went deaf for a whole term."

"You stuck Play-Doh in your ear. When you were seven. And we discussed sleeping arrangements yesterday. Newton was never going to be staying in your bedroom. He's sixteen. There's an age gap. It wouldn't be appropriate or fair for either of you."

"You and Esther share a room. There's an age gap."

"Now you're being daft," he said.

"I still have the dent."

A ram on an isolated crag watched the cars go by. Dave was prepared to bet that ram didn't have to put up with the excuses of hypochondriac lambs.

"Will I be getting less Christmas presents this year?" said Guin.

"Fewer," said Dave automatically.

"So I will?" she said.

"What? No. I was just correcting your— Why would you think you'd be getting fewer?"

"I worked it out."

"Worked what?"

"You used to buy my presents and Esther would buy Newton his. But if we're all together then you wouldn't want to treat us differently. You're a senior paramedic. That's band six salary."

"How do you know this stuff?"

"Internet. And the charity Esther works for doesn't pay her much. I asked her—"

"It's not okay to ask people how much they earn."

"—So if you want to treat us the same, you'd have to spend more on him and less on me."

"It doesn't work like that," he said. "It's not like a tax. It..." The traffic was slowing ahead. Dave began indicating for the train station. "You don't have to be so precise about things. Just soak up the wonder of the season. I think I preferred it when you still believed in Father Christmas."

"I was thinking about that too," said Guin.

"Oh, really. Well, we're here."

***

# 3

Guin Roberts looked up to see they were pulling into a train station car park. She'd been engrossed in the small scale adventures of Wiry Harrison and his quadruped friend Tin-foil Tavistock taking place on the pull-down tray in front of her. The adventures were very small scale; Tin-foil Tavistock had been explaining at length to Wiry Harrison the problems she'd been having with the other year seven girls at the quadruped school. Tavistock, who was formed from scrunched up strips of foil and couldn't decide if she was meant to be a horse or a deer or even a camel, had told Wiry Harrison how the girls at school socialised in wide circles in the school playground – physical circles, presenting their backs to the world and keeping the circle abuzz with gossip about all and any students who weren't part of it. There were several such circles in the playground but it didn't seem to matter which one Tin-foil Tavistock tried to join, she would be told she didn't belong and wasn't wanted.

Wiry Harrison nodded his loopy head of wire and offered what advice he could. Guin listened intently because, by sheer coincidence, she suffered with near identical problems to Tin-foil Tavistock.

"That's them," her dad said.

He swung the car into a parking space and, in a seamless action, put on the brake, slipped out the door and waved to people Guin had not yet seen.

She tried to return her attention to the conversations of Wiry Harrison and Tin-foil Tavistock but she was losing interest. Wiry Harrison seemed to think part of Tavistock's problem was the other girls at quadruped school were mean to her because she couldn't decide if she was meant to be a horse or a deer or even a camel, and Guin couldn't see how this applied to her own, similar problems.

Outside the car, viewable only from thigh to neck through the car window, her dad was wrapping his arms around Esther. Esther tugged at his scarf, the one she had knitted him, and there was the muffled sound of some humorous remark. Esther was wearing her homemade patchwork coat and fingerless gloves. Guin knew she'd knitted those too. Esther's hands were on Guin's dad's chest, patting, stroking. She was a very tactile and touchy-feely woman. Guin approved of the knitting. She didn't approve of all the touching.

Guin's dad shook the hand of the tall boy next to Esther. It was an exaggerated and blokey handshake, like they were making a business deal. Her dad opened the car door.

"—climb in, dude. That's Guin in the back. Guin, say hi."

The boy slid into the back. He was a gawky looking teenager with wild hair that seemed to be trying to cover his face, as though it was embarrassed to be seen with him.

"Hi," he said, smiling. "I'm Newton."

Guin nodded. She knew that. He was Esther's son. And one day — a day she viewed with complete indifference – he might become her step-brother.

Her dad and Esther got in.

"We'll just drive down into Alvestowe," said her dad, "park up on one of the side roads and hit the market. Stollen and mulled wine for everyone." He chuckled to himself. "Well, not everyone. Some of us are aren't old enough to drink."

"And some of us are driving home tonight," said Esther.

"Stollen for everyone and mulled wine for Esther," he corrected himself.

"Or I can drive," she said.

"I thought you didn't approve," said dad.

"Of cars clogging up the roads and the air, yes," said Esther. "But this car's going to be driven tonight regardless, so it doesn't really matter who does the driving."

"And mulled wine for Dave!"

He drove out of the station car park and re-joined the road to Alvestowe. Guin slid Tin-foil Tavistock and Wiry Harrison to one side of the pull-down tray and took out Tim the Robot. Tim was a square metal tube with holes all over it. Into those holes Guin had screwed and bolted an assortment of arms and devices. Timmy had a spanner arm on one side, a picture hook on the other and various glass bead eyes on his front. Tim was always on the lookout for new arms and, one day, she hoped, she might find him some legs, or possibly wheels. Tim wasn't fussy.

"You're Guin, right?" said Newton.

Guin positioned Tim's arms upwards, a sort of a *God, why me?* gesture.

"It's a nice name," said Newton. "Is that short for Guinevere?"

"No. Penguin," she said.

"Guin," warned her dad. "Be nice."

The boy, Newton, leaned over a little to Guin. "Hey. Why would no one bid on Donner and Blitzen on eBay?"

Guin looked at him.

"Because they were two deer," said Newton.

Guin continued to look at him.

"Because there are two of them and they're reindeer," explained the boy, "but they're also too dear, as in—"

"No, I get it," said Guin. "I'm just not laughing."

"Right," said Newton.

***

# 4

On the way to Alvestowe Newton tried out a few more of his better jokes on the girl, Guin, but she just wasn't biting. He wasn't put off; it was a challenge. He also wanted to show his mum he was making an effort. He wanted her to be happy and Dave seemed like an all right kind of guy, and he clearly made her happy, so, until Dave showed himself to be something other than an all right kind of guy, Newton would do what it took to keep them both happy. When other people were happy, Newton was happy.

Lily wasn't happy. That bothered him. He looked at her Instagram page again and flicked between the two pictures, yesterday and today. He could see it in her eyes and the set of her mouth. She wasn't happy.

Newton tried to tell himself that he couldn't make everyone happy all the time. There were priorities. His mum was at the top of the list, the very top with a big gap between her and everyone else. Newton pictured himself at the bottom – well, not quite the very bottom. There were some people who had to be below him. Like Hitler. Or people like Hitler but who were actually alive. And then, in between, there was everyone else. Lily was in there and Yolanda from the farm and Dave and Guin and even Newton's dad, wherever he was and whatever he was up to these days. They were all there in the list. Newton told himself that he couldn't make everyone happy all the time. He wished he could believe it.

"What hides in the bakery at Christmas time?" he asked Guin.

She didn't look up from the homemade toys on the tray in front of her.

"Mince spy," he said.

Guin groaned. Newton could have punched the air. A groan was progress.

***

# 5

The road into Alvestowe town turned sharply before crossing a river via a narrow bridge. Coaches had to take a swing at the corner to avoid clipping the dry stone walls along each side.

"These roads weren't made for this kind of traffic," said Esther.

"I don't suppose so," agreed Dave. "They're kind of constricted by the geography."

Alvestowe sat in a gorge-like cleft between rocky hillsides. The landscape in this corner of the world tended between wind-blasted moors and craggy forested valleys.

"Didn't an RAF jet crash here some years ago?" said Esther.

"I'm sure there was a time when air force planes on 'training exercises' seemed to be crashing every other week," nodded Dave. "I said to Guin, it would be a terrible thing to crash out here, be stuck out here."

Dave considered the traffic and the likelihood of finding a place to park. The narrow pavements between the grey stone houses and the road were already thronged with visitors.

One of the things Dave and Esther told themselves they had in common was a disdain for the activity of shopping. It turned out that what Esther meant was she hated chain stores and conspicuous consumption and unethical production methods. Give her a farmers market or a craft fair and she could spend hours stocking up on organic cheeses, artisanal baked goods and jars of chutney featuring vegetables which no one in their right mind would want to preserve. Dave despised shopping because he despised crowds. He wasn't agoraphobic and he didn't dislike people, but he despised feeling he was just part of the crowd. He didn't want to be reminded that he was a participant in that great big procession marching from birth to death, distracting itself from its inevitable destination with noise and pomp and spectacle. In a crowd, especially in a crowd of shoppers, Dave could see humanity trying to find meaning – trying to purchase meaning – when there was no meaning to be had.

Esther put a hand on his thigh and gave him a squeeze.

"We'll park up, get some food inside you and take a view of things," she said.

Sometimes, she read him like a book. Life might be a meaningless parade but some things made it more tolerable: food, beer, Esther.

Dave turned off the main street as soon as possible, just to get out of the flow of traffic. Ten minutes later, after getting stuck in a cul-de-sac and receiving some seriously evil glares off another driver who had followed him into the cul-de-sac, he found a place to park: next to a stone barn on a lane down by the riverside.

"Everybody out."

They assembled in the lane. The air was cold but there was no wind. There was a closeness to the atmosphere, a stillness too, as though their world was encased in a glass bubble, locked away from everything else.

"Those away," said Dave, pointing at Guin's toys. They vanished into a deep pocket of her duffel coat.

"And that too," said Esther, gesturing to Newton's phone. "He keeps checking Lily's Instagram page," she explained to Dave.

"Lily has Instagram?" said Dave.

"Yolanda helps her with it apparently."

"Yolanda's the nice one, into that Japanese manga stuff, isn't she?"

"It's away! It's away!" said an exasperated Newton.

"Doesn't he like us talking about Lily?" asked Dave. "Or Yolanda?"

"I don't know," said Esther. "We should conduct an experiment."

Newton growled. "Please, can we just..." He waved an arm viciously towards the town. "... go and enjoy the flipping magic of the season?"

"Let's."

Alvestowe was a small town, more of a village with ideas above its station. Situated in an elevated valley, its dimensions were constrained by the steep geography around it. Nonetheless it contained the bare minimum requirements for an English settlement: a church, a pub and a post office. These and the few shops were all close to a wide square at the centre of the town which was currently filled with the Christmas market. The market over spilled the square and extended some distance along all the roads leading in. Wooden stalls that were part-shed, part-Alpine chalet ran back to back up the centre of the roads, blocking them off to all motor traffic.

Christmas lights hung from all the stalls and in a criss-cross web across the streets from drainpipes to gutters to lampposts. They were turned on, even though it was daytime and their weak multi-coloured glow was sickly and pathetic.

There was an *"Oof!"* Dave turned to see Guin on the floor and a long-haired woman in big glasses and a Russian army surplus hat with furry earflaps standing over her.

"Sorry, I didn't see her," said the woman.

Newton had offered Guin a hand up but she was ignoring it.

"Watch where you're going," Dave told Guin.

"Me?" said Guin and pointed at the open hardback book in the woman's hands.

"No harm done," said Dave. The woman moved on, continuing to read as she went. "Come on. Up you get."

"I could have broken bones," said Guin.

"You're fine."

"Some paramedic you are."

"Oh, look," said Esther. *"Zwetschgenmännle."*

"The what-the-what now?" said Dave. Guin was on her feet and joining Esther at the stall. Zwet-thing-thingy was apparently German for *people made from dried fruit.*

"They use wire for the skeleton underneath," said Guin knowledgeably.

"They've been made this way for over two hundred years," said Esther. "It's very authentic."

Ah, authentic, thought Dave. That word was like catnip to Esther.

"Which ones do you like?" Esther asked Guin.

"I thought we were getting food first," said Dave.

"Technically, these are food, dad."

"Okay, food without a face."

Esther gave him a look and took her purse out of her bag. "Newton, take some money and buy this man some—"

"Hey, I've got money," said Dave.

"Please don't argue," muttered Newton.

They weren't arguing, not even bickering, but Dave knew the lad had a low tolerance for arguments. The boy's Pavlovian response was to make everyone a cup of tea and offer them a biscuit; a sort of physical manifestation of the *Keep Calm and Carry On* spirit. Newton would be an absolute godsend if the Second World War came round again.

"Not arguing. Flirting," said Dave with a wink for Esther. He slapped a hand on Newton's shoulder. "Come on, let's go find something that could kill a diabetic at fifty paces."

It wasn't difficult. Soon enough, he was munching on a giant chocolate-covered pretzel and looking at the Christmas tree dominating the centre of the market. It was wrapped in spirals of fairy lights, dotted with candy canes, sleigh bells and baubles and its base was surrounded at by silver Christmas present boxes.

"S'good," said Newton, waving his pretzel.

"At a fiver each, they ought to be," said Dave.

"Supply and demand, squire," said a stout man next to him who was also looking at the tree. Underneath an expensive-looking wax jacket he wore a cable-knit cardigan and a patterned cravat. Dave found himself thinking that you didn't see many men wearing cravats these days. Those who did were either middle-aged thespians or, possibly, twats.

"People demand five quid pretzels?" said Dave.

"They're prepared to buy them," said the man. "It's the golden quarter."

"Is it?"

"October through to December. Key sales period for retailers. It's all ebb and flow, my good man. It's the sea I sail on."

Twat then, thought Dave.

Something rustled in the boughs of the Christmas tree, shaking the sleigh bells. Dave wondered if there was a bird or squirrel in there. The bough weighed heavily. A fat bird or a tubby squirrel.

"It's this season that keeps the retail industry afloat," said cravat and wax jacket. "Importing Black Friday from the US was the best thing to happen to this country."

"My mum supports Buy Nothing Day," said Newton, taking another big bite of pretzel.

"And what's that about?" said the man, unimpressed.

With a mouth full of chocolatey pretzelness, Newton attempted to explain. Since everything you needed to know about Buy Nothing Day was pretty much contained in the title, Dave thought he did a brilliant job.

The cravat man looked appalled, as though Newton had just displayed the symptoms of a terrible, contagious disease. He shook himself, turned up the collar of his coat and looked up at the tree.

"You know who turned on the lights this year?" he asked.

Dave shook his head. How could he?

"It's an important job," said cravat man. "Very symbolic. Marks the start of the season. You need an important dignitary. A local celebrity." The man looked about him as though to check who was listening in. "I would have done it if they'd asked. I can turn on lights."

Dave frowned. "I ... think we all can."

The man laughed. It wasn't a natural laugh. "I mean I bring the kudos, squire. The gravitas."

He looked at Dave expectantly. Dave looked back. The man waited. Dave didn't know what to say.

"Duncan Catheter," said cravat man.

"Yes?" said Dave.

"The king of construction. I'm a black belt in housing development. Not yet met a green belt I can't conquer. You get it, squire? I've put more roofs over people's heads than anyone this side of Skipton. And I've got graphs to prove it. I tell you—" Duncan Catheter was warming up to his theme, "—if I'd been around at that first Christmas and young Mary and Joseph had come to my door, I'd have said, 'No room at the inn? No room at the inn? Why are you bothering with inns? I can get you a small but reasonably priced starter home, two down, two up plus a box room for your boy Christ. Five percent deposit, no problem. Handy for the shops and the better kind of schools, if you know what I mean.'" The king of construction nudged Dave in the ribs.

"Not sure that I do," said Dave and smiled politely.

"You can tell your friends." said Duncan, oblivious. "And, if you see the organisers of this thing, point out that they've missed a trick."

"Oh, yeah. I will."

The tree rustled again. The tubby squirrel had apparently moved on.

Duncan Catheter slapped his own belly contentedly. "A bloody good Christmas tree. All the trimmings. All the goodies. Reminds us what life's all about, eh?"

"Yeah," said Dave, wondering if he meant life was like the shiny empty boxes under the tree, all surface and no content, or if he meant the tree itself, ripped out of its natural setting, dressed up in gaudy colours and presented to the world to ultimately die in a pot – a small but reasonably priced starter pot – that was too small to support it.

"Are you enjoying your pretzel?" said Newton.

"What?" said Dave.

Duncan Catheter, the king of construction, had moved on. Dave looked down and realised the chocolate coating was melting on his fingers. Newton had scoffed his.

"I can get you something else if you prefer," said Newton.

Dave put on a smile. "No. This ... this is great. Might need something to wash it down with."

***

# 6

There must have been a hundred or more stalls in the market, tightly packed to create a twisting maze of lanes across the town square. In the jostling tide of day-trippers and serious shoppers, Esther made sure she and Guin stayed close.

They were ostensibly looking for the boys, but each stall was a distraction. Esther and Guin were both creators. Esther had scored a lot of brownie points with Dave's girl when she'd given her free access to her craft boxes. Their personal crafting philosophies diverged strongly. Esther loved to make with a purpose: to follow a pattern or set of instructions, preferably an authentic one that meant she was continuing a grand, preferably ancient, tradition. She had dyed her own yarn with collected onion skins. She had subjected her loved ones to meals that followed medieval recipes. She had created vast quantities of Seminole patchwork according to traditional plans.

Guin, on the other hand, was not one for following plans. For her there was no pleasure to be gained from seeing a crocheted blanket completed, no joy in knowing the yarn she was using had been dyed with onion skins. She crafted without aim, with no concept of rules. The little crocheting Guin had done had been sporadic and random pieces, malignant tumours worked in wool. She was not at all interested in studying a craft and producing something in the style of anything. Guin looked at crafts only with the intent of seeing what she could cannibalise for her own little projects.

By midday, Esther and Guin had progressed only a short way into the market and were currently standing in front of a stall selling traditional nutcrackers, nearly all stylised as soldiers. Guin picked one up and worked its mechanism, watching its little jaw move.

"They are very beautiful," said Esther. "Although I'm not sure I approve of military toys."

"Isn't toy," said the stallholder, propelling himself bonelessly from his stool and coming closer. "Nutcracker."

"Sorry, yes," said Esther. "Military nutcracker."

"Just nutcracker," said the stall holder.

"Oh, yes, I do understand," said Esther. "And I know this is an authentic design. I'm just never happy with toys – or any items – that glorify warfare. Just one of my things."

The stallholder frowned, uncomprehending. "Not for warfare. Nutcracker." The man seemed to have a limited vocabulary. He looked tired. Esther could easily imagine that a week or however long of dealing with Christmas shoppers from morning till night would rob anyone of the power of rational speech.

"Of course," said Esther. "I'm just talking about the design."

"Can I buy one to take apart?" asked Guin.

"I don't think that would be appropriate," said Esther.

"Nutcracker," said the stallholder. "Peanuts." He produced a knobbly peanut, popped it in a bearded nutcracker's mouth and cracked it. "Nutcracker!"

"Got it," said Esther.

"Hazelnut," said the stallholder. He put a hazelnut in the nutcracker's mouth.

"Here comes dad," said Guin.

"Oh, good," said Esther, edging away from the stall. "Maybe we can move on..." But Dave and Newton were too quickly upon them.

The stallholder smashed the hazelnut. "See. Nutcracker."

"We've been looking all over for you two," said Dave. The carrier bag at his side clinked heavily.

"Looking really hard?" said Esther.

"Walnut," said the stallholder, putting in another nut.

"You definitely weren't by the mead stall," said Newton. "We spent a lot of time looking there."

"We?" said Esther.

"Me," said Dave. "Not sure what he was saying half the time but he was very insistent and—" he took one of the bottles out to peer at the incomprehensible angular writing on the label "—I'm sure this is full of meady goodness."

"My dad also likes mead," Guin told Esther.

"I was thinking," said Dave, "I could do with a new hobby."

"Alcoholism?" said Newton.

"Home-brewing," said Dave, "but I'm willing to branch out."

"Even brazil nut," declared the stallholder, even though no one was listening.

"Snowflake!" said Newton abruptly and pointed at a drifting flake. "They said it would snow today."

"One snowflake doesn't necessarily mean it's snowing," said Esther.

"How many snowflakes do there have to be?" asked Guin.

"And if a snowflake falls and no one is there to see it, has it really fallen?" said Dave.

Guin put on a deeply thoughtful expression. "Wow."

"Even almond!" said the stallholder.

"Okay, Confucius." Esther herded the family away from the stall. "Time to move on."

"See!" the stallholder called after them. "All the nuts! Nutcracker!"

***

# 7

They ate gingerbread men and drank hot chocolate. They wandered down every lane and cut-through of the market and discovered whole sections they had entirely missed. The rest of the world shuffled and squeezed through the alleys, while tinny music from hidden speakers competed with the grumble and natter of a thousand visitors. A few more brave flakes of snow wafted about here and there.

Newton bought a blanket for Lily that his mum clearly thought was too expensive but didn't say. Guin bought herself a wooden box painted with a cheery arctic scene that she declared would be used for 'things'. When her dad asked her what things, she repeated, "Things!" Newton's mum found a stall selling hand-thrown earthenware pots. She eagerly questioned the stallholder about their production methods until the stallholder pretended another customer needed his attention and wandered off. She seemed not to notice. Dave bought everyone foot-long hotdogs. Newton thought the supposedly pork sausages didn't quite taste like any pork he'd eaten before but said nothing, not wanting to make a fuss. They stood and ate them between a carousel ride and a large nativity display near to the town post office.

The human figures and animals in the nativity, all only slightly smaller than actual life size, appeared to have been carved from single pieces of solid wood. It gave their faces angular, severe expressions. Newton found those expressions disconcerting.

"Now, that could be a good hobby for you," his mum said to Dave.

Dave glanced at the nativity. "Messiah? I think it's been taken."

"No, my love. Wood carving. You're good with your hands."

Guin scoffed.

"You work with your hands," Esther corrected herself, suddenly breathless.

"Have you seen my bed?" said Guin. "It slopes so much I have to hold on in the night."

"Exaggeration," said Dave.

"Beds are big things," said Esther. "Tricky."

"It's from IKEA," said Guin. "There's instructions."

"I like making flat-pack furniture," said Esther.

Newton watched Guin take her little robot figurine out of her pocket. He saw several of its limbs were made from the interlocking bolt and screw components of flat-pack furniture. No wonder her bed sloped if it had all those bits missing. Guin opened the box she had just bought and laid the metal man inside it like it was his bed, or a coffin. She closed the lid firmly.

Newton looked at the polar bears on Guin's new box and asked her, "Why don't polar bears eat penguins?"

"Depends," she said.

"On what?"

"If this is an excuse to tell me a fact everyone knows or if it's a really bad joke."

He inhaled deeply and plucked a fresh joke from his memory. "Okay, what did one snowman say to the other?"

"I don't know," she said.

"'Can you smell carrots?'"

She tried not to smile. She almost succeeded. "Are you trying to make me like you?" she accused him.

"I'm trying to make you happy."

"Don't I look happy?"

"I don't know."

"Don't you know what happy looks like?"

"Sort of like this," he said and smiled widely.

"I think that's more mad psychopath."

"They're easily confused," he said.

"There's some lovely hand-carved cuckoo clock house things on a stall down there," Esther said to Dave.

"If I can't make an IKEA bed, I can't make a cuckoo clock."

She tutted at him. "I'm just saying, come take a look. I like them."

He raised his eyebrows. "You like them. Aren't they a bit—?"

"Teutonic," suggested Newton.

"Good word," said Dave, impressed. "I was going to say kitsch."

"I know," said Esther, "but they're so—" She scrunched up her face and waggled her fingers closely together to somehow indicate the tiny, intricate nature of things.

"Cuckoo clocks it is then," said Dave.

"I wanted a go on the ride," said Guin, pointing at the carousel.

"You've not finished your hotdog."

She passed it to her dad. "It's too big and it tastes funny."

"Fine," he said. "Carousel, Newton?"

"No, thank you," said Newton.

"It's not like riding a real horse, is it?" said his mum, patting his arm.

Newton liked real horses but he always thought there was something sinister about carousel ones, with and their fixed, sharply painted mouths, and cold eyes.

"I can watch Guin while you two go and look at cuckoo clocks," he said.

"Thanks, dude," said Dave.

"We're just down there," said Newton's mum.

Dave dug in his pocket and gave Guin some change. He remembered the hotdog he'd been given, looking briefly around for a bin, before deciding to eat it instead.

***

# 8

Guin took her dad's money and ran to the carousel. The earlier crowds at the market had thinned and there was no queue. Guin found a horse with a purple saddle and the name *Pokus* painted in jolly script across its bridle. A man came round to collect the money. He walked with a wobbly gait, never looking in the direction he was going. Guin guessed if you spent all day working on a spinning carousel, you would end walking with a wobbly gait.

She handed over the coins and when the pipe organ struck up, held on tightly. The mechanical pipe organ had little figurines on the front, one with a conductor's baton, another with a pair of cymbals. As the carousel started to turn, she watched them and their precise little movements.

More interesting still, far more interesting than being on a jiggling wooden horse, was the mechanism above her head. Guin watched the rotating crankshafts and arms and daydreamed what she could make from components such as these.

However, several circuits of looking up made her feel queasy and Guin had to look down, focus on the world beyond the carousel mechanism before her hotdog made a unpleasant encore. Her dad and Esther had already wandered off. There was Esther's son, Newton, standing by the nativity scene. He saw her looking and gave her a wave. Next turn round, he pulled a silly face at her. She scowled and determined not to look next time.

Snow was falling steadily now and it was a blurry screen against the wooden stalls and lights of the market. Through it, Guin caught a glimpse of long hair, big glasses and a hat with furry earflaps. It was the woman who had knocked her to the ground earlier. Guin felt a surge of anger. The bump had been an accident but that didn't matter. Guin was eleven and bearing grudges took little effort at that age.

The woman was still walking round with her nose in a book! She wasn't even looking at the stalls! Guin tutted. People had no right to go wandering blindly around Christmas markets, not buying stuff and being a general hazard. The woman should buy something or go home.

Angry though she was, Guin couldn't help but wonder what was so interesting about a book that could hold the woman's attention completely. Guin suddenly wanted to know. The curiosity was threatening to overcome her anger, which made her angrier still. There was nothing an angry mind hated more than having its anger reasonably eroded by a more positive emotion.

\*\*\*

# 9

Newton gave up trying to catch Guin's eye. She was too busy staring at something else. Whatever it was, she didn't look happy about it, but what did he know? Guin had a furiously private intensity about her. Maybe that expression was her version of sheer delight.

Newton looked at the nativity figures. The scene in front of him was fairly traditional: Mary, Joseph, baby Jesus in the manger (this one so thoroughly swaddled in blankets that its ugly little face and staring eyes were barely visible), shepherds, three wise men, various donkeys and sheep and something that couldn't decide if it was meant to be a horse or a deer or even a camel. The story of Christmas was one he'd had repeated to him, performed to him, had performed in so often that he hardly ever stopped to think about its meaning.

It was mostly, he reflected, the story of a holiday slash business trip gone wrong. Joseph had to go to Bethlehem. This was complicated by his wife being pregnant with a baby that they knew wasn't his. Their accommodation plans had fallen through and they'd ended up staying somewhere appalling. The wise men had only turned up because they'd been reading cryptic messages in the stars. The shepherds didn't even have a choice; they'd been bullied into attending by an angel while they were in the middle of their night shift. Even the animals were probably wondering what these people were doing in their barn and why there was a baby in their food trough.

It was, thought Newton, a story without a single happy moment. Less a story than a collection of anecdotes which, if they happened to modern Brits, would have them phoning consumer watchdog programmes or trying to get compensation from their travel company.

The Virgin Mary certainly looked pissed off, almost cross-eyed in her fury. Or maybe she, like Guin, had an odd way of expressing happiness.

\*\*\*

"Cuckoo clocks!" said Esther, arms spread.

"So, I see," said Dave.

They pressed forward under the shallow eaves of the stall to be more out of the briskly falling snow. The side walls and back of the stall were crowded with intricately carved clocks – chalet house shapes, covered with carved trees and fruits and animals, pine cone weights dangling on long chains beneath. On tiny balconies and in tiny doorways, varnished figures stood, some fixed, some poised to spring out at the chiming of the hour.

"I don't like them," said Dave.

"Why not?" said Esther.

"I don't know. They always look ... sinister to me."

She looked up at him and smiled.

He kissed her on the forehead. "I look at them and all that super detailed carving and I think 'that's what happens when you're cooped up all winter with snow piled outside your door and nowhere to go.'"

"Really?"

"Cabin fever as an art form."

She shrugged. "I guess people did need something to keep them occupied through the winter months."

He looked back the way they'd come. "They'll be all right together?"

"Newton will keep an eye on her."

"I'm more concerned about him," said Dave. "No, I meant long term. Them. Us. A new life."

Esther gave him a reassuring hug. "Taking it slow. Let's see how Christmas goes, all four of us at your place. And if that works out..."

"Oh, crap."

She pulled away. "You don't want it to work out?"

Dave patted his coat pockets before putting a hand in each.

"What?" said Esther.

"Keys. Car keys."

He took out his wallet to check the inside pocket. He looked inside the carrier bag of mulled wine.

"When did you last have them?" asked Esther.

"Definitely in the car."

"Obviously."

He shot her a tetchy took. "I had them at the car. I went into *that* pocket to buy pretzels and mulled wine. I might have..." He mimed a hand out of pocket action and then looked round as though the keys might magically be on the ground somewhere nearby.

"Maybe fallen out near one of those stalls," she said. "Let's go look."

He held out his hands. "You stay here. The kids will come to you. I'll go check." He sighed. "Buggeration," he said and hurried off.

***

# 11

The carousel slowed to a stop. The automaton conductor gave a final jerk of his baton. The cymbal player froze a centimetre from one final clang. Guin slid off Pokus the horse and down the wooden steps. Newton stood staring glumly at the nativity scene.

The woman with the heavy book trudged past Newton, each oblivious of the other. The woman had something dangling from the fingertips of the hand supporting the book. It was a five-pointed star, but no Christmas decoration. Even from a distance, Guin could see it was constructed from twigs and string, neatly bound and tightly secured.

The woman stopped to check something in her book, glanced at the dangling star, then seemed to stare at the ground in search of something before slowly moving on.

That was curious. Guin decided to follow her. "I'm here," she said to Newton as she passed.

"Good. Good," he said, still looking at the carved nativity. "Have fun?"

"Sure," she said. The book woman was moving off through the crowd. "I'm just going to look at something for a minute."

"Okay," said Newton.

In the crowd, following the book woman was difficult. Guin was not tall and the afternoon shoppers pressed in closely, but glimpses of that flappy-eared hat drew her on. She saw the woman, cut away from the stalls and down a side route. However when Guin reached where the woman had been, she was gone. There was just a set of footprints in the settling snow.

Guin hesitated because she was not an idiot.

She knew she had wandered off from Newton, but reasoned she hadn't gone far and she knew the way back. If she got into any trouble of the 'stranger danger' variety, she wasn't afraid to scream for help. She put her hand in her pocket, felt the reassuring shape of Wiry Harrison, and followed the footprints.

They led up a dark and narrow alley between two houses. Here the snow had only fallen in a narrow strip down the centre of the alleyway. Above, the sheer white sky was a thin line between rooftops.

There was thump and a muffled sound up ahead. Guin pressed on. At the top of a short flight of steps, the alley joined onto a path which ran behind the houses. On the far side was a wall and a shadowy wood. The footprints went right. Among them were smaller, wedge-shaped depressions, like animal prints, or holes melted in the snow. They followed the book woman's footprints, and so did Guin.

She wondered what the new prints were, and was so focused on them she didn't see the book and the star on the ground until she'd almost stepped on them. The book lay open on the ground, collecting snowflakes in its pages. The star made of twigs and string lay next to it, like it had been dropped.

Guin turned about. The woman had gone. There were no people in sight at all. The footprints in the snow continued for a couple of steps before becoming confused and oddly spaced. Then they became a pair of gouged lines in the snow.

"That's weird," she said to Wiry Harrison. She picked up the book and the star.

***

# 12

Newton had looked at the nativity scene far longer than its crude artistry demanded, but there was something peculiar about it that bothered him. He couldn't work out what. It wasn't the stern expressions on the people's faces. It wasn't the animal that couldn't decide if it was meant to be a horse or a deer or even a camel. When it struck him, he had quite a start.

The ugly baby Jesus's eyes were closed. They had been open. He was sure they had been open.

"Hey, Guin," he said, turning. "This baby. Its eyes—"

He continued to turn, eyes scanning the thinning crowds. His brain told him to not panic even before he realised he was panicking.

"Guin!" he called.

He dashed to the nearest stall, then the next and the next. He turned to the carousel and watched it go round half a dozen times before he could admit she wasn't on it. He saw the carousel man watching him and gave him a desperate look which he foolishly hoped would cause the man to leap into action and produce the girl like a rabbit from a hat.

"Guin!"

People looked at him as he called out.

"It's short for Guinevere," he told one, which wasn't a useful thing to say. He added, "She's about this big. Pale looking. Bright coloured mittens," which was moderately better.

He pulled out his phone, the automatic response in a moment of alarm. He would call his mum. She would never forgive him but he had to call her.

The phone had no signal. They were out in the wilds, snow closing in thickly. No signal.

"Guin!"

He ran down the nearest lane of stalls.

\*\*\*

# 13

Dave retraced his steps to stalls where he might have dropped his keys. They were not at the hot dog stand. The floppy-limbed woman at the pretzel stall shook her head when Dave asked if any keys had been handed in. The man at the mead stall, who had been so encouraging this morning, now seemed to struggle understanding English. Many of the day visitors had left and Dave was able to kick through the snow around the stalls with little fear of bothering others. But the snow was now falling fast and although the market stalls' overhanging roofs kept the worst of the snow away, it had been building up millimetre by millimetre for some time. He was not going to just see the car keys lying around somewhere.

Cursing himself, Dave continued to retrace his steps, away from the market and back down towards where they'd parked the car. It was possible he had dropped them the moment they'd parked. It was even conceivable that he'd left them in the ignition all day long.

Dave didn't think he was old enough to be so forgetful. He wasn't the kind to wonder where his glasses were, only to discover they were on his head – he didn't wear glasses for one thing – but finding he'd left the keys in the car would be a win at this point.

There was the hiss of brakes and he pressed himself against a wall as a coach full of departing day-trippers trundled past the narrow pavement, its headlights on full beam. It was not even four o'clock but night fell quickly in midwinter and the snow, whilst catching and reflecting the light from the lampposts and Christmas lights, obscured any dying daylight.

With night falling and the weather closing in, they'd need to be away soon.

***

# 14

Holding the homemade twig and string star and the book, Guin followed the rapidly disappearing trail in the snow and wondered where the woman had gone to.

It was possible she had simply dropped her book. People dropped things all the time. Guin had once found a whole box of buttons and beads in the park near their house. She'd collected tools, old toys and odds and ends which no sensible person would deliberately leave behind.

But this was definitely just weird.

She held onto Wiry Harrison for moral support. Out of all her creations, Wiry Harrison was definitely the best for moral support. Tinfoil Tavistock was made of flimsier materials and had distracting issues of her own. Tim the Robot was made of sterner stuff but he was really only a child, very unworldly. The others, Bertie O'Cork, Scampious and Cliptoria had varying qualities but, when you needed a dose of bravery, Wiry Harrison was the one you should turn to.

"Just a little way," she said, under her breath, "and then we'll go back and find Newton."

She walked on. The path behind the houses ran up to a drystone wall and a narrow gate leading into a churchyard. There was something on the ground by the wall: a flat shape draped over the wall. It was hard to make out in the gloom.

Guin made towards it. The shape began to move, sliding slowly over the wall. Guin hurried.

When she got close enough to see what it was, she couldn't understand what she was seeing. Dangling from the top of the low wall was what appeared to be an arm-length glove. It was a peachy pink, skin coloured. It wasn't an actual human arm: it was floppy and rubbery and quite lifeless. But if it wasn't an arm-length glove, in a perfectly realistic skin tone, what was it?

There was something else: fat and round on the ground in front of the wall. Guin recognised that.

As she hurried closer, the arm-glove slid away over the wall as though pulled from the other side. The hand bit seemed to wave goodbye before disappearing. Guin crouched by the fat round object.

It was a big winter hat with furry earflaps. She picked it up. There was something red and sticky on the brim.

Guin heard voices on the other side of the wall. No, not voices exactly, but high-pitched chittering chattering noises that were very much like speech. She stepped closer. Between the top of the low wall and the sweeping boughs of the trees there was only a black-green darkness.

"Hello?" she called.

There was no reply.

"You left your hat here," she said to the darkness.

There was nothing for several seconds and then *"Villast, útlendingur."*

The voices sounded close, like they were just over the wall, down by the mossy trunks of the nearest trees. Guin leaned nearer.

***

# 15

Esther leaned close to the cuckoo clock stall as the snow came down in thick, tangled clumps. There was still virtually no wind but there had to be a point at which heavy snowfall automatically became a blizzard. Wherever that point was, surely they were close to it. She pulled her collar about her neck and continued to look at the range of clocks.

She wasn't sure cuckoo clocks were the way to go but she was confident Dave would enjoy a creative hobby if the right one could be found for him.

"So, are all these clocks hand-carved?" she asked the old man behind the stall.

The old man grunted ambiguously. He was packing clocks away in wooden crates lined with straw. It was late; the fairground rides still turned and there were still people drinking and eating but this man had probably sold his last cuckoo clock of the year. And it was the last day of the Christmas market. Esther supposed the clocks that went unsold would resurface in this market or another next year.

"I just wondered," she said. "They are very beautiful. Does someone carve them all?"

"Yes, yes," he said and waved to the unseen space behind the stall. "All carved."

He continued to pack clocks, spooling the weight chains in his hands before laying them flat. He moved sluggishly, failing to co-ordinate left hand and right.

"You make them back here?" said Esther. There was a narrow space between this stall and the next, little more than a crawlspace but, looking round, Esther could see a dim light and hear the sounds of industry.

"Yes, yes," said the old man, waving. "All carved."

"I mean, if you don't mind me looking—"

The old man didn't seem to care. She took a step towards the little cut-through. Newton and Guin would be coming along soon. They might miss her if she wasn't standing out front. Then again, Newton could just phone her if there was problem or they failed to spot one another.

"I'll just—" She slipped down the space. There was a surprising amount of room: the stalls weren't arranged precisely back to back. A surprisingly wide alley was laid out between them, covered over with sheltering canvas, in parts lit by an inferior sort of fairy light.

The sounds of construction came from the dim shanty town. There was almost no light here and Esther stepped carefully, waiting for her eyes to adjust. There were low tables – roughly made things – little more than split logs laid across trestles. Worn hand tools, too dark to make out clearly were strewn around.

Workers sat at the benches. She could not make them out properly, although they seemed happy enough in the near darkness. She guessed, purely from the sounds they made, there were three or four or them; no more than five. They must have been cramped: there couldn't be room for more than two people to sit comfortably in that space. Suggestions of hands moved across their materials. A chisel glinted here, a saw there.

"Hello?" she said. "I didn't mean to interrupt but the man said it was okay."

The work stopped instantly.

"If you don't mind," said Esther.

Five pairs of eyes turned to regard her. Eyes set widely in round faces, far lower down than she expected.

***

# 16

Newton checked his phone for the umpteenth time. Still no signal.

Unconsciously he'd begun to make a methodical search of the market, spiralling out from the place he had last seen Guin. He'd taken to asking every passer-by he met but they were growing fewer by the minute.

When he came by the church, something made him stop. There was a lane, a driveway of sorts, running up the hill, churchyard on one side and a thick line of fir trees on the other. He wouldn't have been able to articulate what drew him to that driveway but he felt it was somewhere Guin might have gone. There were small footprints in the snow, along the side of the driveway nearest the trees. Perhaps too small to be Guin's, but then again...

He followed them, sick at the thought something terrible had happened to Guin, that he would have to face his mum and Dave and face the unbearable anguish, the guilt and the disappointment of what he had done.

The little footprints drifted nearer to the line of trees before disappearing under the low boughs.

"Guin!"

He did a three-sixty, looking across the driveway, the churchyard and back to the town square. He called again.

There was silence. The tinny music playing over the Christmas market had ended. A grey, dead hush had fallen over the town.

He looked at the footprints. They entered the trees. For whatever reason, perhaps this was where Guin had gone.

He crouched next to the trees and tried to see what was on the other side.

*\*\*\**

# 17

Dave hurried to the riverside and to where they'd left the car. Departing traffic was queuing on the narrow bridge out of town. Definitely time to leave.

He was almost running by the time he got to the lane where they'd parked: a kind of shuffling jog full of high-shouldered arm actions and evident urgency, which wasn't actually any faster than a brisk walk. It was a gesture of intent – "Look, I'm in a hurry" – rather than an attempt to go faster.

The snow had fallen heavily in the lane, banked up against the short wall by the riverside and the stone barns on the other. Dave saw the car but did not immediately recognise it. The bonnet was up, and in the blue-white gloom of dusk he saw a large, broad figure leaning over it.

"Hey!" Dave called. "What are you doing?"

The figure ignored him and continued pawing at the engine.

"Hey!"

Dave stopped jogging. He stepped forward in slow, careful footsteps. He didn't want to be a statistic, stabbed to death in the act of confronting a car thief. The figure held up a curve of piping, inspected it – seemed to sniff it! – and then tossed it away.

"Get away from that car!" commanded Dave in his best manly voice (which he considered to be quite manly indeed). He waved his hands firmly in a gesture he'd seen demonstrated on a nature documentary as a way of driving away a grizzly bear. "That's my car!"

The figure, hunched and black, shifted as though to look at him and then went back to ripping things out of the engine.

Well, that was just rude!

"Oi!" Dave squeaked, losing much of the manliness he had mustered earlier. "I'm going to call the police, you know!"

The figure took note of that. It turned, coming apart as it moved, splitting and collapsing. It wasn't one large person. It was four or five much smaller people. Children? Dave held his hands up against the obscuring snow to see better.

It was children, he guessed. Children or a travelling band of circus dwarfs.

"What the hell are you playing at?" he demanded, advancing towards them.

\*\*\*

# 18

The craftsmen – no, they were too small to be craftsmen – the individuals in the makeshift space behind the stalls watched Esther.

*"Stinga henni með hníf"*

They were no bigger than children; small children at that.

"Do you work here?" she asked in her most gentle, mumsiest voice.

They said nothing, merely looked.

"Are you ... are you children?"

There was an utterly obvious explanation. This was some sort of child labour sweatshop. Children forced to make traditional cuckoo clocks by the cruel taskmasters of a travelling market. She could see it so clearly: an itinerant community, undocumented children, always moving from place to place so that even in the enlightened West, child slaves and indentured labourers could go unnoticed.

"My name's Esther," she said.

"Esther," said one of them.

"Yes, I work with a charity that helps families and children. I can help you."

"Help?"

"Yes," she said. "If you want to come with me." She held out her hand. "I'll keep you safe."

There was a scrape on the table top as a shining chisel was picked up. Another small figure swapped its saw for a sharp-edged carving knife. They moved towards her slowly, but even in the dark she could see it wasn't fearful caution. She sensed something more purposeful, the slowness of a crocodile drifting towards an unsuspecting wildebeest.

"Or maybe you don't need my help," she said faintly.

The chisel was raised up high, ready to strike down.

\*\*\*

# 19

A branch creaked and snapped beneath the trees. It could just have been the snow, weighing the trees down, shifting as it settled.

"Guin, are you there?" hissed Newton.

There were rustles and definite movement.

He had a sudden mental image of an injured Guin, stuck under there somewhere. He crouched right down and pushed aside the nearest branch so he could crawl in. Something chittered in the dark; something that was not nice.

"What are you doing?"

He whipped round. Guin stood a short distance away, down the lane. "What the—?"

"Did you see something?" she asked. She stood with her wooden box and a thick book clutched to her chest. Snow stuck to her fleecy collar in mounding clumps.

He stood quickly, taking two jittery steps away from the edge of the trees. "I was looking for you," he said. He'd meant to sound angry and accusatory, but he was so overcome with relief it came out as a higgledy-piggledy jumble.

"I'm here," she said.

"I can see that."

"Our parents are going to be wondering where we are," she said, as though it was his fault.

"I was looking *for you*," he pointed out.

"Good job I found you then," she said. "Come on."

He crunched through the snow towards her. At the bottom of the driveway, he looked back at the line of trees. Close to where he had just been, the heavy bottom boughs swayed.

***

# 20

Esther ran, clutching her injured hand, squeezing against the pain. She collided clumsily with a wooden wall. On the other side, something fell and banged with a clockwork *sproing* and a plaintive *cuckoo*. She rebounded and ran on, looking for the turning, the channel that would lead out into the lanes of the market.

It had only been a few feet from where she had stood, but somehow she had missed it, and now she was running between the backs of what felt like endless stalls. She jumped over trailing electric cables, clattered past neatly stored gas heater canisters.

The child in the darkness had stabbed her! They had actually stabbed her!

She knew in her heart of hearts the poor kid was a victim of trafficking or forced labour or something, and that whatever they had done it wasn't their fault. Just a reaction to circumstance. She couldn't blame them. Although right now, with a sharp pain gripping her hand and blood seeping through her fingerless gloves, she was finding forgiveness a little difficult to come by.

Something made a noise behind her. Something was chasing her!

"Oh, God," she whispered. "I didn't mean to—"

She didn't look back. She didn't want to.

Seeing a gap between two stalls she thrust herself down it. It was far narrower than the one she had come through. She had to force herself sideways between two walls of slatted panels, her thick coat catching on both sides, at least two buttons snapping off. The space narrowed further. She propelled herself the last few feet by digging in her heels.

Something touched her elbow. Something grabbed for her elbow.

She couldn't look back now if she wanted to. There wasn't even room enough to turn her head. She keened with anguish and pushed on, scraping knees and pulling her shoulder, exploding out into the market.

"Oh, God! Oh, God!" she panted.

"There you are," said Newton.

Newton and Guin were coming towards her, along the avenue of mostly closed up stalls. The last few stallholders were drawing the shutters down on their little chalet huts.

Still breathless, still bewildered, Esther looked back at the space she had squeezed through. There was nothing to be seen and little light to see by. No one had followed her. She had imagined it. Nonetheless, her coat was ripped and studded with pine splinters along the one side. Her hand—

She carefully uncurled her hand, gasping at the sight.

"Mum, what have you done?" cried Newton.

The palm of her glove was saturated with blood. She winced just looking at it. "I went back there to have a look. I shouldn't have and I—" She hissed as the cold air brought sensation back into her hand.

"Here's dad," said Guin. "Dad!"

Dave jogged up the lane towards them. He had Newton's suitcase in one hand, Esther's big ancient rucksack in the other and a grave look on his face. "You'll never guess what's happened," he said tersely.

"Mum's hurt herself," said Newton.

"What?" Dave dropped the bags.

"It's nothing," Esther said automatically, immediately hated herself for saying it. Clearly it was not nothing. That was the kind of stupid thing people said, the kind of stiff upper lip nonsense that got people killed. "I mean, I've cut my hand."

Dave had a first aid kit in his hand, magicked from nowhere. Before she'd met Dave, Esther had briefly dated a teacher. The man had carried a green biro with him at all times. He had used it to correct spelling mistakes and misplaced apostrophes on restaurant menus. Paramedic Dave and his ever-present first aid kit was the same sort thing, only much less annoying. The relationship with the teacher had ended quickly, after an argument in a pub over the correct placing of the apostrophe in *shepherd's pie*. One of the last things she heard him shouting at the barman before she quietly slipped out and blocked his number on her phone was, "But how many shepherds, huh? Huh? Is that a pie for one shepherd or are several of them sharing it, eh?"

The much more sane and lovely Dave calmly peeled off Esther's glove, inspected the narrow cut in the fleshy heel of her hand and removed the excess blood with a wipe. She sucked in at the tingle.

"What did this?" he asked.

"A chisel, I think," she said.

He sprayed something onto the cut, something cold and wonderfully numbing. He produced a dressing. "And how did that happen?"

"I just wanted to have a look at how the clocks were made," she said.

"Clocks."

"Cuckoo clocks."

He gave little smirk.

"It's not funny," she said.

"No, it's not," agreed Newton.

Dave wrapped sticky blue gauze over the dressing. "It's not deep, but we'll have to get it checked to make sure you haven't damaged any tendons." He kissed her on the cheek. "I didn't mean to laugh, it's just been a weird—"

"Why have your brought our bags, dad?" asked Guin.

Dave looked to the heavens and shook his head. The look on his face wasn't a good one.

"What?" said Esther.

"Some b—" Dave's mouth stiffened, unable to find a 'b' word he was willing to say in front of his daughter. "Some *people* have broken into our car."

There were universally shared groans and "Oh no!"s.

"Stolen anything?" said Esther.

"Engine parts, if you'd believe it," said Dave. "Caught the b—"

"Criminals," suggested Esther.

"Ne'er-do-wells," offered Newton.

"Bastards," said Guin with gusto.

"I caught them in the act," said Dave. "I challenged them and they ran off, but that car's going nowhere." He sighed. "I brought the bags because I didn't want to leave them. I was going to call the police and the RAC but—" He took out his phone. "—no signal. Any of you guys?"

Newton had his out. Esther found hers.

"No."

"Nope."

"We should find a phone box," said Newton.

"Huh. When was the last time you saw one of those?" said Dave.

---

43

Esther looked round for a stallholder. They'd know where to find a phone. All along the lane, stalls were closed or in the last seconds of closing. There was still light and an open front at one at the far end.

"Let's go ask," she said.

Newton hurried to pick up the bags before anyone else could. The pull-along suitcase dragged a deep furrow in the snow. The shutters on the final stall were drawing down as they approached.

"Wait up!" called Dave but this only made the shutters close all the quicker. He rapped on the shutters. "We just want to find a telephone box."

"Busy," said a rasping voice from within.

"We've broken down," said Dave.

"We need to call the cops," added Newton.

"Try pub," said the rasping voice.

Dave huffed. Esther put a comforting hand on his back and then led the way to the pub. Which also turned out to be closed.

"What kind of pub closes at tea time?" said Dave. "Pubs should be open all hours!"

"Alcoholic," whispered Guin.

Dave gave his daughter a sharp, tight-lipped look.

The town was closed for the evening. Apart from the fairy lights strung between buildings and stalls, all life and activity had gone from the market. There were no traders or visitors, no open stalls, no sounds. The early winter night had come and shut everything down.

"There," said Newton. Hands occupied with luggage, he pointed with a nod of his head. There was an open doorway and a warm yellow light a few doors down. Esther scurried ahead.

A woman stood in the doorway. She wore horn-rimmed glasses on a chain, her ash-blonde haired tied up in a bun. On her face was the kind of expression which declared she didn't approve of snow and was trying to drive it away with a good hard glare. That expression softened a mite as she saw Esther and family approaching.

"Oh, come in, come in," she said, waving them over.

"Thank you," said Esther. "We were just wondering if you had a telephone. We—"

"Come in, come in," she repeated.

The porch way between the outer and inner front doors contained a huge upright hoover. As Esther squeezed past it loops of tubes and pipes fell outwards her. The woman wrestled silently with them, kicking the huge and ancient vacuum cleaner they were attached to for good measure as the family squeezed past.

"R2-D2's let himself go a bit," said Newton.

"Stamp the snow off your boots and then you can put them over there," said the woman.

Esther was already in the hallway before she registered the sentence. "No. We just wanted to use your phone, if we could."

"Of course," said the woman, shutting the door on the defeated vacuum cleaner. "Time enough. Boots there. Are there four of you?"

"Is there a phone?" Dave asked.

"We are fully complemented with all modern services," said the woman. "Tea *and* coffee making facilities."

"Sorry?"

"No, you're fine. You're fine. You've not booked, but I do have a family room available."

It was a hotel, Esther realised. A small hotel. Maybe a bed and breakfast. There was a tiny reception desk but the hall was big enough to suggest a large grand house with lots of bedrooms. The visible décor, dark and heavily patterned, reminded Esther of guesthouses she had stayed in when she was a child.

"Ah, no," said Dave. "We don't need a room, we just want to use the phone."

"I did say," said Esther.

"And is that all your luggage?" asked the woman. "People carry so much of it these days."

"The phone," said Dave. "Our car's been vandalised."

"Well, no one's going anywhere in this weather, are they?" said the woman. "Come in. Boots there. You too, little miss."

Guin slid her shoes off.

"No, we're not staying," Esther tried to explain. "We need to call the police."

"Nearest is over in Great Eccles. Has something happened?"

"Our car," said Dave.

"Ah, so it will wait."

"I'd rather be the judge of that," he said with forced reasonableness.

"Now, dinner is in thirty minutes."

"No dinner," said Esther.

"Should I put my shoes back on?" said Guin.

"Have you got somewhere else booked?" asked the woman.

"It's not that—" said Dave.

"I didn't think so. This close to Christmas. But we're always open for guests. Otherwise it's just my husband and I, and King Leopold of Belgium. And the cats, of course."

"Cats?" said Newton.

"The phone," said Dave.

"Of course," she said and stepped aside to reveal an old dial telephone on the reception desk, next to a hideous and misshapen statue of a horse.

"Right," Dave said, picking up the receiver to dial 999.

"Are we staying here?" Newton whispered to Esther.

"I hope not," she whispered back.

"Did she say she lives with the king of Belgium?" whispered Guin.

Esther pulled a helpless face.

"There's no tone," said Dave and rattled the receiver cradle.

"Snow on the line," said the woman. "Always causing problems."

"Isn't that trains?" said Newton.

"It'll sort itself out soon enough. And, besides," the woman smiled, "no one's going anywhere in this weather. Now, let me take your coats and hang them up to dry while you get settled."

Esther sighed and shrugged out of her coat.

"We're staying?" said Dave.

"Are we?" said Newton.

"Is the car driveable?" said Esther. "If you can't get through to the breakdown people…"

"Can't we call a taxi?" said Guin.

"Same phone," said Dave. "How much is the room for the night?" he asked the woman.

"We have so few guests this time of year," she replied. "What seems reasonable?"

Dave laughed faintly. Esther could hear a note of hysteria in it. "Let's sort that out later," she said, taking off her coat.

The woman opened a large cupboard door, hanging up Esther's first coat and then the others as offered.

"As I was saying, dinner is in thirty minutes. None of you have any of those special dietary requirements." It was said as a statement not a question. "My husband would normally help you with your luggage, but Mr Scruples is out at the moment. You are welcome to inspect your room, or you can relax in our guest lounge."

"Yes, the room," said Esther.

"Of course," said Mrs Scruples in a tone that suggested they had picked the wrong option. "I will just go and get the key."

***

"But I don't have a bag!" Guin pointed out as they tramped up the stairs behind Mrs Scruples. "I'm not packed for a night away."

"Well, we weren't planning this," said her dad in a low voice. "And, if we're lucky, we might still get away tonight. I wouldn't have exactly picked this place."

He looked up and around. The staircase was a broad U-shape, a spiral with only one turn and a grandfather clock placed on the large step of the turn. The high walls around were lined with tartan wallpaper and deep shelves. Mrs Scruples had said she had cats. The shelves were lined with them; gingers, tortoiseshells, fluffy white things, black cats with yellow eyes and fur like midnight. Guin counted at least twenty of them. All were dead and stuffed in straight-backed upright seated poses.

"My, that is a lot of cats," said Newton politely.

"Were they all yours?" asked Esther.

"I didn't steal them," snapped Mrs Scruples. "Here."

She rattled a key in the lock  Guin followed the others into a room. It was large, larger than any room they had at home. There was a big double bed, high like it belonged in *The Princess and the Pea* or some other fairy tale. There was a set of bunkbeds on the near wall between the sink and a wardrobe so huge and old it probably led to Narnia. A further door led to a little bathroom. On the furthest wall, a tall Georgian window bordered by heavy curtains overlooked the town square. There were the dots of fairy lights and the swirl of heavy snow. Everything else out there was black.

"Now, I must show you how the bath and shower work," said Mrs Scruples. "We have one of those American mixer taps and they can be quite confusing if—" She faltered. There was the sound of a doorbell, playing Westminster chimes. "Another guest? We are popular tonight."

"Maybe it's your husband," suggested Dave.

"No," she said, soft and sombre. "No, it won't be him. I'll leave you to settle in." And, with that, she was gone.

Guin stood in the centre of the room. A double bed and bunkbeds. Four beds. Four of them.

"We're not staying, are we?" said Guin.

Her dad closed the door. "It's not ideal," he agreed.

"We discussed this." Guin glared at him, jerked her head at Newton, pointed at the bunkbed and glared at her dad again. Through this silently furious pantomime, she hoped it was perfectly clear she was not okay with sharing a bedroom with the new boy.

"You promised," she said between gritted teeth.

"It's not ideal," her dad repeated which was useless and very much a dad answer.

"Top or bottom, Guin?" said Newton, testing the mattresses.

She wanted to answer "Neither!" loudly and angrily, but that might mean Newton got to pick. She rapidly weighed up the pros and cons: having to climb past him while he watched if she was on top, the thought of having the big lump of a boy directly above her if she took bottom.

"I don't snore," said Newton, smiling.

"Top," she said, immediately stomping up the little ladder and throwing herself on the mattress. The springs creaked like a mechanical donkey being tortured. At least she was elevated above them all. If she tried really hard, she could pretend they didn't exist.

She laid out the few possessions she had with her. She opened her new wooden box and took out four of her creations. She placed them along the guard rail around the top of the bed – Bertie O'Cork, Scampious, Tinfoil Tavistock and Wiry Harrison. Tim the Robot stayed in the box because he was tired and in no mood to explore this stupid room in this stupid hotel.

The five pointed star fashioned from twigs and string which she'd been careful not to break she hung on the corner of the bed. She then opened the book she had found, the one which the silly woman in the big fur hat had clearly dropped.

There was no title on the cover but on the first proper page inside it said:

CHARGE OF THE SPRITE BRIGADE– THE ORIGINS OF LITTLE FOLK IN
EUROPEAN FOLKLORE
DR EPIPHANY ALEXANDER
SHEFFIELD ACADEMIC PRESS

Underneath was written in biro:

*Property of Elsa Frinton, <u>B.A. Hons!!!</u>*

The B.A Hons bit was added in a different colour pen. Clearly, this Elsa Frinton (probably the woman with the flappy hat and no sense of who was around her) was very pleased with her B.A. Hons, whatever one of them was.

"There's no wi-fi," said Newton from the bottom bunk.

"We can ask the hotel manager about it when we go down," said Esther.

"No, mum," he said. "There's literally no wi-fi. No networks of any kind."

"Wow," she said, faintly sarcastic. "It's like we've travelled back in time to the nineteen nineties."

"More like eighteen nineties," said Dave, inspecting the décor. "You've picked a fine place here for us, Esther."

"What did you want us to do?" she said.

"Don't argue," said Newton.

"We're not arguing," Esther and Dave said as one.

"Just don't."

"Look, we're not arguing. We're getting on just fine. Isn't that right, smoochy-poos?" said Esther in a simpering lovey-dovey voice.

"It certainly is, pumpkin," said Guin's dad in an equally drippy tone.

Guin didn't look up from her book – she didn't want to – but when they began to make overly dramatic kissing noises she made a sharp and angry sound.

"Get a room, you two!" she said. "Everyone. Get a room. Not this room. Another room."

"All right, all right," said her dad. "Hey, Newton. How about we give these girls some space. Allow them to relax and freshen up before whatever delights Mrs Scruples is serving us for dinner. There might – might! – even be wi-fi downstairs."

"Unlikely," said Newton.

"Hey, it's Christmas, Newton, the time of miracles."

***

# 22

When they stepped out onto the landing, Newton could hear the sound of music from downstairs. It was Christmas music, kind of like that old *White Christmas* song but not that one.

Dave heard it too and smiled. "Can't beat a bit of Bing."

"You could try," said Newton.

"Ah, makes it feel all kind of Christmassy," he said, heading for the stairs. "All of us snug inside. Snowing outside. Music. The smell of overcooked vegetables. The decorations."

"Twenty stuffed cats?" said Newton.

"Sure. They're in the extended version of *The Twelve Days of Christmas.*"

Newton loved animals and he loved cats. He wasn't sure how he felt about them dead and stuffed and staring at him from on high.

"Look," said Dave, "they've got an elf on the shelf. That's Christmassy."

He was right. On one of the lower shelves, tucked between a cross-eyed ginger and a fluffed up moggy was a little Christmas elf, dressed in red and green. At the end of his floppy striped legs were pointed boots with fur trimming.

"So, it is."

Its round face was turned to look at them, its big blue eyes wide.

"Not at all creepy," said Dave.

They went downstairs and followed the hallway as it turned right, and along the considerable width of the building. Behind a potted plant Newton saw a dumbwaiter built into the wood-panelled wall next to the guest lounge. He'd never seen one outside a Hollywood movie. He was about to point it out to Dave when there was as prolonged crash of pots and pans from behind a door at the far end of the corridor.

"You all right in there?" called Dave.

There was no reply.

Dave pushed open the door. Steam and a fug of boiled potatoes and sprouts rolled out into the hallway. Amongst multiple hobs and ovens and industrial kitchen equipment, Mrs Scruples battled against a cascade of oven trays and a wide scattering of roast potatoes.

"You all right?" Dave repeated.

Mrs Scruples plucked the roasties off the tiled floor one by one, dropping them back in the pan and trying not to burn her fingers. "Three second rule. Ow. Three second rule. Ow."

"Let me help," said Dave.

"I'm fine, I'm fine," insisted the hotelier.

"I can help," said Newton.

"Too many cooks," said Mrs Scruples.

"You'll burn yourself," said Dave. With a glance towards Newton of the 'go on, I'll deal with this' variety, he slipped into the kitchen.

"I could have helped," said Newton to no one. He went to explore.

Back along the hall a bit was the guest lounge. It was empty, of people at least. It appeared to have been entered into a how much furniture could be crammed into one room competition. There were eight over-stuffed armchairs and two sofas. All of them covered with blankets and those doily-type headrest covers. The thick carpet was layered with three overlapping rugs. Even the television in the corner had a table cloth over the top of it. To top that, every flat surface had ornaments on it. There were five table lamps. There was a china shepherdess, a pottery shire horse – the twin of the one on the reception desk – palely-glazed willowy women and forlorn children. There were three potted plants. And amongst all of that, room had been found for a Christmas tree, sprawling over the two sofas it had been planted between.

In the eye-watering detail of the crowded room, Newton forgave himself for not spotting the parrot sooner. It sat in a bell-shaped cage hanging from a heavy metal stand in the corner. It was a massive bird, bigger than any parrot he'd seen before. If a turkey went to a fancy-dress party as a cockatoo it still wouldn't come close to the bulk of the thing.

Newton knew that parrots were intelligent creatures and lived a surprisingly long time. He wasn't sure if they also grew bigger with age. This one certainly looked old. It was grey and blue and slowly regarded Newton.

"Hey, boy," he said in a chirpy voice to see if he'd get a response.

The parrot repositioned itself, foot to foot, on its perch.

"Who's a pretty boy then?" Newton tried in his best parrot squawk.

Nothing.

He approached cautiously. The bars of the cage were widely spaced. Not wide enough for the parrot to escape through, but enough for a hungry-slash-angry bird to lunge through and attack an unwary finger or nose.

"Let me guess," said Newton. "You're King Leopold of Belgium."

It was a rational conclusion and allowed Newton to dismiss the possibility their host, Mrs Scruples, was a raving nutter. Unless King Leopold of Belgium was one of the dead cats. That didn't seem any less mad.

Newton tried a few more "Hello"s and "Who's a pretty boy then?"s, but the parrot was having none of it. It flexed its beak a little and gave him its full attention, one eye at a time, but did not indulge him in any parrot-speech.

"Well, it was nice meeting you, your majesty," said Newton, who felt that politeness should be extended to all living things. "I'd best see if we're staying for dinner." He turned to leave.

"Stumid bmmy bfftrd," muttered the parrot.

Newton looked back.

"Sorry?"

The parrot looked at him dumbly.

"Right," said Newton and walked towards the door.

"Slly blmmy twrrt."

Newton whirled. The parrot looked nonchalantly away. Newton squinted at it. King Leopold whistled a jaunty and innocent tune.

"It's not polite to swear at people behind their back," said Newton and left.

"Dffft bgger," muttered the parrot.

***

# 23

Dave tried to assist Mrs Scruples in the kitchen but she firmly ejected him. He resisted momentarily, curious to know if she intended to serve up roast potatoes that had been thrown all over the floor.

"Bang the gong, if you must," she said, "then take your seat."

"Gong?" He found it back by the dining room, near the reception area. It was burnished brass, the size of a dustbin lid, and looked like an oversized pound coin.

"A gong to summon the diners," he murmured. "How—" Quaint? Old-fashioned? Ridiculous? Very Fawlty Towers?

He struck it with enthusiasm, because there were limited opportunities in life for gong hitting. Newton appeared almost instantly.

"Good gong that," said Dave and led the way into the dining room. There was one long table, laid out with silver cutlery and white crockery and one diner already seated. He recognised the cravat and the cable-knit jumper, but couldn't quite place him. The man had called him "squire" several times, Dave remembered that much.

"Evening," said Dave.

The man's face at once became ebullient and alive. "And good evening to you! Not mein host is it? Fellow travellers perhaps? Also lodging at Madame Scruples hostelry."

He stood and offered Dave a chubby hand. As he opened his mouth to introduce himself, Dave remembered his name.

"Duncan Catheter."

"My reputation precedes me, squire," said the man with a humble blush.

"We met," said Dave. "Earlier."

"We did?"

"We were eating pretzels," said Newton. "Five pound ones."

"'Tis the season," said Duncan Catheter.

"And then I told you about my mum supporting Buy Nothing Day."

"Oh, yes," said Duncan Catheter, the horror of the memory returning. "I'd be fascinated to discuss that with her," he added, although Dave suspected 'fascinated' wasn't quite the right word.

"This is her," said Newton as his mum and Guin entered.

"Did someone actually hit the gong?" asked Guin.

"I did," said Dave proudly.

"I want to hit the gong," she said.

"Another time. Two gongs might mean double the dinner."

"Did you tell the woman about my allergies?"

"You don't have any allergies."

"That you know of."

Esther nodded in greeting to Duncan Catheter.

"The Buy Nothing mother," said Duncan. "Delighted to meet you, m'lady."

Esther gave Dave a confused look as she shook his hand.

"Ah, this is Duncan Catheter," said Dave. "The construction king."

"Guilty as charged," said Duncan.

Esther shook his hand. "Duncan...?"

"Catheter," he said.

"Catheter. As in...?"

Duncan chuckled. "Yes. Fine old Scottish surname. The catheter was invented by an ancestor of mine, a great-great uncle, and named after him."

"What's a catheter?" said Guin.

"Well, it's a—" She caught herself doing hand gestures. "It's a medical matter. Ask your dad."

"Thanks," said Dave.

"The gong was rung some minutes ago," said Mrs Scruples sternly from the doorway. She had a tray laden with ornate glass dishes of prawn cocktail. "If no one is seated, how am I going to serve them?"

In the face of such chastisement, the Woollbys and the Roberts hurried to find their seats.

***

# 24

Newton picked at the prawns in his dish. They were grey, tightly curled things and very chewy.

"I met King Leopold of Belgium," he said. "It's a parrot. In the lounge. I think it swore at me."

"Esther and I saw an elf on the shelf," said Guin. She had the book on her lap, below the edge of the table, and didn't look up when she spoke. Apparently she wanted to compete in the unspoken competition of 'things that had been seen'.

"Yes, we saw that too," said Dave.

"But it's not a proper elf on the shelf," said Esther.

"How is it not?" said Newton.

"I meant it's just an elf toy on a shelf. Elf on the shelf is a thing. It's a copyrighted toy and a book."

"Really?" said Guin.

"I thought it was an old Christmas tradition," said Newton.

"Not at all," said Esther. "It's only a few years old."

"Huh!" said Dave, pleasantly surprised. "I never thought about that."

"But you can't copyright an elf," said Newton.

"Canny bit of marketing there," said Duncan Catheter.

"But it's just two words that rhyme. Something on a something. You can't copyright that."

"You'd be surprised what you can copyright, squire."

"So, like ... Troll on the Pole?"

"If you like. Getting people to buy it. That's the trick."

"I don't like them," said Esther.

"That's okay. Trolls on poles are unlikely to catch on," said Dave, topping up his wine before offering the bottle first to Duncan and then Esther.

"The elf on the shelf I mean," said Esther. "It's like the robins."

"What?" said Dave.

"My mum used to tell me that robins were sent by Father Christmas to spy on us to see if we'd been good or bad, and if we deserved any presents. Same thing."

"Makes sense," said Duncan. "He's making a list and checking it twice and all that."

Esther sipped her wine. "It's the surveillance state," she said.

Newton recognised his mum warming to a theme. The surveillance state. Any moment now, she was going to mention that there were more security cameras per person in the UK than any other country in the world. Newton decided to stay out of it and tried to think of other mythical creatures that could rhyme with things they sat on. Minotaur on the floor?

"The elf on the shelf is a toy you're supposed to have in your house but aren't allowed to touch," said Esther.

"Is that right?" said Dave.

"It's one of the rules."

"There's rules?"

"Of course there's rules," said Guin, nose in her book.

"It sits in your house and watches you," said Esther, "and every night parents move it somewhere new but, allegedly, if the child touches it then the magic is gone and the elf won't come back."

"It's a bit of fun, dear," said Duncan.

"Fun? It's conditioning us to be obedient. Did you know that there are more CCTV cameras per capita in this country than anywhere else in the world?"

Bingo, thought Newton. Cyclops on the worktops?

"I thought it stood to reason that good children should be rewarded. Perhaps I'm wrong," said Duncan, very much in the manner of a man who knew he wasn't wrong but thought it better to indulge the little lady at the table.

"We should all be good, Mr Catheter," said Esther. "But not because we hope to be rewarded. I raised Newton to be a good person but he's not good because he thinks he's going to get something for it."

Newton smiled at his mum. No, he wasn't good because he expected something in return. He was a good person because of the crippling fear of disappointing others, his mum most of all. Of course, he didn't say this and pondered whether Griffin on your Tiffin was sufficiently good.

"What did you raise me to be, dad?" asked Guin.

Dave gave it some thought. "'Raise' is a strong word."

Duncan swilled his wine, sniffed it, sneered but drank it anyway. "In the old days, naughty children were given lumps of coal or sticks to be beaten with. What's that goaty creature they have in Germany who comes to steal wicked children at Christmas?"

"Krampus," said Newton.

"Right," said Duncan, clicking his fingers. "Put the fear of God into them. If we're rewarded, then we know we've done good. If we are punished or deprived then we know we've done wrong. That's what the good book says."

"That's what the rich tell the poor," said Esther. "And themselves."

Duncan pulled an expression of disgust. Dave put a hand on Esther's and Newton felt the sudden tension. Duncan had pressed Newton's mum's political buttons; they were easy buttons to press. Dave had reached out to calm Esther, which she would definitely take the wrong way. Dave was probably irritated they'd wound up staying the night in this weird bed and breakfast that Esther had seemingly picked on a whim. No one wanted to be here and it was all somebody else's fault but the little irritations would creep to the surface and Newton knew his mum was going to say something snappy and Dave would weigh in and then there'd be an argument and—

"Krampus on a hamper!" Newton said very loudly.

Everyone stared at him. Even Guin looked up from her book.

"Pardon?" said Dave.

"Krampus on hampers," Newton tried again. "Kramper-s on hamper-s. It almost works."

Duncan pushed his prawn cocktail away and dropped his screwed up napkin on the table.

"Lovely pair of children you have, Esther," he said.

"Thank you," said Esther, polite if nothing else. "Except Guin's not mine."

"I'm not," agreed Guin.

"Guin's mine," said Dave.

"And Newton's mine," said Esther.

"Oh," said Duncan. "I just thought..."

"We're not yet," said Newton, doing a big circular, all-inclusive motion.

"It's complicated," said Esther.

"Life is, m'lady. Life is," grinned Duncan Catheter. "Course, I discovered the secret to peace and simplicity years ago."

"Oh, really?"

"Two simple words. Thai brides."

\*\*\*

# 25

The *Little Folk in European Folklore* book fascinated Guin. Not just the contents (which were really interesting) but the manner in which it had been written. It was, basically, a collection of different fairy stories and accounts of meetings with 'little folk' but it had been padded out and added to with difficult and flowery words to make it seem far more impenetrable than it really was. For example, on the topic of a creature called Jenny Greenteeth, the author had written:

> *Synonymous with the duckweed and algae which perpetually covers deep, stagnant pools with their luminous green sheen, Jenny Greenteeth is a witchlike creature of faerie who preys on careless children and unwary travellers. Akin to Peg Powler and the Grindylow (she also goes by the names of Ginny Greenteeth, Jeannie Greenteeth and Fowl Jenny), Jenny Greenteeth is a river harpy, enticing children and the elderly into the depths where she drowns and devours them.*
>
> *However, unlike other enticing water sprite (c.f. neck, nacken, nix, mermaids) this siren is far from pulchritudinous. Her piscine looks, green skin and weed-like hair make her quite a ghastly prospect.*

It was almost as if the author, this Dr Epiphany Alexander, was worried people wouldn't take her seriously if she just wrote a really interesting book about fairies and elves and felt the need to stick in big words willy-nilly. Pulchritudinous indeed! Nonetheless, once she'd realised the difficult language was just a trick of sorts, and that the meaning was almost perfectly clear if she simply skipped over any words that were too big for her to understand, Guin found herself reading the book at speed. And there were illustrations every few pages, of sharp-faced and sly-eyed creatures executed in scratching pencil, harsh inks and gloomy watercolours.

Fairies and pixies and ancient gods were all the same to Dr Alexander. It was all part of something that she more than once referred to as the 'rich tapestry of folklore'. This imagery was compounded by Dr Alexander's mention of the Norn, witch/god/fairy creatures who wove the fates of all people. And it was while reading about these that Guin had one of those minor epiphanies that children had far more than adults, in which she realised that the word 'yarn' had two meanings: that although yarn (a thread) and yarn (a story) were quite distinct concepts, in the hands of the Norn, they were one and the same.

The hotel woman, Mrs Scruples, made a disapproving noise as she came to collect Guin's starter plate. "We never read at the table in my day," she said. "Or played with our devices."

"I'm reading about changelings," said Guin. "That's when fairies swap babies for evil fairy babies. And reading is a good thing, not like playing on your phone."

Newton, who had been waving his phone around as though he might magically scoop up some missing data signal, blushed and put it away. "I was just seeing if there was any update from Lily."

"I'm sure she'll be fine without you for the next couple of days," said Esther.

"Ah, young love," said Duncan Catheter.

Dave and Esther smiled at that. Newton did not.

"I'm going to try the phone again," said Dave, getting up. "See when the breakdown people can come."

Esther patted his hand as he excused himself from the table. As he left, he held the door for Mrs Scruples to come in with plates of roast turkey.

Duncan refilled his glass. "What did you do to your hand there?" he asked Esther.

"Oh, cut it. My own fault, I guess. But Dave's patched it up for me. He's a paramedic."

"Fine job. Damn fine job. Don't let anyone tell you otherwise," said Duncan, as though there was a very real danger people might tell Esther it wasn't a damn fine job, and only people like Duncan could say otherwise. "And what line of work are you in, m'lady?"

"I work for a women's refuge charity," she said. "I find new homes for women and their children fleeing domestic abuse."

Duncan made thoughtful noises. "Very noble. Very noble."

Mrs Scruples all but slammed Guin's plate down in front of her. "Eat it while it's hot. I'm sure there's nothing so important in that book that can't wait."

In fact there was. Guin had found a picture of a five pointed star, fashioned from sticks and twine, like the one she had picked up earlier. It was, the description explained, an elf-cross. They were originally from Scandinavia (which Guin vaguely recognised as being somewhere near Norway and Sweden and those countries). In Scandinavia elf-crosses were called Älvkors and used to protect homes and livestock from elves. Scandinavian elves, it appeared, caused disease and bad luck and homes needed protecting. Guin traced a five pointed star on the tablecloth with her fingertip.

"Women's refuges. Busy line of work then?" asked Duncan.

"Endless," said Esther. "There's never enough accommodation for those who need it."

"I think it's a shame," said Mrs Scruples, placing a steaming bowl of vegetables in the middle of the table.

"It can seem quite bleak at times."

"I just think if people made more effort to keep their families together, there wouldn't be the need for these refuges and whatnot."

"The women we help are escaping from violent and abusive partners," Esther pointed out.

"Well, no one said marriage was easy," said Mrs Scruples. "You have to work at it, don't you? People should learn to stick together."

Her gaze drifted to the window. The world outside was black. Snowflakes occasionally drifted close enough to the glass to be caught in the light before falling away again, tiny ephemeral ghosts.

"Christmas is a time for families," she said faintly.

"Hear, hear," said Duncan.

"*You* have family?" said Esther. Guin guessed that Esther didn't mean to sound so surprised.

"I do indeed," said Duncan. "Indeed I do. Tangmo, my oriental queen and my two little princes, Gamon and Joe are waiting for me at home. I've just got to wrap things up here in the morning and then it's off homeski."

"Wrap things up?"

Duncan started to ladle sprouts and carrots onto his plate. "Top level talks with the local bods about opening up some of their brownfield sites for property development. It's taken me an age to get my foot in the door, but I got a letter last week, arranging a meeting. Tomorrow morning, Christmas Eve. Unconventional but strike while the iron's hot, says I."

Guin read on.

Mrs Scruples put roast potatoes on the table. As Guin looked up, her dad re-entered.

"No. Nothing but static on the line," he said.

"Give them time," said Mrs Scruples.

Guin's dad spooned vegetables onto her plate for her. He made a surreptitious neck slicing motion as Esther reached for the roasties. Esther frowned.

"Oh, I forgot!" said Mrs Scruples and dashed out.

"Don't eat the potatoes," whispered Dave.

"Why ever not?" asked Duncan.

"She dropped half of them on the floor."

"Which ones?"

"I didn't take photos," said Dave.

"This one's got a footprint in it," said Newton.

"I'm just asking how many," said Duncan.

"Does it matter?"

"I like roast potatoes."

"*Some.* Some fell on the floor."

Duncan grunted. "I'll take a piece of that action," he said and grabbed half a dozen.

"I'll risk it," said Newton and reached for the bowl.

"Germs," said Guin.

"People are too fussed by cleanliness these days," said Esther.

"Everything in moderation," agreed Duncan.

"Crackers!" declared Mrs Scruples, returning.

"Totally," said Guin before she realised the old woman was carrying a bundle of shiny red Christmas crackers.

"It's not Christmas Day yet," said Esther.

"It's near enough," said Mrs Scruples, handing them out. "They're locally made."

"You like things locally made," said Newton and held one out to Esther to pull.

Esther put one finger in her ear as she pulled. The crack of the explosive snapper was loud and there was even a whiff of smoke. Newton caught the little toy and the paper hat as they fell out. Esther picked up the dropped joke.

"What's the difference between snowmen and snowwomen? Snowballs."

"See?" said Dave. "Locally made *and* recycled. Come on, Guin." He waggled a Christmas cracker at her. "Put the book down now."

Guin closed the book, slowly so her dad could see it was a major inconvenience, and dutifully pulled the cracker. The toy was a little plastic jumping frog. Guin quickly spirited that away to a pocket. Her dad unrolled the joke.

"Help me! I'm being held prisoner in a Christmas cracker factory!" he read.

Duncan chuckled.

"Marginally more original," said Newton.

Dave scratched at a red, inky fingerprint in the corner of the joke. Guin poked at her turkey with a fork. It looked dry. She poured some gravy on it. The gravy was the colour and consistency of marmite. It didn't enhance the turkey much.

Guin saw Duncan looking at Esther's joke lying on the table. A dark expression crossed his face. His hand went involuntarily to his chest, as though feeling for something in his breast pocket, when he caught Guin watching him.

"So, princess, what are you reading?" he asked. Princess apparently meant Guin.

"A book about fairies," she said.

"Fairy in a dairy," said Newton.

"What?" said Guin.

"Elf on a shelf. Fairy in a dairy," said Newton. "Work in progress."

"Ignore him," said Esther. "Bad jokes and puns are his speciality."

"Medusa on a juicer," said Newton.

"Fairy princess stories, eh?" said Duncan.

"Not really," said Guin. "It's about elves and spirits. Like, did you know, that at Christmas time, there was this thing called Yule—"

"It's an old word for Christmas," said her dad.

"—Yule," said Guin, ignoring the interruption, "when this thing called the Wild Hunt came riding through the land. Some say it was led by Odin and some say it was the elves, coming through to steal people away."

"What people?" asked Esther.

"Unbaptised babies mainly," said Guin, doing her best to remember. "But there was this one called, um, Dando. This man called Dando who needed a drink so much that he said he was willing to go to hell for it." She gave her dad a special look, just so he could understand the significance of that. "And the Wild Hunt of elves and things, came along and took him."

"God bless the old yuletide traditions," said Duncan. He raised his glass and drained it. He looked at the near empty bottle on the table. "Will I have to go to hell to get another drink round here, eh?" He laughed at his own joke. "Course, my grandpa used to say he saw piskies when he'd had a pint or two. Or three or four."

Guin didn't know about piskies but she'd seen the illustrations in the book and the elves there didn't look much like the woodland pixies in her story books at home. Storybook elves and pixies wore flouncy see-through dresses and lived in mushroom houses, and they all had wings and looked like they were on starvation diets (probably because they couldn't achieve take-off with those little wings if they were a single gram overweight). The elves and pixies in *Little Folk in Folkore* were equally thin, but not because they were on a diet. Those ragged fairies looked like they had to kill and steal for every scrap of food they got and would do so willingly.

Guin glanced at the corners of the room and thought about the whispering voices she'd heard under the trees earlier in the day. She wished she had the elf-cross in her hand and hadn't left it in the room upstairs.

***

# 26

At some point, the distant Bing Crosby Christmas album was replaced by a distant Elvis Presley Christmas album.

The main course was dry, Dave thought. The turkey was wood dust shaped into turkey-shaped lumps. The vegetables had been so thoroughly boiled that even water hadn't survived the process. Even the gravy, through some arcane process that defied science, left a dry and dusty taste in the mouth. Dave piled cranberry sauce on his pre-Christmas Christmas dinner but that was tart and did not help. The temptation to wash it all down with copious amounts of wine was strong but, despite what his darling daughter might tell him, he was not a devotee of the gods of wine and drunkenness. If there was still a chance they could drive out of there tonight, he wanted to be sober enough to take the wheel.

He suspected it was already too late, and the snow far too thick but, as Mrs Scruples cleared away the plates in preparation for pudding, he excused himself from the table and went out into the hallway to try the telephone again.

He picked up the receiver and dialled the emergency services. Instead of the dead tone as before, there was some sound on the line. It crackled and swirled as though the snow had got inside the telephone system itself.

"Hello?" he said.

"*Khhorrrzzxx...*" hissed the line. "Hello?"

"Hello?"

"Hello? *xeeeeek-k-k.*"

"I'd like report a crime. Someone's broken into my car."

"Broken... car... *khhoorroo.*"

"Yes," he said. "I'm in Alvestowe. We're currently staying at ... damn, I don't know its name."

"*Eeeeeff.* Damn."

"At this number anyway. I'm sure you'd be able to look it up. Will someone be able to come out and help us? We'll need a mechanic for the car."

"Mechanic... *wwwweeee...* car?"

"Will someone be able to come out tonight?"

"Zzhhhh... come out."

"Will it be tonight?" He had raised his voice to be heard over the awful static.

"Tonight."

The line hissed and howled.

"Okay, then," said Dave eventually and hung up, not a hundred percent sure what he had actually achieved.

Thoughtful, he went back into the dining room. Mrs Scruples had brought in two desserts. An cut glass bowl filled with the red, yellow and white layers of a rich trifle, and a plate bearing a huge domed Christmas pudding with a traditional spring of holly jammed in the top.

"Any luck?" Esther asked him as he sat.

"I think so. Hard to tell with that line."

"No one will be travelling in that weather," said Mrs Scruples.

"Is your husband not coming back soon?" said Esther.

Mrs Scruples faltered. "Oh. Oh, yes. He will. I'm sure. They said."

"Sorry? Who?"

Dave could see Mrs Scruples' expression had driven down a dead end street and with tremendous awkwardness and restraint she was trying to back it out again.

"Christmas pudding or sherry trifle?" she said, attempting a decent enough smile.

"Is there lots of sherry in the sherry trifle?" asked Dave.

"Lots."

"Christmas pudding for me and Guin then." He gave his daughter a playful look. "Don't want to turn Guin into an alcoholic too."

"Too?" said Mrs Scruples.

"Ah," said Duncan, leaning over conspiratorially and nodding towards Esther. "Is m'lady here fond of the sauce?"

"No. I was joking and—"

"Cos I also wondered if the princess's real mum was a bit of a—" He gave a cuckoo whistle and swill of his glass.

"No, she wasn't."

"Wasn't?"

Dave set his lips and lowered his voice. "It was ovarian cancer. Guin was just a baby. Long time ago."

"Ah," said Duncan as though he just been told a heart-warming tale. He looked at Esther. "And did your...? The boy's father...?"

"No, Mr Catheter," she said coldly. "He didn't die of ovarian cancer. He's still alive, somewhere."

"My daughter thinks I'm an alcoholic because I enjoy a drink," Dave explained. "That's all."

Duncan laughed. "How do doctors diagnose alcoholics? It's anyone who drinks more than they do. Fortunately, my doctor's an old soak. Trifle, Mrs Scruples! A big dollop. Let's see how much sherry there is."

Desserts were doled out. Dave poured a healthy splurge of semi-solid custard onto his Christmas pudding and dug in. He coughed on the first mouthful.

"Does – *kof! kof!* – does this have alcohol in it?"

"A sprinkling of brandy," said Mrs Scruples.

"A sprinkling?" It tasted as if the pudding had spent the last decade at the bottom of a cask of brandy. He could get drunk just breathing in the fumes.

He poured a thick layer of custard over Guin's pudding.

"Stick to the custard," he told her.

He ate round the pudding, only nibbling the edges of the spirit-soaked lump of dark Christmas cheer. As he ate, he looked at the 'joke' he had pulled from his cracker. He scratched again at the red splodge that partially obliterated the words *held prisoner in a Christmas cracker factory!* It looked like a thumbprint. It looked like blood.

\*\*\*

# 27

Newton barely touched his Christmas pudding and was not encouraged when Mrs Scruples told him that there might be a shiny sixpence waiting for him at its centre. Nonetheless, he was born to please and was prepared to choke down the chemical mess when he saw that, with the exception of the loud and unashamed Duncan Catheter (who had wolfed down two and half bowls of trifle), the others had hardly eaten theirs either. He might have been born to please but he wasn't about to show everyone else up in front of Mrs Scruples.

"You're full then, I take it," said Mrs Scruples accusingly as she cleared away four uneaten puddings and Duncan's cleaned out bowl.

"Quite full," said Newton.

"Couldn't eat another bite," added his mum.

"Then I shall leave you to your own devices. And your devices," she added as Newton tried to covertly take out his phone. He felt instantly guilty.

She paused at the doorway with a stack of custardy bowls in her hands. "The guest lounge is at your disposal but I will retire to my rooms at the back of the hotel if it's all the same to you. The door is marked private but knock if you must. But, fair warning, I do crank up the gramophone volume to mask the noises, so knock loudly."

"Mask what noises?" Newton said to Guin.

The girl shrugged and went back to reading her book.

Duncan stood. "Ladies and gentlemen, mesdames et messieurs, Damen und Herren. I need to stretch my legs." He gave a shake of his foot, let out a fart and then departed.

Esther and Dave looked at each other.

"So," he said.

"So," she said.

"I don't think we're going to see a police car or a repair truck tonight."

"No."

"So, we're staying here," he said. It wasn't a question as such and it wasn't really a statement. It was a hopelessly resigned comment, one that begged to be contradicted.

"Looks like it," she said wearily.

"Then I'm going to bed," said Guin.

"I might go see if the TV works," said Newton.

In the hallway, Newton pointed out the dumbwaiter to Guin.

"Know what that is?" he said.

"A little old fashioned lift thing," she said.

"It's a dumbwaiter. And do you know what were they used for?" he asked.

"Well, if films have taught me anything, it's to enable smart and resourceful kids to escape stupid villains."

"Um, yeah. Pretty much it," he said.

Guin went upstairs. Newton went into the guest lounge.

King Leopold of Belgium eyed him beadily from his cage.

"Evening, your majesty," said Newton. The parrot said nothing.

Newton crouched in front of the TV. It was an old television with actual buttons on the front. He turned it on and static washed across the screen. Newton could not recall ever seeing static on a television in real life. Modern screens had the decency to put up a black screen and a polite *No Signal* notice.

He tried all the channels. Static howled at different pitches and swirled with different rhythms. Something like a human figure appeared to stagger through the electric blizzard for a moment but then it was gone.

"Come on," he said. "Show me something."

"Y'll nnt gtnuttin, ye dffft prkk," squawked King Leopold darkly.

***

# 28

Guin eyed the elf on the shelf as she climbed the stairs. Its stripy legs dangled over the edge, curly-toed boots swaying ever so slightly. In the stairs' stark upward light, its face was heavily shadowed and looked down on her with what felt like stern judgement.

Back in the room, alone, she thought about changing for bed. She had no change of clothes with her but there was a white robe hanging from the bathroom door. She stripped down to her underwear and put the bathrobe on. It was the only one in the room, but it was first come first served as far as she was concerned. No one had told her they'd be staying the night. No one had the intelligence to foresee it and tell her than bedclothes might be needed. As she saw it, the bathrobe was her right, given how shoddily she'd been treated. (And, yes, she knew she was being grumpy and selfish and inwardly reprimanded herself for it but kept the bathrobe anyway).

She went into the en suite bathroom. Esther had put out her toiletries bag before going down to dinner. Guin looked through it for toothpaste. She found the toothpaste and also a tub of cotton bud sticks which she put on the side of the sink.

Guin cleaned her teeth with toothpaste and her finger and read the signs taped to the wall between the sink and the toilet.

THE SINK IS FOR HANDS ONLY.
THE WATER HERE IS NOT FOR DRINKING. NOT SANITARY.
SANITARY PRODUCTS IN HERE.
TO SAVE WATER, PRESS SMALL BUTTON FOR SMALL FLUSH. PRESS LARGE BUTTON FOR SOLIDS.
DO NOT FLUSH SOLIDS DOWN THE TOILET. VERY HOT.
THE TOILET IS FOR TOILET PAPER ONLY, NOTHING ELSE.
NOW WASH YOUR HANDS.

Guin re-read the signs and concluded she wasn't sure what she was meant to do if she needed the toilet. The toilet and the surrounding plumbing looked like they were a relic of Victorian times and she didn't want to break it by flushing the wrong thing. She needed the toilet but decided to hold on until later.

She took the cotton buds and *Little Folk in Folkore* to her top bunk.

Wiry Harrison, Tinfoil Tavistock and the others were where she had left them along the guard rail. She silently told them about the rubbish dinner and the family decision to stay for the night. She then showed them the elf-crosses in the book and told them they were going to make some more. Tinfoil Tavistock asked why and Guin explained it was the season for the Wild Hunt and 'little folk' – and the Krampus too! she added, remembering – to come riding through and kidnap children, and she didn't like the look of the snow and the darkness outside. What she *didn't* say was that if there were dangerous creatures out and about, the elf-cross had done little to protect Elsa Frinton B.A. Hons. *Whatever* had happened to her.

With the bendy cotton bud sticks and short lengths of cotton thread, Guin constructed several five-pointed elf-crosses. She hung them from the sash window latches, two in the bedroom, one in the bathroom. There was a loft hatch in the centre of the room, a slatted panel of painted white. If she could have hung one there she would have done but it was too far away to reach and there was nothing to hang it on. Instead, she hung one on the back of the bedroom door and, for good measure, tucked one under the double bed where her dad and Esther were going to sleep.

"There," she said, climbed back up onto her bunk and, with her homemade friends around her, continued reading the book.

\*\*\*

# 29

Through the door with *Private* written on it came the muffled sounds of Christmas crooning. If pressed, Esther would have said it was Michael Bublé, but it was possible Michael Bublé was her default guess when presented with any kind of crooning lounge-singer. It was more likely to be Dean Martin, or Frank Sinatra, or any one of those crooners through the ages who were indistinguishable to her ears.

Esther popped her head round the lounge door. Newton crouched in front of the television, redundantly flicking between stations.

"No joy?" she said.

"It's not picking up anything."

"That's one of them old analogue TVs. You know, wotsit ray tubes. I think they turned the signal off for them years ago."

"Bggroff 'n' lvvvimalone," screeched the parrot in a cage in the corner.

"My, that's a big bird," said Esther.

"That's King Leopold," said Newton.

"Course it is."

Newton sighed irritably at the television and turned it off. "No TV. No wi-fi."

"Oh, it's like the dark ages round here." Esther smiled sympathetically. "You'll have to engage us in conversation."

"While we're all tucked up in our beds. Ugh."

"It'll be like *The Waltons*," she said. "'Night, John Boy. Night, gran'ma.'"

"What's *The Waltons*?" said Newton.

Esther rolled her eyes. "It's a different world these days, huh?"

A score of stuffed cats watched them as they climbed the stairs to their room.

"What *did* you do to you hand, mum?" Newton asked.

She looked at it and felt the itchy tension in the injury. "Stuck my nose in where I shouldn't have," she said.

"But it was your hand."

"Ha, ha. No, I surprised someone ... something..."

"Something?"

She shook her head. "Someone."

Newton nodded at the elf on the shelf. "Who treats elves when they're injured?" he said.

"I don't know."

"The National Elf Service."

"That's a good one, son."

***

## 30

Guin flicked through *Little Folk in European Folklore* after everyone had finally gone to bed. They had made a big show of being quiet and unobtrusive, even though it was clear Guin was still awake and very publicly ignoring them as they took turns in the bathroom to dress for bed. Her dad turned up ten minutes later, belching and wheezing and making whispered complaints to no one that he had eaten too much of that Christmas pudding and he was (to used his own vulgar phrase) "Pissed on brandy fumes."

Half an hour later she was the only one awake and reading about elf-bolts by the light cast from a lamp which had been left on. The lamp featured a jaunty cartoon squirrel leaning against the centre post of the lamp stand. Guin kept reminding herself that it was a squirrel, because she'd seen it earlier in better light. Right now it looked like a malevolent, buck-toothed troll, cast in shadow. Guin was mildly unnerved by the sight, but the sighs, snores and occasional farts from the others in the room was somehow reassuring. Guin glanced up at Wiry Harrison perched on the guard rail of the bed and shared a few thoughts about the squirrel lamp with him.

The light was just about enough to read the book, but there was an occasional distracting flicker, just discernible from the corner of her eye. Guin looked up as it happened again. The wiring was probably ancient, but the tiny disturbances were accompanied by a small, stealthy sound – definitely a non-electrical sound. She put the book down and watched. A few minutes later she saw something fly from the open doorway and collide with one of the elf crosses hanging on the back of a chair. Wasn't the door closed when they all went to bed? The elf cross swung briefly on its paperclip hanger. Guin couldn't see what had hit it, but there was a scattering of tiny objects – wads of paper, fragments of wood - on the carpet to indicate the elf cross was definitely the target. She lay perfectly still and watched as another three tiny projectiles shot from the doorway. The last of them succeeded in dislodging the elf cross, and it fell to the floor.

Moments later, Guin saw the door open a little further. She held her breath, wondering who was there. She watched as a head came around the door, but it was much lower down than she'd expected. It was the height of a toddler, but with an air of subtle cunning that was something else altogether. The head turned from one side of the room to the other and Guin realised it was wearing a hat with a tiny bell, the tinkling almost too faint to hear. The face had sharp features and eyes that shone in the lamplight. The rest of the figure slunk around the door. It was skinny in a very familiar way. Guin realised she had seen a picture of it in the book.

It was an elf.

Guin watched the eyes swivel round to regard her bed. She tried to shrink back with the least possible movement, avoiding its attention. She began to wonder if she was dreaming – this was a familiar nightmare: the invading presence, the need to keep perfectly, perfectly still.

The elf crept into the room and Guin realised it was carrying something at its side. The lamplight gleamed off a shiny, wickedly pointed blade, as misshapen as an icicle, the grey of winter sky.

Guin felt her heart banging in her chest. She wanted time to figure this out. She wanted to consider why her mind would conjure such a terrifying dream. Was this simply a result of falling asleep while reading the book of fairy folklore?

The book was in her hands. She glanced at it, fearful that even eye movement would draw the creature to her. She looked at the page, at the words.

*Elf-bolts or elf-shot, (which modern scholars have rationalised as the cutting implements and arrowheads of early Britons) were thought to be the weapons with which elves hurt livestock.*

She could read. She could read and the words stayed the same. She could never normally read in a dream. Which meant—

"Oh, hell," she whispered.

The elf looked up at her contemptuously before moving purposefully towards Newton in the bottom bunk. Guin realised doing nothing was not an option. She reached out for the nearest thing, which turned out to be a coat hanger on the end of the guard rail, and vaulted to the floor with a loud thump.

The elf hissed and turned its knife towards her. It smelled of old things in boxes, of cinnamon and sugar. Guin thrust the coat hanger forward. It was one of those rubbishy wire ones which would bounce off if she tried to hit it over the head. She jabbed instead, which was equally useless. She dodged a knife thrust, and then she made her move. Over its head went the coat hanger and she twisted, using a corkscrew to tighten the coat hanger around its throat. It swung its knife at her but, coat hanger in hand, she kept it at more than arm's length.

"Some help here!" she shouted.

The elf wasn't giving up. It stabbed and jabbed at her and she pulled away. It never thought to stab at the hands holding the coat hanger, going for her belly every time. The elf's face turned red as it choked, but Guin's arms were tiring. A wild swing of the blade snagged the edge of her bathrobe. It tried to haul her closer. Guin twisted, letting the robe slip from her arms.

The elf was like a wild animal, she thought. Its attention was centred on the robe it had speared, like a bull in one of those horrible bullfights taking all of its anger out on the cape, not the horrible matador. It dragged the robe closer, gathering it up, entangling itself. Guin swung the coat hanger, the elf still firmly clamped by its neck, up and over, slamming it down against the floor with all of her might. The elf made a tiny *Oof!* Sound, and went slack beneath the bathrobe.

Guin prodded it with her foot. It didn't move.

She looked round. "Did no one wake up?" she demanded.

"Wah?" said Newton, groggily.

She thumped her dad. "How are you all still asleep?" She turned on the main light. There were grumbles from three sleepy individuals.

"What's the time?" said her dad, turning over.

"No idea," said Guin, wondering why the hideous clutter of this building included no useful features like clocks. "That's not important."

"What's the time?" mumbled Esther as though needing confirmation.

"I just killed an attacker."

Her own words hit Guin hard. She had just taken a life. It was a murderous elf, but it was still slightly overwhelming. It was either horrific and deeply traumatic, or ever so slightly cool. She would decide later.

Everyone was sitting up now, bleary and incredulous.

"What?" asked her dad. "Did you...?"

"Did she say killed an attacker?" said Esther.

"Yes. With a coat hanger," said Guin. "It was an elf."

"It was an elf and you killed it with a coat hanger," said her dad slowly. He scanned the floor. "Nightmare, honey?"

Guin sighed and pointed at the bundled bathrobe.

"It's a dressing gown," he said.

"Inside the dressing gown."

It was his turn to sigh. He swung his legs out of bed, scratched himself in a way Guin wished he wouldn't in front of his daughter and began to unroll the bathrobe.

"You see," he said patiently, "sometimes, particularly when we're sleeping in a strange new place, we see things and we think that they're – Oh, my God! It's a dead elf!"

Newton scrambled from his bed to look.

"What is it?" said Esther.

Guin rolled her eyes silently. How many times did she have to explain?

Newton got out of bed. At least he was wearing proper pyjamas, unlike the boxers and T-shirt combo her dad was in.

"Bloody hell," said Newton. "You've murdered the elf on the shelf."

"It's not a doll," she said.

"It's so small," he said, in the voice of someone who was thinking about picking it up and cuddling it.

"It was heading for you with a knife in its hand," said Guin.

Her dad prodded the elf and shook his head.

"It's a tiny man," he said faintly, like he didn't believe it. "You killed a tiny man in an elf suit."

"Otherwise known as an elf," said Guin.

"But there's no such things," said Newton.

Her dad picked up the elf's knife and tested the blade with his thumb. He winced. "Maybe ... maybe it's a midget burglar who like dressing as an elf."

"That's totally un-PC, Dave," said Esther. "You can't use the 'm' word to describe little people."

"It's an elf!" said Guin.

"No such things," Newton repeated numbly.

Esther stepped into her jeans. She knelt by the elf and touched the edge of its stripy trousers. They were probably meant to be red and white but time and dirt had turned them to mucky purple and urine yellow. "Right," she said. "This is either an elf, or it's not."

"What?" said Guin's dad.

"We either re-evaluate everything we thought we knew, or we rationalise it away. But there's no denying this ... individual is here."

"No."

"And so we must act accordingly."

"Right."

She looked up at the open door and the dark landing beyond. Guin shivered.

"I'm sure it was alone," said her dad.

"Are you?" said Esther.

"The ones that killed Elsa Frinton weren't," said Guin.

"The what? Who?" said Newton.

"There aren't any more of these," said her dad, trying to sound confident, rather than actually sounding confident. "It's just one man."

"Elf," said Guin.

Her dad went to the door but to Guin's dismay, he didn't close it. He opened it wider and looked out.

"The ones in the market weren't either," said Esther.

"Weren't what?" he said. "Wait." He scrunched up his eyes and along the landing. "I think I—"

There was the sound of a pattering feet. Esther was already up, pushing the dumbstruck Dave out of the way of the door and slamming it shut.

"What is it, mum?" said Newton, a quaver of fear in his voice.

Esther turned the key in the lock and stepped back. She held up a finger for quiet. "I saw some of these things," she whispered. "In a workshop. I thought they were children."

"When?" said Dave, confused.

"At the market. There were several of them. They—"

There was a thump at the door then a series of knocks. Guin wasn't the only one who noticed that the knocks were coming from near the bottom of the door.

"They want to hurt us," said Newton.

"No," said Dave.

"They hurt me," said Esther and held up her bandaged hand.

The door handle rattled violently.

"They chased me and stabbed me with a chisel," said Esther, no longer even trying to whisper. "I think one of them had a knife as well. It might even have been the one Guin killed."

Guin ran to her bunk and grabbed Wiry Harrison from the guard rail – not because she was scared but because he might be. She reached up and grabbed the *Little Folk in European Folklore* too.

"Elves are real?" said Newton, still trying to take it in.

"Elsa Frinton thought so."

"Who's Elsa Frinton?" asked Esther.

Guin waved the book. "I can't be sure, but I think she was trying to track down these things,. I think they got her first. I saw her hat and it had blood on it."

"All right, all right," said her dad. "I think we're all getting a little bit spooked."

"There's a dead elf at our feet, Dave," said Esther. "That came into our room with murder on its mind."

"Yes, now we're making small mundane encounters seem downright sinister. I'm sure these things aren't *really* after us. I mean we'd have noticed if there were loads of tiny—" He stopped and stared at his feet.

"You've seen them too, haven't you, dad?" said Guin.

He shook his head. "Earlier, when I saw someone messing with the car, it was the strange way that they looked when they ran away. I thought I saw one tall person breaking apart into—" He laughed. "It sounds ridiculous when I say it out loud."

"You think it was elves all standing on top of each other to look like a person?" said Guin and placed the fallen elf cross on the door handle.

The thumping at the door subsided. From outside came a fiercely dark chittering sound, words in a language that Guin didn't recognise.

"I have no idea what to think," said her dad. "This is utterly beyond me."

"The elf crosses seem to help," said Guin. "Our room was protected until they knocked one of them down."

"Can we make more?" said Newton.

"I made these out of cotton buds and string. They're five-sided stars and I copied the design out of the book." She held it up.

"Have you got any more cotton buds and string?" asked Newton.

Guin shook her head.

\*\*\*

# 31

Esther crossed to the window and pulled the curtain aside.

Outside, on the narrow ledge, stood two elves, their sly faces pressed against the window, their palms flat. Snow was mounting on their shoulders and on the tops of their pointy shoes. Their faces were small and round, too small to be human faces, too sharp to be children. They looked cold and they looked hungry.

The pair of them glanced at Esther and then pointedly looked at the window catch and the elf cross hanging from it, imploring her to remove it.

"Nah," she said and closed the curtain. "We're sitting ducks. We need to get out of here."

"They can't come in with the elf crosses there," said Guin.

"Do we sit here until daylight?" asked Dave. "Will they go when it gets light?"

"That's vampires," Guin pointed out.

"They're afraid of crosses," said Newton.

"Elf crosses."

"Could we make elf crosses out of this stuff?" asked Newton. He was pointing at the seat of a chair. "If we unravelled it, maybe?"

"Looks a bit stiff," said Guin, flicking it with her fingers.

"It's cane," said Esther, stabbing it with a finger. "It will become perfectly pliable if we soak it in hot water. Run the tap, Dave."

"Oh, good," he said. "I'm really glad in this time of crisis we're going to do some crafting."

Esther stood on the bed and launched herself, feet-first onto the chair seat. She expected it to pop out with her weight on it, releasing the cane for them to use. What she didn't expect was for the chair to explode around it. She picked herself up off the floor and released the seat from the shattered wood. She picked at the edges to expose the strands of cane.

"I could have just used my pen knife to cut it out," said Dave.

There was a penetrating screeching noise from the window, and the sound of more tapping from the door.

"They're just trying to scare us," said Newton.

Esther beamed at her son, in an effort to convey a lack of fear. Her shaking hands were fooling nobody.

Guin took charge of elf crosses and supervised the construction of another five. Her practised fingers made two while everyone else struggled to make one.

"Two nuns were walking along one day," said Newton, his fingers fumbling. "Dracula leapt out at them from behind a bush. One nun says to the other, 'Quick, Sister Mary! Show him your cross!' and the other nun frowns and shouts, 'Sod off, Dracula!'"

Guin just looked at him.

"I don't get it," said Esther.

"Show him your cross. It's a joke. It's—" He looked down. "I think I might have seen the elves too," he said. "I definitely heard something in the trees near the church. And, at the nativity, I saw the baby Jesus in the nativity open and close its eyes."

"I've seen dolls that can do that," said Guin.

"I think they've been following us all over town."

"So, if elves are real, what does that mean for all the other stuff?" asked Dave. "The reindeer with red noses, the flying snowman and goodness only knows what else?"

"Aren't you forgetting the man in the big red suit?" asked Esther.

"No, I'm *ignoring* the man in the big red suit," said Dave. "Apart from the fact that my brain's about to explode, I know very well where all of the presents in our house have come from over the years, and I've never received any threatening letters from the North Pole claiming copyright infringement or whatever."

Esther gave a small shrug of agreement. "No, of course not." She swallowed the natural follow-up, which was to say that would be ridiculous, because it was all ridiculous. Utterly and completely ludicrous.

"But," Guin said slowly as she finished her third elf cross in as many minutes, "does this mean we've been bad?"

"No," said Dave automatically. "How so?"

"You know, the naughty list and the nice list. That man at dinner was talking about the Krampus."

Esther thought for a moment about Duncan Catheter. There were elves in the house. Had they already got him? And Mrs Scruples?

"We've not been bad," she said firmly. "And no one gets to pass judgement over us except, you know, us. These little fascists got a problem with my family then they have to go through me first."

Newton huffed. "I think mine looks more like a really rubbish hat" He tried his elf cross on his head.

"Nonsense," said Esther, "it's a great job."

"So what are we going to do with them now?" asked Dave.

Guin fetched her new box and took out the little robot figure. She unclipped a safety pin from its side.

"Dad, you've got more safety pins in your first aid kit, right?"

*\*\**

# 32

They quickly took the sheets off the bed and, pinning them together, turned them into a protective shield. Dave decided it looked like a cross between a bird hide and a family-sized body bag. Elf crosses were strategically placed around the outside, and each person held up a side. They had dressed, or at least thrown on trousers and shoes and such clothes as they thought necessary to do battle with Christmas elves. Dave had his smallest first aid kit stuffed in his back pocket. Guin had insisted on bringing the folklore book and pockets stuffed with her little toys. In this situation, Dave wasn't going to deny his little girl anything.

"Try to keep it level," instructed Guin.

They had decided there needed to be little port holes to enable each person to see out, but that the protection needed to extend to the top of Dave's head, as he was the tallest.

"How are we going to get anywhere?" asked Esther. "If we're all standing back to back in the middle. Only one person can walk forwards at a time. It could get very tricky. What if someone walks slower than all of the others? Who will decide where we go?"

"Esther's in charge of steering," said Guin. "Dad, you're lookout. You're tallest."

"And me?" asked Newton.

Esther thrust a weapon into her son's hand. It looked very much like a toilet brush.

"What's that?" asked Dave.

"Toilet brush. With added elf cross," said Esther.

"If it doesn't work as a protective ward, you might be able to pass on some nasty germs," said Guin, disgusted.

Dave took a deep breath and tried to focus on their goals. "We're going downstairs and straight outside so that we can get some help, yes?"

"Absolutely," said Esther. "It's not that far, if we concentrate and don't let them distract us."

"Stairs will be tricky."

"Which is why we need to concentrate," said Esther firmly.

Dave felt for the door handle through the sheet, peering through his porthole. "Everyone ready?" He unlocked the door, pulled it open and looked outside. At first glance, the landing was empty. Even so, he was pretty sure the elves were not far away.

The lights flickered. Dave prayed that whatever antique wiring illuminated this place would hold up for a few more minutes. "All clear."

"To Dave, to Dave," said Esther.

"ONE two three four, TWO two three four," said Guin as they shuffled forward in time.

The group stepped out onto the landing. Dave looked all around. He saw an elf lounging against the wall, next to their door. It had a lazy, arrogant air about it. This one had a smear of white beard on its chin, unlike the other beardless elves they had seen. It looked like an evil Papa Smurf.

"ONE two three four!" hissed the elf, in a mocking but recognisable parody of Guin's time-keeping chant.

Guin faltered. Esther didn't miss a beat and picked up the tempo with a bout of, "We shall overcome! We shall overcome! We shall overcome some da-aa-aa-ay!"

It wasn't a song Dave normally enjoyed, but at that moment it was perfect. Esther was able to bellow it at the top of her lungs, drowning out the elf. Dave had to admit it was rousing in the way only a protest song could be.

The elf peeled itself off the wall and feinted at them, but mainly for show. It was clearly reluctant to go anywhere near the elf crosses.

They were making a lot of noise. How was it possible nobody had woken up and come to see what was the matter? He wasn't sure whether he'd caught the faint strains of a saxophone coming from somewhere. Presumably Mrs Scruples was still playing her music. He remembered she said she played her gramophone loudly to "Mask the noises". A chilling thought struck him.

"Evil cow," he whispered to himself.

"What?" said Guin.

The Woollby-Roberts (or possibly Roberts-Woollby) steered towards the top of the stairs. Dave had the unenviable task of going down backwards, last of the group. He was grateful Esther altered her singing to indicate the change in terrain.

"We shall overcome! *Step down.* We shall overcome! *Step down.*"

Dave glanced down to see where he needed to tread. He made the first step, and the second, without incident. The elf on the landing lounged against a wall, watching them with a disconcerting half smile.

"Where are the others?" Dave asked.

"You're meant to be lookout," said Newton.

Now the whole family were on the stairs, and nobody had tripped or knocked them down like bandage-wrapped dominoes. The appalling stuffed cats were right above them; compelling, in that car crash way bad art always was. Dave dared to hope they all might make it to the ground floor unscathed. As he twisted round to look at Esther and give her an encouraging smile he caught sight of movement above.

"Oh no—!" The rest of the sentence was lost in a screeching of gleeful hatred. The stuffed monstrosities toppled forward into the shield.

Dave tried to understand how a stuffed cat had come to land on the step directly behind him, then its head peeled open. Tufts of long-dead fur were cast aside. The cat's ears slid down and an elf face popped out and leered at him. Another two stuffed cats messily exploded into elves. The family's protective shield suddenly felt like a very confined space. They tried to move back from the elves, but the sheets held them in place. There was a ripping sound. Guin shrieked and stumbled backwards, falling down the stairs inside a length of bed sheet.

"Guin!"

Esther was already running downstairs after Guin.

An elf dropped onto Dave's shoulder. He ducked and yelled, trying to dislodge it.

"Elf-crusher!" yelled Newton and swung his toilet brush.

It wasn't the invincible weapon Esther had originally planned. Perhaps, she'd pictured it working like Thor's hammer, frying elves with its super powers. Even though it clearly had the power to repel them, it didn't actually damage the elves in any significant way. To make matters worse, it was clearly a very cheap toilet brush. The end broke clean off when it clipped Dave's shoulder. Something wet sprayed Dave's face, and it wasn't elf blood.

"Come on!" Esther shouted to Guin. There was a definite, if woozy, response from Guin further down the stairs.

"Esther!" Dave called as he ripped the elf from his shoulder, tearing its sharp nails from the fabric of his T-shirt.

"We're fine!" she shouted back. "Help Newton!"

The only advantage Dave had was elevation: he was further up the stairs. He kicked out at the elf and sent it flying – immediately horrified he'd made things worse for Guin and Esther.

"Newton! Grab my hand!"

He pulled Newton up onto the landing, so there was less chance of him falling down the stairs. Dave knew the drill. The first thing you did in an emergency was remove whatever danger you could from yourself and the victim; and a fall from height was a classic risk. He grabbed hold of an elf clinging to Newton and pulled it off. His initial plan was to use the momentum to get in a really good swing: bash the little bastard's brains out on the wall opposite. But Dave had forgotten the beardy boss elf who'd been leaning against the wall outside the bedroom. He was reminded when a voice rasped behind him.

"ONE two three four!"

It grabbed Dave's arm on the count of four,. Dave was like a hammer-thrower who'd been interrupted mid-spin by someone hanging a bag of groceries off his arm. He tottered about the landing, clumsily holding two elves.

Newton came at them, holding up a torn section of sheeting. Dave hurled the pair of elves into the sheet.

"Tie it up!" yelled Newton.

They tied it, corner to corner, the elves wriggling inside. Newton found another piece of sheet and they double-bagged the elves. "It's not gonna hold, is it?" he said.

At that moment another stuffed cat burst off the shelf. Dave watched in horror as the elf discarded its disguise mid-air, with moves resembling martial arts kicks and twists. It landed on Newton's head, digging its tiny hands into his face and bracing its legs on the back of his neck. Newton reached up. He was unable to dislodge the elf. Instead he twisted long strands of his own hair into a makeshift noose.

Dave wanted to help, but was all too aware the elves in the improvised sack would not improve the situation if they got free. Newton tugged tighter and tighter. The elf made choking noises and went slack, sliding down Newton's shoulders.

"Is it dead?"

Dave half-nodded, half-shrugged. Paramedic training didn't cover the vital signs of mythical creatures.

"Incoming!" called Newton, pointing at another pair of elves climbing the stairs.

Dave hurled the bagged elves downwards, intending to bowl over the climbing ones. One of them reached out a hand and clawed the bag open, mid-flight. The bagged elves tumbled out, righting themselves. Now there were four elves advancing up the stairs.

"Back to the bedroom!" said Newton.

Dave hesitated. His daughter and his girlfriend were out of sight, downstairs somewhere. The beardy boss elf spat something in a scratchy language. Knives appeared in hands.

"Right. Back to the bedroom," agreed Dave.

***

# 33

On the ground floor, Esther had her own problems. She had an elf by its ears and was swinging it around at arms' length.

"I've banged my head," muttered Guin.

"You said that already," said Esther. She flung the into the guest lounge and slammed the door.

"Maybe I've got amnesia," said Guin.

"One problem at a time. Behind you!"

An elf was dangling from the bannister by its spindly arms and preparing to jump onto Guin.

Esther wouldn't say she consciously decided to hit it with the gong. It was heavy and unwieldy and really not the ideal shape for an offensive weapon. But it was a gong.

Without a thought (because that thought would have been "Use something else"), Esther yanked it from its stand and slammed it against the dangling elf, pinning it to the staircase. The elf made an understandably surprised *"Urk!"* sound and its limbs went limp.

"This way," said Guin, pushing open the door to the kitchen.

Esther dashed after her, gong still in hand, although it was really, really heavy and she might have to put it down soon.

Guin closed the kitchen door and slowly dragged a steel table across to block it. The table legs screeched hideously.

"You injured?" said Esther.

Guin shrugged and worried she hadn't absorbed enough of her dad's first aid knowledge. "I'm fine. Did I mention I bumped my head. Where's dad?"

"They're still upstairs. I think." Esther breathed out heavily. "We need to figure out how to get back to them. We all need to work together."

"Well, they're probably trying to get to us," said Guin. "We shouldn't go back."

"No?"

"Never run back into a burning building. That's what dad says. Let the dog drown."

"Pardon?"

"It's our family motto."

Esther's arms and brain, coming off an adrenaline high, finally decided to put the gong down. As it touched the table top, something peeled off and flopped onto the surface.

"You brought the elf with you?" said Guin.

"I didn't mean to!"

"Quick! Put it in here." She pointed at the orange juicer a contraption with metal arms and paddles for juicing whole oranges. More importantly, it had a large transparent reservoir on top where the elf could be dumped and kept under observation.

Esther scooped the elf up – entirely weightless – and dropped it inside. She closed the lid and locked the catch. The elf woke almost immediately.

With the elf safely under glass, the woman and girl studied it closely. It had a floppy felt hat and a green tunic in the traditional Robin Hood style, but this one didn't have striped trousers. Instead they were an earthy brown colour. Its face was bordered by two huge pointy ears. It blinked. small and beady eyes, like raisins in uncooked dough. It wore a grin that made Esther very uncomfortable. She tried not to let it show.

"It looks like Dobby the house elf's stunt double," she said.

Unnerved, Esther put a large cast iron saucepan on top on the machine to weigh it down further. The elf angrily considered the confines of its tiny prison.

"Now what?" said Esther.

Guin drew a chair up, facing the machine. "Now, I think we should talk."

\*\*\*

# 34

The bedroom door rattled and banged as it was barged and kicked from outside.

"Are they allowed to do that?" asked Newton. "Don't they know there's an elf cross on the other side?"

Dave shrugged. Then he leaned forward and whispered to Newton. "I have an idea."

He gestured up at the ceiling on the far side of the room. Newton saw there was a white loft hatch in the centre of the ceiling. Dave performed a complicated mime which Newton understood to mean they should both climb into the loft space, move to somewhere else in the house and then sneak down, avoiding the elves.

Newton gave him a hearty thumbs up. He knew how important it was to keep everyone's spirits up, and he didn't want to point out how difficult and risky this was likely to be.

"So," said Dave loudly. "We'll wait for a few minutes, then we'll try to battle our way out of the door. They're only small, we can crush them if we try."

As an accompaniment to this monologue, Dave laid out his plan in the form of large gestures. He pointed at the dressing table and indicated they would move it underneath the loft hatch. They would need to put a chair on top of it in order to climb up. Dave went on to mime they would need to be very careful. He seemed obligated to stress this point by ostentatiously mouthing most accidents that occurred in the home were due to falls.

Newton didn't point out they could avoid the risk of falling altogether by not doing it, mainly because he didn't have a better plan. The two of them crept across the room to move the dressing table. It took them several minutes to clear all of the ornaments, mirrors and trinket trays off the top first.

"Can you tell what they're saying?" asked Dave. "Sometimes it almost seems as though they might be speaking English, but it's not quite right."

"I know what you mean," said Newton. "Like it's Chaucer or something."

"Is Chaucer that YouTuber that Guin likes?"

"Possibly," said Newton, unwilling to pursue the conversation.

They lifted the dressing table, and one of the legs on Dave's end toppled away. He nodded frantically that they should put the dressing table back down. They lowered it to the floor and Dave picked up the stray leg, putting it on top. They shuffled underneath the loft hatch, giving Dave a chance to re-insert the leg into its correct position. He leaned carefully on the top to test how secure it was.

"Should be all right as long as we're careful," he mouthed.

Dave fetched a chair and placed it on the top. He used the dressing table's stool as a step up. It looked as badly-made as the dressing table. Dave turned it over. The legs were screwed into the base, so he attempted to tighten them. The legs turned round and round, with no sign of tightening. Dave sighed and placed it back down, bedding it into the carpet to give it the best chance of remaining intact. Newton gave him another thumbs-up to show he was sure they could do this.

They both stood and surveyed the rickety tower for a moment. Newton pointed to himself, indicating he should go first, as he was smaller and lighter. Dave nodded, and grabbed hold of the chair to stabilise it as much as he could. Newton pictured himself climbing easily up the stack, treading lightly and precisely. What he actually found was the whole thing wobbled in a terrifying threat of imminent collapse. Once he'd shoved the loft hatch aside, he hauled himself up at lightning speed just to feel something firm beneath his feet.

Dave followed seconds later. It seemed to Newton that he made a lot more noise, as he heard the chair scrape loudly across the dressing table. Newton helped pull Dave into the loft, just as the whole stack collapsed with an unholy racket. He peered through the hatch: the leg had come off again, and the dressing table lay on its side, broken. He couldn't see the chair.

"Job done," said Dave quietly, dusting off his hands.

***

# 35

Esther watched Guin scribbling in the back of the folklore book she had found. There was no doubt the girl had real patience and dedication. Esther glanced at the captive elf and felt a twinge of guilt. It looked like a malevolent little gremlin, but she knew better than to judge someone by their appearance. She knew some sort of unconscious bias was making her feel that way, so she tried to set it aside and think about what had made the elves so angry. Was it a territorial issue? If Guin succeeded in understanding them, perhaps she could make sense of this situation and end it amicably.

"*Einn, tveir, þrir,*" said Guin to the elf, holding up fingers to indicate one, two and three. "Hey, Esther, I can count up to three in their language!"

"Great job, Guin," said Esther. "Can you get it to explain what they want?"

"I'll keep going."

"I'm sure it's just some horrible misunderstanding..."

Horrible misunderstanding. Esther found herself unhelpfully wondering what elves would want. Picturing Christmas elves, beavering away in Father Christmas's proto-capitalist workshop, was one thing. Imagining small fey creatures creeping into one's room at night was something else entirely. Nothing good ever came of fairy creatures sneaking into your home.

"Maybe it just wants to mend some shoes," she said.

"What?" said Guin.

"Nothing. Carry on."

While Guin expanded her elf vocabulary, Esther explored the kitchen. She wasn't doing it just to distract her from the simmering fear of what had happened to the two most important men in her life. No, sirree.

The kitchen was a single-storey extension on the original building, running its entire length. The ceiling was a large skylight with several open vents. As a consequence, it was quite a chilly place to be in the middle of the night. There was a sizeable industrial range and a pair of microwaves. Steel preparation surfaces between the sinks made Esther think about autopsies on the TV. She shuddered and gave herself a stern talking-to. If Guin could buckle down and try to solve this then so could she.

"Esther, come here."

Esther hurried over. They both watched the captive elf as it beckoned and smiled – as far as it was able, with its face smooshed against the plastic sides.

*"Við numpa dreþ einog svín!"*

Guin looked puzzled. "I might have misunderstood, but I think it just said it would slay us like swine—"

The elves that dropped from the ceiling vents did so with a gleeful screeching sound. There were three of them; they moved in on Esther and Guin in a loose semi-circle. Their knives were small and sharp, but Esther reckoned their grubby fingernails and tiny teeth could be equally harmful.

"Swedish people are terrified of badgers," said Guin.

"What?" said Esther, wishing she had made another elf-fighting toilet brush for herself.

"I read it in a book," said Guin. "Just saying. It's a matter of perspective."

There was a hammering from inside the juicer, as the elf demanded to be released.

Guin produced a meat tenderiser from behind her back. She swung at the nearest elf – a wallop to the cheek with the flat side of the meat hammer – and then backswung at a second – spikey side to its chest. Esther felt blindly around. Her hand closed around a chopping board, not her first weapon of choice.

Guin used the meat tenderiser without mercy: flat side, spikey side, flat, spikey, flat, spikey. Esther's weapon was less deadly, but she swung it, edge-first towards the nearest elf. She heard a satisfying "Oof!" and smacked it over the head.

The elf inside the machine danced with rage as he watched his colleagues collapse unconscious, or the least constricted parts of him jigged and twitched.

"On the griddle!" said Esther.

"The what?" said Guin.

"Put them on the hob thing!" Esther picked up the weighty gong. Guin caught on.

There was a large griddle of a similar size to the gong. Guin scooped one of the elves off the floor. It groaned and she recoiled in horror, quickly dropping it onto the griddle. She swiftly laid the other ones next to it and ducked out of the way as Esther placed the gong on top to weight them down.

Esther and Guin stood side by side and looked at the tiny limp boots and hats hanging out from underneath the gong. Guin voiced the thought that was in Esther's mind. "Elves crushed by a giant chocolate coin."

"Christmas destroyed by rampant greed and consumerism," nodded Esther sagely. "A fitting metaphor."

"Whatever," said Guin. "I'd eat a chocolate coin that big."

***

# 36

Once he'd found the pull-on light switch above the hatch, Dave saw the attic space was enormous. There were some partition walls at the sides, with a tiny crawl space which Dave felt no inclination whatsoever to explore, but the main body of the loft would have accommodated a barn dance, if it hadn't been quite so full of accumulated junk.

"Should we look for weapons?" asked Newton.

"Fine idea," said Dave. He wasn't sure there would be anything useable in terms of weapons, but it was good to keep busy. They stood and surveyed the boxes, cupboards and dust covers. Where to start?

Newton opened the nearest box and peered inside, Dave turned to a heavy wooden trunk with brass fittings and lifted the heavy lid. It was filled with children's toys from another era.

"How are you doing?" he asked, as he sifted through.

"Me? Completely fine. Really. Don't worry."

Their gazes met for an instant. "We have a bit of breathing space, I reckon, so we'll rest for a moment and then figure out a way to get downstairs."

Dave picked out a tin car from the trunk.

"Not much of a weapon," said Newton, who was holding an ancient wooden tennis racquet, clamped in a storage press.

Dave contemplated the tin car. "Dangerous for a child. Sharp edges like these and they'd need a tetanus shot."

Newton pulled the dust cover off an old-fashioned mangle. He gave the handle an experimental rotation and grunted in satisfaction when the rollers turned. "Once we're tooled up, we need to find mum. And Guin, of course."

"They can look after themselves," said Dave. "Your mum will get Guin out, and I'll do the same for you. Your mum knows that."

He moved on to another box. He pulled out an electric iron and set it aside in case he needed a blunt weapon at some point. Underneath was a selection of vinyl records.

"Carole King," he said, surprised. "I used to own this album."

"You're not going to rescue them then?" said Newton.

Dave put the record down. "Who says they need rescuing, Newton? No good will come of running around looking for them. Get away from the danger. Never return to a burning building."

"The building's not burning."

"Okay. Never return to a building full of savages elves. We don't fix things by putting ourselves in more danger. Let the dog drown."

"Let the ... what?" Newton looked horrified. "What dog?"

Dave shook his head. "Doesn't matter. It's just something Guin and I say. Family motto."

"About drowning dogs?"

Dave paused in his search of the boxes. "You hear certain news stories. A dog jumps in a river and the owner jumps after it. What happens? Half the time, it seems, the dog swims ashore, safe and fine, and the owner gets pulled under by a current and ... yeah." He sniffed. "We instinctively leap into a situation, thinking we must do something, anything. But it's rarely the right thing. Basic personal safety rule."

"But the dog—"

"If it lives or dies isn't going to be changed by a fully-clothed idiot jumping in after it, dude. Hence the phrase."

"Let the dog drown. And that's your family motto?"

"Yup. If we had a coat of arms, that's what we'd put on it."

Newton shook his head. "That's cold..."

"Sorry," said Dave. "I just didn't want you to worry about your mum."

"Well, that worked because all I can think about now is dogs drowning—" He went silent for a moment. "Um, Dave?"

"Yes, mate?"

"Can you see something hanging from the rafters?"

Dave looked where Newton was pointing. Something ragged and dirty hung from the apex of the roof. Folds of cobwebbed grey dangled in the shadows, as if the contents of a vacuum bag had spilled through a hole in the roof. Was it a filthy puppet, hanging up so that its strings didn't tangle? A desiccated bat?

As they both peered at the thing, an eye popped open and it grinned at them, upside down. Another eye opened and another mouth grinned.

"Elves!"

Three of the creatures dropped to the floor, tittering maniacally.

Dave automatically threw the iron. Two of them dodged it easily but the third, pulling cobwebs from its hat bell, looked up too late. The iron slammed into it, knocking it through the plasterboard floor. From below, something smashed. As Dave looked for another heavy item to throw, Newton began to hurl records at the creatures.

"Not the Carol King!" Dave heard himself say.

Newton skimmed records like Frisbees. The sharp edge of one caught an elf on its arm. Dave joined in; trying to save any records was ridiculous . He threw them by the handful. They weren't particularly effective weapons, and the elves dodged and wove their way closer.

"Tennis racquet!" yelled Dave. Newton picked up the racquet and prepared to meet the elves.

"Knees bent!" said Dave. "Handshake grip. Eyes straight. And swing!"

Newton howled with rage and caught an elf in a powerful forehand. The elf flew back and hit the toy trunk's raised lid. The elf fell inside, stunned. The hinged lid wobbled.

The other elf came at Dave. He grabbed for the nearest item, an ugly pottery lamp with a fabric shade, and smashed it over the creature's head. He pushed the lampshade over the elf, pinning one arm to its sides. Not its knife arm unfortunately. Dave tripped over a carved hat stand as he tried to get out of knife-range. The elf advanced, abruptly stopping just short.

Newton had hold of the lamp's flex and was hauling it back!

For a tiny creature, it had surprising strength. As Newton fought to reel it back, Dave had to wriggle on the floor to stop the damned thing stabbing him. The tassels on the lampshade cascaded dust as the elf struggled for purchase.

Newton was hauling with both hands, his feet digging in against the floor timbers. He was thoroughly occupied and Dave knew he hadn't seen the elf in the toy trunk pull itself up. It raised its knife to attack.

Dave kicked the at the hat stand. By luck as much as anything, it fell onto the trunk. The lid tipped forward. The elf, halfway out, looked up, but it had no time to dodge. The brass-bound lid slammed shut and an elf head bounced onto the floor.

"He'll need a bit more than a tetanus shot for that," grunted Dave.

The lampshaded elf was startled enough by the sight of his decapitated companion that Newton managed to haul in a vital foot or two of lamp flex.

Dave grinned.

The elf saw the grin and looked round.

Newton started to turn the mangle, gaining momentum. The light flex was squeezed between the rollers, shortly followed by the elf. There was the snap of bones breaking and the crackle of the heavy mangle grinding them to dust.

"I think it's dead now," said Dave.

Newton gave the mangle crank a final heave. The elf's head popped in a shower of bloody pulp. "Is now," he panted.

They turned at a noise. The iron-struck elf was hauling itself back up through the hole in the floor.

"Hit it with something! Anything!" yelled Dave, grabbing at boxes and flinging them blindly. Newton scrabbled inside the nearest box. He pulled out an accordion. The bellows fell open with a tuneless honk. Newton grabbed the strap as the elf dived to attack. Newton squeezed the bellows. The noise that followed was horrendous as the accordion sound was joined by the elf's squealing: like a herd of cows in a car crusher. In the following silence, Dave and Newton stared at each other. The elf hung limply from the accordion's insides.

"I think what you meant to say," said Newton, standing, "was he was an elf hazard."

***

# 37

Guin and Esther sat on top of the gong, so any elves who tried to escape could be dealt with. They could hear a muted grumbling beneath them, but they'd stopped trying to get out. Guin had spent some time reading the book and listening to snatches of elves' conversation.

"I really don't know what they're saying," she said. "But none of it sounds nice."

"No," Esther agreed.

"I think we're going to have to fight our way out of here."

Esther nodded. She jumped down off the gong and hauled a sack of potatoes on top to keep up the weight. "How about the bottles of spirits? We can make Molotov cocktails."

Guin stared at her suspiciously. "Are you an alcoholic too?"

"No, a Molotov cocktail is a primitive bomb where you set fire to some flammable liquid in a bottle and throw it."

"Oh, that," said Guin, making out she already knew. "Yes, definitely those. There are quite a few knives in here," she added, rootling through a cutlery drawer.

Esther tore up a tea towel to stuff into the ends of bottles.

"We should find the heaviest thing we think we could swing in anger as well," called Guin, banging pots around in a cupboard. "Try that frying pan." She nodded at a cast iron pan hanging from a hook over the cooker.

"I'm a bit uncomfortable with violence for its own sake," said Esther. "Perhaps we could find some strong bin bags and concentrate on immobilising them?"

Guin gave her a withering look.

***

# 38

Dave knelt on the attic floor, bent over as if in prayer.

"What are you doing?" asked Newton.

"I'm seeing what we can see," said Dave.

Newton approached the splintered laths and torn insulation around the holes they'd punched in their fight.

"If we stand on the joists then we should be safe from going through," said Dave. "Watch where you put your feet."

Newton tried to look down, but the hole offered only a ragged view of some dusty pink carpet, deep in shadows. "I can't see. Perhaps if I get down and put my head through?"

"I think it ought to be me," said Dave. "Don't want to put you in harm's way."

Dave knelt on the joist and lowered himself carefully forward, his hand on another joist for balance. Behind them, the fatally damaged accordion gave a discordant *squonk*. Dave turned in alarm. Newton stepped back.

A timber splintered, the plaster and lath gave way beneath them both. They fell through the ceiling, scrabbling at thin air, into the bedroom below. Dave bounced on a spongy mattress and rolled noisily onto the floor.

The plaster dust made it hard to see for some time. It made it hard to breathe as well. Dave was relieved to hear Newton coughing. At least it meant that the boy was still in the land of the living.

A light came on, a bedside lamp. Through the dust he could see Newton on a double bed, covered by a pink bedspread and a cascade of plaster. Next to him was the very surprised Duncan Catheter.

"Would you care to—" Duncan broke down in a fit of coughing. He gulped at a glass of water on the nightstand to clear his throat, immediately spitting it out again, along with a lump of plaster. "Would you care to explain what the heck is going on?"

Dave nodded tersely. "Yeah, there's a dangerous problem in this house."

"I can see that much."

"A real problem. We can explain but I need to check for immediate danger first."

Dave's training kicked in. He could assess any potential injuries just as soon as he'd made sure that the area was safe. He stood, chunks of ceiling crunching under his feet. He switched on the main light and checked under the bed. Then he checked behind all of the furniture in the room.

"Wouldn't have happened in one of my houses," said Duncan, inspecting the hole in the ceiling. He turned to Newton. "Young squire. I'd appreciate it if you got off my bed."

"Sorry," Newton coughed.

Dave turned his attention back to the teenager. "You hurt, dude?"

Newton shook his head.

"What about me?" demanded Duncan. He swung out of bed and pulled on a dressing gown. Not one of the towelling bathrobes which came with the room, but a thick thing covered by a paisley pattern in red and gold. It even had gold knotted tassels on its belt. "A man does not expect to be assaulted in his sleep by attic-creeping idiots. I have a good mind to complain to the management."

"Get in line, there's a queue," said Dave darkly. "Are you hurt, Duncan?"

"Apart from my pride?"

Dave gave him a look.

"I am shaken," said Duncan. "I don't mind telling you that."

Dave leaned against the wardrobe. "There's something strange going on."

"Somewhat of an understatement, squire."

"Elves," said Newton.

Duncan gave Dave a look to indicate he thought the boy was quite mad. It was understandable, given the situation and the fact that Newton's hair was still full of chunks of plaster.

"Tell me, Duncan, have you noticed anything strange at all during your time here?" asked Dave.

Duncan puffed out his cheeks. "Stranger than this?"

"In the town. Odd people. Peculiar behaviour. Any unsettling encounters, for example?"

Duncan considered for a moment. "Someone mentioned something about a Buy Nothing Day. I find that more than a little worrying."

"The baby Jesus opened his eyes!" said Newton.

"Oh dear me. Clearly, the boy needs help," said Duncan. "I think you need to pop back off to bed now. I wish I could do the same, but I think I'd better see if I can get hold of Mrs Scruple. She'll need to find me another room."

"She's not going to find you another room," said Dave. "There's something going on. Something weird."

"Elves," said Newton again, which really wasn't helping.

Duncan shook his head but, for a moment, Dave saw his eyes linger on pieces of paper on the dust-covered bedside table. Dave took a step towards the table but Duncan was swiftly in front of him, blocking the way.

"What have you seen?" said Dave.

"Nothing," insisted Duncan, too quickly. "Nothing. Wild imaginings brought on by too much of Mrs Scruples' sherry trifle."

"It's not the trifle, it's elves," said Newton.

Duncan scoffed.

Dave sighed, exasperated. The thick plaster dust in the air caught in his throat and made him cough. When he'd recovered, Duncan had three pieces of paper in his hand. One looked like folded architect's plans. Another was a creased letter. The third— Dave realised it was one of the Christmas cracker jokes from dinner.

"Well I'm sure it won't be long before you see what the problem is," said Dave, "but right now, you need to believe in elves, because that's what we're dealing with here."

Duncan snorted, although he never looked up from the papers.

"Listen to me," said Dave. "The danger here is very real. If we split up, there's a good chance it will prove fatal. I need you to trust me for a few minutes."

"I'd say your track record has hardly lent itself to gaining trust, sirrah. I'm more inclined to report you to the police for endangering my health."

"Oh, I'd welcome police involvement right now!" growled Dave. "The phone lines have been down all evening. Seriously, don't you think I might—?"

There was a knock at the door.

"Well, really!" declared Duncan, peeved. "It's like Piccadilly Station in here! All I ask is a little peace and quiet to get some rest. I don't think any of you realise how hard I work on behalf of the local community. I refuse to continue with this absurd pantomime!" He crossed to the door.

"Don't!" yelled Dave, but Duncan, a man of considerable bulk and filled with the power of his own importance, pushed him aside. He opened the door.

On the landing stood a mass of elves, a dozen at least. They looked up at Duncan with hungry little smiles. Duncan made a strangled noise that was half-annoyance and half-disbelief. He looked at the letter in his hand. "Would any of you gentlemen happen to be Mr – er – Bacraut? Bacraut, is it?"

One of the elves shouldered its way to the front. From behind Duncan, Dave saw it was the one with the wispy white beard who had jumped him on the stairs.

The elf thumped its chest. "Bacraut," it growled.

"Very good," said Duncan. "I believe you and I have a meeting scheduled."

He waved the letter at the elves as evidence. They craned forward. The written word appeared to have a mystical hold over them. There were numerous mutters.

"Perhaps," Duncan beamed, warming to the sound of his own voice, "we could have that meeting now. If you'd care to join me in my office? Um…" He gestured to the room off to the left on the landing.

Newton looked at Dave. "Are we actually going to have a meeting with murderous elves?" he whispered.

Dave was lost for words but, if nothing else, Duncan had the elves' attention. They hadn't attacked yet.

"Mr Catheter believes he is," he whispered back. "I think I'm inclined to let him do that on his own."

But as Duncan moved into the next door room, numerous pixie faces turned to look at them. Dave was suddenly aware of their sharp knives and shining eyes.

"Yes, yes, we're just coming," he said.

The room had once been an upstairs dining room. Perhaps it had been called the 'banqueting suite' or something equally pretentious. There was a decrepit oval dining table in the centre of, several equally decrepit chairs around it and a dumbwaiter hatch in the corner. However, the room had clearly become a storage space over the years. There were heaps of towels on a side table, a wonky hostess trolley under a pile of sheets, and a trouser press next to the door.

Duncan sat himself at the head of the table, tugging at his dressing gown and stripy pyjamas as though he was wearing the finest business suit.

"We have a situation, I can see that," he said, nervousness barely showing through his glib businessman attitude. "So, let's get around the table and see what needs to be done here. Never yet found a scenario that couldn't be resolved by talking it out."

The elves, sniggering and whispering, clustered around the table.

"Please, take a seat," said Duncan. "We can discuss this like civilised human be— Like grown-ups, I'm sure." He gestured to the chairs. The bearded Bacraut leapt onto the end of the table and sat cross-legged.

Duncan steepled his hands in front of him and smiled around at the whole room. Dave imagined he practised the gesture in front of the mirror. "I received your letter," he said, placing the papers flat on the table. "And I had no idea the civic leaders of this town were such distinguished – gentlemen – as yourselves."

An elf pulled the letter closer to look at the writing on it. Hand to hand it made its way round the table.

"Shall we begin by all stating what we'd like to get out of this meeting?" asked Duncan. "As you know, I wrote to the local business forum with suggestions for a mixed usage building project." He unfolded the plans he'd brought with him and laid them flat on the table. "A project that utilises some underdeveloped brownfield sites within the town proper, extends through the churchyard and into the woodlands behind."

Bacraut and several of the other elves hissed.

"Do not worry yourselves unduly, good sirs," said Duncan. "I have initiated projects like this before. I'm a dab hand with building on consecrated ground. We'll soon have those stiffs swiftly – but sensitively – relocated. We can even make a decorative feature using the headstones. And, hey—!" he spread his arms warmly "—what's better for Alvestowe, eh? A graveyard for sixty, seventy unproductive corpses, or an estate of affordable starter homes and mover-onners for two hundred locals? And with that avenue created we can spread into that under-utilised wood."

The elves hissed again.

"It's just trees, my friends," said Duncan. "We're not talking about the Amazon rainforest here."

At the back of the room, near the door, Dave leaned in to whisper to Newton. "I don't think they want him to cut down the trees, do you?"

"Eco-terrorist elves?" murmured Newton.

***

# 39

"I'd just like to know what they want?" said Esther, as she stuffed a rag into the top of a bottle.

They had scoured the kitchen for flammable materials and Esther spent too long dithering which alcoholic spirits burned and which did not. She suspected some of their Molotov cocktails were more likely to make things smell like a New Year's party than set fire to them.

"I think they want to kill us," said Guin.

"Yes, but perhaps we've got it all wrong," said Esther. "Maybe elves are an endangered species."

"Like orangutans?" said Guin.

"Exactly. And this is the last little enclave of them. No wonder they're desperate, they're fighting for the survival of their entire species. Imagine if the orangutans of Borneo had the means to fight back against the humans who are taking their habitat? I bet they'd behave in just the same way."

Guin opened her book on the counter next to them. "No. I think they just like killing."

"What? That's a terrible thing to say, Guin. Sometimes we need to put ourselves in someone else's situation. If we can truly understand and empathise with them, maybe we can find a way through this. Violence can't be the only way."

Guin flicked through the book purposefully, watched by the creature in the orange juicer. "I think I need to show you some of the pictures in this book," she said, holding up *Little Folk in European Folklore*. "This is what elves do to people they catch."

Esther looked at the image. It involved a bent willow tree, lots of rope and some improbably positioned spikes. She swallowed hard and stared at the elf that was trapped in the juicer reservoir, glaring out at them.

"Point taken," she said.

\*\*\*

# 40

"So—" said Duncan, after his initial offer had met zero response from the elves, apart from some unhappy hissing, "—perhaps you can tell me what you're after, Mr Bacraut?"

The elf stared at him, unblinking. The light in the room was bright, but still the elf's eyes were dark and malevolent. Dave tried to look at the elf with a detached and professional eye. Did it have a similar physiology to a human? What did elves eat? How did they reproduce? How easy was it to make one bleed?

Duncan's smile faltered slightly, but he pressed on. "I feel that your outward hostility is a sign of frustration. Has it been difficult for you, negotiating with humans? I want you to know that I'm the man who can make things happen for you. Do you understand?"

The elf inclined its head by a fraction. It was a tiny gesture, but managed to be both supercilious and dismissive at the same time.

"Oh, you don't think that's true?" said Duncan. "Well, why would you? I haven't proven myself to you yet. Let's try something. Is it money you want? I can get you a great deal of money if that's what you need."

The elf stared back, unimpressed.

"No," said Duncan, with a small nod of understanding. "I can see that you're not motivated by money. Let's think harder. I gathered by the tone of the gentlemen over there that there's been some level of violence this evening?"

Elf eyes flicked to Newton and Dave for an instant. The beardy Bacraut was smirking.

"Yes!" said Duncan. "I see I have struck a chord. Interesting. I'm working hard here, trying to put myself in your shoes. I hope you appreciate the effort I'm putting in."

"Psst," said Dave.

"What?" said Newton, who was trying to keep one ear on the meeting, keep one eye on his own personal safety and keep his brain from squirming out of his ears in anxiety over where his mum was right now.

Dave nodded at the table. The letter had worked its way from the table, from one uncaring elf hand to the next. It was now just in front of them, scuffed and torn around the edge.

It was hand-written, which was a rarity these days. Only grandmas sending birthday money wrote letters anymore. Furthermore, it looked like it had been written by a grandma who'd learned to write from medieval monks. The lettering was all long and scratchy and surprisingly familiar. Yes: caught in a fold was one of the Christmas cracker jokes, written in the same hand.

Duncan had seen the joke and at some point realised that it was the same writing. What had that meant to him? Did he know about the elves?

"Why did they invite him here?" Newton whispered.

"What would you do if an aggressive property developer wants to turn part of your elfy town into a housing estate? What if he's never going to take no for an answer?"

Newton thought about it. He knew what he would do (probably a strongly worded yet polite e-mail). But elves? "They just wanted to get him here," he said.

"Mmmm," nodded Dave. "Up close."

"So," said Duncan to his audience, "it's the violence that excites, is it?"

Elves grinned.

"I totally understand. Rode with the Goathland hunt a couple of times myself. Fine tradition. Nothing like tearing across the countryside in pursuit of quarry, man and beast."

Bacraut jiggled up and down, whether in excitement or a mime of horse-riding, Newton couldn't tell. He suddenly thought of the stables back at the farm, of Lily and, yes, Yolanda too and realised there was a strong possibility he would never see them again.

He tapped Dave with his hand. "We need to escape."

"Mmm-hmm," agreed Dave but seemed to have no idea how they were going to do it.

"So, a spot of hunting is the order of the day," said Duncan. "You are talking to the right chap! I know all the local hunts. Do business with most of the huntmasters. Stirling fellows. Real animal lovers. I can set you up, I promise, and Duncan Catheter's word is his bond. Now, what do you fancy, eh? Fox, is it?"

Bacraut shook his head slowly.

"Partridge? Grouse? A bit of old bang-bang on the Glorious Twelfth?"

Bacraut raised his knife. A couple of elves giggled. Duncan was undeterred.

"I can – on the hush hush – get in touch with some fellows who do a spot of hare coursing. No, I know what you're thinking, but the hare enjoys it! Really does! No? Then badger baiting? I think I know a man in Pickering who knows a man who knows a man."

Bacraut was on his feet now, standing at the centre of the table, blade held tightly.

Duncan's face twitched in a confused nervousness. "Unless, of course," he said hoarsely, "it's ... people you like to hunt?"

Bacraut nodded.

"Penny drops," muttered Dave.

Duncan licked his lips. His eyes darted to and fro. Newton could almost see the cogs whirring in his brain.

"Humans. Humans," Duncan muttered. He cleared his throat. "And what would you do with those humans when you have them?"

Bacraut performed a rapid and very expressive mime in which he pretended to slit open his belly and poured out handful after handful of guts. This delighted his companions. More than one reached over to grab the imaginary innards and shove them into their mouths.

"My word, yes," said Duncan. "And how many humans would you like?"

Bacraut raised his arms up and round, a rainbow to encompass the whole world.

"All of them?"

Bacraut shrugged.

"Well, it's nice to have a goal," said Duncan. "Now, this is where the art of negotiation and compromise comes in. You want people. I want houses. You can't have all the people. No, I'm sorry, you can't. And, similarly, I can't build all the houses I want. It's just the way of the world. So, I say to you, yes, I can probably get a number of people for you – er, ten? – and you say, 'Thank you, Mr Catheter, that's lovely. We'll sign over our land to you now.'"

"Ten?" growled Bacraut.

"Yes. Er." Duncan struggled to focus on his own hands and held up ten fingers. "Ten. I know where the rough sleepers can be found in Scarborough and York."

"*Vilgé* ten-ty," said Bacraut and every elf at the table held up a hand with tiny wiggling fingers.

"Tenty?" Duncan blew out hard. "That's a tall order. Although I do know a care home or two with a few residents who are just not value for money. You okay with, um, older specimens?"

The elves looked at him blankly.

"Very good then," said the businessman. "Tenty it is. Now, I will go and make the arrangements and we'll draw up plans of which portions of Alvestowe I can—" As he stood to leave, the elves pressed in closer, weapons raised.

Duncan held out his hands. "I do need to leave. I can't just magic them here."

"Ten-ty," snarled Bacraut.

"Yes! Yes. Tenty it is, but I don't have them on me."

"Ten-ty!"

Duncan huffed, irritated. "Do I have them in my pocket, eh?"

The elves actually leaned forward to see if he did have tenty hidden people in his pocket. Dave tapped Newton and flicked his hand surreptitiously towards the door. All the elves were close to Duncan now, none looking back. Newton shuffled quietly towards the exit and Dave followed.

"I haven't got them on me," protested Duncan. "You'd be fools to think I did."

Elves hissed angrily.

"If we're taking about humans I have on me then it's a different ball game, my friends. You're talking about much smaller numbers and a much higher price per unit. Now, if I were you, and the sight of human blood excited me, I think I would value the slaughter of children above adults. For example, we have fine a specimen over there." He pointed at Newton, who was within a foot of the door. Newton froze.

"There are two plump young individuals in this very building."

"What the hell—?" hissed Dave.

Bacraut grinned gleefully.

"I'd say I've hit upon a real point of interest there," said Duncan. "Now my colleagues are likely to have some issues that we need to work through, but I think I can safely say that we can deal with those. The offer that I'm going to put on the table is that we give you the two children in return for the safe passage of the adults. How does that sound?"

The elf continued to smile, but blew a small raspberry and then laughed.

"Not enough?" Duncan asked. "Well, that is easily remedied. Two children, one adult. The mother or the father. Your choice which."

The elf hooted with laughter, rubbing its belly with mirth.

"You rat," spat Dave.

"I'd go for the father trying to sneak out right now," said Duncan, his expression cold and desperate.

"Ten-ty," insisted Bacraut.

"Oh, they're just a down payment. What do you say, squire?"

Bacraut advanced on Duncan, a knife in each hand and its face now a solid mask of murderous intent.

"No? Then how about two children *and* all of the other adults in the house? If you just let me go safely out then you take the rest. How does that sound?"

The offer clearly didn't appeal to Bacraut. He twirled his blades, forcing Duncan back.

"Wait! Let's not be hasty, I can't help thinking that there's an aspect we haven't explored. Shall we sit back down and try to find some common ground?" He backed against the window as the elf moved forward.

"Can't we help him?" whispered Newton.

"You want to help *him*?" Dave whispered back.

Duncan grabbed a chair and whirled around, smashing it into the wide window. As soon as the glass shattered, he climbed onto the windowsill with a loud grunt of effort.

"Honestly," he said indignantly. "Do you have no idea how business meetings are conducted? I'm hoping we might work a little harder at our communication skills, but I'm going to climb down the fire escape to the ground for the moment so that we can all cool off!" He turned round. "Oh. Is the fire escape on the other side?"

The elf lunged at him and Duncan toppled out of the window with a prolonged scream. There was an extravagant smashing sound accompanied by more screaming. Elves poured out of the window after him.

\*\*\*

# 41

Guin had once broken a vase at home, and was surprised by the amount of broken glass that resulted, and how far it travelled. It seemed as though they were finding pieces for months afterwards, even though she and her father had carefully cleaned it all up. She now knew that a glass roof made a much, much bigger mess when a human body fell through. It bounced off a counter in a shower of glass and snow and sprawled onto the floor.

She recognised the odious businessman who had alternately ignored and insulted her at dinner, although he wasn't quite the same cocky, strutting businessman after he'd come through the roof.

"Is he dead?" she said.

Esther stared wordlessly, then looked up at the shattered skylights. Guin wished her dad was here, at least he would have known.

The question was answered when Duncan lurched to his feet with an incoherent grunt. His face was fifty-fifty glass and blood. He seemed to have left some of it behind in a pile of gore on the floor. She would remember that phrase for Newton. Gore on the Floor. She recognised panic bubbling up in her mind and reached for Wiry Harrison.

"Oh, no." Esther was looking up. In the darkness above, beyond the smashed skylight, elves were climbing rapidly down the exterior of the hotel.

Duncan Catheter staggered forward. He seemed incapable of walking, or seeing where he was going as his face was a pulped mess. Guin wondered if she should help him. She hadn't read anything in *Little Folk in European Folklore* about elf-related injuries being catching, like zombies or vampires, but it might be wise to take care.

Duncan lurched forwards, his arms banging into things, and the bloodied mess of his hands flapping uselessly. He howled with something like pain and fear and anger all jumbled up. He fell against the juicer with the elf inside and pressed what must have been his one good eye to the glass.

He whirled – blood sprayed out in an arc across the counter and Guin would have vomited if Wiry Harrison hadn't been there to comfort her.

"You!" he bellowed, spraying spittle, blood and little fragments of things that might have been glass or teeth. He was addressing the elves who had dropped like mini-SAS soldiers onto the kitchen table. "Another – *ssffffp!*—" He spat out a gobbet of loose flesh from his mouth – "—Another step and your friend is gonna be a smoothie."

The elves peered round to look at their trapped companion in the orange juicer. The trapped elf made worried noises and pleading eyes.

"Smoothie," said the lead elf, coming at Duncan.

The injured man thumped the switch on the machine.

A high-pitched motor started up, stuttered, whirred again. The lights flickered in the kitchen, strobing across the room and highlighting the colour change in the transparent hopper. The contents had gone entirely red, but significant chunks of white bone hopped within the soupy mess, making the machine judder violently. Each time the motor paused, the lights flickered again.

"Don't look!" called Esther. Guin thought it was perhaps a little late for that.

***

# 42

Several elves ran to the door, ignoring Dave and Newton in their urgency to get to wherever Duncan had fallen. Suddenly the room was empty but for the two stunned humans.

Dave turned to Newton. "We need to get out of here."

"Ya reckon?"

The lights flickered both in the room and on the landing outside. As Newton looked up, Dave realised he had been wrong. They weren't alone in the room.

The white-bearded Bacraut leapt up from his position under the table and latched onto Newton's leg. Newton swung round, yelling, grabbed the little git and hurled the elf away.

The elf tumbled, rolled and came up facing the wrong way. Dave had a free run at the lone elf and he booted it as hard as he could. His foot connected with such a satisfyingly powerful kick that Dave thought he'd re-join his five-a-side team if he made it out of this nightmare place. The elf connected with the open door and slid bonelessly to the floor. Dave opened the trouser press, inserted the elf and stood on it so that he could clamp it shut. The elf made small grunts which diminished after a few moments into a final-sounding sigh. Dave propped it upright and wondered if the elf would be able to revive itself and escape. He picked up the plug and pushed it into a nearby socket to be sure.

"I think you made an impression on him," said Newton and pulled the little elf's hat down to hide its face.

***

# 43

Duncan roared as the juicer gave up its fight against hard-to-blend elf bits. The motor gave a loud electric bang and died. The lights went out completely for a long moment and then came back to life, accompanied by a dangerous-sounding fizzing noise. Appliances across the kitchen sparked.

Duncan whirled on the elves, near blind and deranged. "Who's next?" he screamed. "I took on the Bridlington chamber of commerce and won, you little bastards. You think I'm frightened of some bloody pixies? Eh?!"

Guin knew the power of words. When girls in the playground banished her from their circles with harsh language, it hurt deep. She and Tinfoil Tavistock had had deep conversations about how she felt when the other students at quadruped school called her a "Spaccy alpaca". Guin reckoned the elves didn't take kindly to the use of the *p* word at all.

As the first one leapt at Duncan he grabbed at the lined up Molotov cocktails on the counter, swept one up and smashed it powerfully into the side of the elf's head, dashing it to the ground. Another elf, another bottle. A third. A fourth. In the strobing light of fusing electrics, they fought, man and elves, like the weirdest and most violent silent comedy ever.

Guin wanted to angrily point out that she and Esther had spent ages making those cocktails.

"You're meant to light them!" Esther shouted.

Duncan grunted and fumbled with the hob. He twisted knobs to turn on the gas but couldn't see how to ignite them through his bloodied vision. He grabbed up a big bottle of clear spirits and tried to feel around in his pocket, presumably for a lighter (but who carried a lighter in their dressing gown pocket? Guin didn't know).

"Come on – *pfff!* – come on!" he spat. "Try take me down! Bridlington tried and look what happened to them!"

He tossed the barricade against the door aside with pain-fuelled adrenalin and backed out of the swing doors. Spirit-soaked elves picked themselves up and chased after him.

***

# 44

Esther stared at the mess in the kitchen. The spilt drink, the smashed glass, the trail of blood Duncan Catheter had left in his whirlwind passage through the room.

"I don't know about you," said Esther, picking up the two remaining alcohol bombs, "but I am fed up of waiting around for someone to kill us. I say it's time to go on the offensive."

"What about understanding their point of view?" asked Guin. "Like the orangutans."

"You've tried to tell me these things are evil," said Esther, "but I don't usually see the world in that way." She looked at the two bottles. She kept the brandy and passed the certainly non-flammable Malibu rum bottle to Guin. "But I know I hate these bloody things."

"Good," said Guin.

There came the sounds of distant shouts and struggles. Esther picked up a disposable lighter from beside the oven. "With me," she said and led the way.

They ran, crouching low. Esther wondered if they ought to be moving alternately, shouting "Clear!" at every doorway. There was a crashing further off.

"Heppe! Now!" came a plaintive cry from the guest lounge.

Esther gestured to the side of the door. Guin flattened herself against the wall, in the classic buddy cop pose, while Esther squared up to the doorway, Molotov cocktail at the ready, lighter ready to strike.

The room was empty. The only light came from the fairy lights on the Christmas tree wedged between two sofas. They, like every other light in the place, were flickering. Something just out of sight sparked dangerously.

"Heppe! Now!" called the parrot from his cage.

"Damn," said Esther, passing her brandy bottle to Guin. She tried to unhook the cage from its stand but it was far too heavy.

"Gerramovon yum idjit!"

"I'm trying!" yelled Esther.

"Esther!" warned Guin.

Esther turned. Duncan Catheter came stumbling through the door, locking in a deadly embrace with two elves. The three of them were slick with blood and alcohol, struggling to get a purchase on each other.

Duncan tore off one that had its teeth clamped onto his throat. It came away with more of his neck than was healthy.

"*Gn-argh!*" yelled Duncan and hurled it away. The vodka-soaked elf arced into the Christmas tree; both crashed to the floor. There was the sound of dozens of popping baubles, followed by a fiery *whump*. Electrical fire plus accelerant plus wood. Sap filled pine needles exploded like a million tiny firecrackers.

Esther raised her arm protectively against the blooming fireball.

"*Sddn hlll!*" squawked King Leopold of Belgium.

Duncan staggered back. The elf on his chest took the opportunity to leap higher and bury its bone handled knife up the hilt in Duncan's eye.

"Is that all you've got, Bridlington?" Duncan mumbled and dropped, dead before he hit the ground.

"Sodding hell," said Esther.

She yanked open the bird cage door. The huge fat parrot barrelled out, dipped momentarily and flew straight out the door. Esther was only a second behind it. The elf swung at her as she passed but she hurdled over it and out the door, slamming it shut behind her.

"Can you smell gas?" said Guin.

***

# 45

As he and Dave ran downstairs, Newton snatched up the most solid looking elf cross from the mess of sheets and stuffed cat remnants. There were shouts and thumps from downstairs and a dull background roar that might have been the snowstorm outside. Newton suspected it wasn't.

A shape flew up into their faces. Dave gave a startled yelp.

"Shttn lil bfftrds!" squawked King Leopold, banking at the top of the stairs and turning.

Dave put a hand to his chest and gave the bird an evil glare.

"Did I mention it was a very rude parrot?" said Newton.

"I can smell smoke," said Dave. "We need to get out."

"Bout brurrytime. Pairra gommin iddits."

At the bottom of the stairs, Newton made immediately for the front door.

"What do you think you are doing?" came a strident voice.

Mrs Scruples stood by the little reception desk. She was wearing something like a lightweight turquoise coat made of quilted polyester. A flannel nightdress peeked out at the hem.

"Mrs Scruples!" gasped Newton. "We've got to get out of here! You won't believe it but there's elves in the house!"

She strode forward. "I heard a good deal of noise for the middle of the night. Why are you up and causing so much disruption?" She took in the mess and wreckage littering stairs and hallway. "Breakages must be paid for."

"But Christmas elves!" said Newton. "Real ones! And—" He stopped, seeing the shotgun in the old woman's hand.

"I think Mrs Scruples knows all about Christmas elves," said Dave softly.

She raised the shotgun. "Nobody is leaving unless I say so."

She called over her shoulder. "Wee folks! Come here!"

"Wee folks?" said Newton, terrified and incredulous. "Why are you trying to make them sound cute? They kill people. Mr

Catheter. He…" He shook his head. "But wee folks? Really? Shall we get the china cups out and make a little tea party for them?"

Newton caught Dave's gaze and the little shushing motion that he was making.

"But they're murderers," said Newton.

"I've seen no evidence of that," said Mrs Scruples. "I see plenty of violence perpetrated by the two of you, mind. Right here under my roof *and* staining my carpet to boot."

"Where's Mr Scruples?" asked Dave. It was an odd question and Newton couldn't quite see the relevance.

Mrs Scruples' head jerked. Her face twitched unhappily. "He's still around. I've seen him in the distance a couple of times."

"Have you? Really?"

"I'd know his waistcoats anywhere. He was always good with his hands, was Mr Scruples. He's valuable to them. That's why they want to keep hold of him."

"They?" said Newton and then understood.

"And you?" said Dave. "Is your role to lure us in? Is that why you're 'valuable' to them?"

Newton wasn't sure why Dave was so keen to chat when there was some serious escaping to be done. Then he realised Dave was trying to keep Mrs Scruples talking because he'd spotted Newton's mum, dirty and bedraggled, creeping up behind the woman.

"Mum!" It came out in a blurt of shock and delight.

"Mum?" said Mrs Scruples.

Esther grasped the massive pottery horse from the reception desk and smashed it over Mrs Scruple's head. The woman flopped lifelessly to the floor.

"Oh, poor horsey," said Newton.

Guin ran forward to her dad. "We put an elf in a blender!"

"Um, trouser press," Dave replied.

Esther planted a smooshy kiss on Newton's forehead. "We need to get out of here." She pulled open the inner door, squeezed past the monstrous vacuum cleaner in the porch and battled futilely with the outer door. "Locked!"

Keys," said Dave, whirling to look at Mrs Scruples.

"Uh-oh," said Newton quietly. A small band of elves was advancing towards them down the hallway. Each carried a weapon. One looked as though it had a carving set, a matching fork and knife with horn handles. Another had something like a small garden tool with a clawed end. Another held a hammer. They each had a face that was scrunched up with determined malice, expressions deepened by the fact they had been variously thumped, cut, burned or trampled.

"Yrrr scrrwwed!" screeched King Leopold, flapping around the ceiling.

"I've got this," said Newton, grabbing the hose of the vacuum cleaner. It was already plugged in. As he brought it to bear, the wheeled body trundled behind him, like a baby Dalek. He stabbed the switch; nothing happened.

"The body needs to be shut," said Esther and leaned heavily on the wobbly casing. She had to sit on top to force it shut.

The vacuum cleaner's head bucked in Newton's hands. He thrust the pipe at the nearest elf. It disappeared up the fat pipe and into the body of the vacuum cleaner with a series of thumps. Newton swept it round and bagged another.

***

# 46

Dave had run forward and put his fingertips to Mrs Scruples' neck. "She's still alive," he said.

"Yeah?" said Esther. "Try focusing on the lives of the four people who aren't in league with evil elves!"

It was perhaps a little callous but Dave took the hint. He went through the pockets of her housecoat.

"Watch out! Elf on the shelf!" yelled Guin.

"On it," said Newton.

An elf dropped down with a lusty war cry. Newton sucked it up the pipe with a snarl of fury.

"Hey, suckers!" called Newton. He hoovered up the last two elves. The last one got caught up somewhere in the hose and the motor hesitated. A lump in the hose wriggled. Esther gave it a sharp kick and it vanished with a hollow *thwump!*.

"Here!" said Dave as he pulled out a key ring, triumphant.

He tossed it to Esther and then hooked a hand under Mrs Scruples' armpits and hauled her along the hallway.

"What are you doing?" said Esther.

"I am not leaving her in a burning building."

"I can definitely smell gas now," said Guin. "Did that man leave the hob on in the kitchen?"

Newton took the keys from Esther and hurriedly unlocked the outer front door.

"Out. Now!" said Dave.

King Leopold was first out, flapping into the night sky with a cry of "Bggrit! S'frrrzzing!"

Newton and Guin followed. Esther took hold of the evil old lady's legs and helped her far too public-spirited man carry her out into the snow. They laid her down in the centre of the road.

"I should go back for that shotgun," said Esther.

"Why?" said Dave.

"What if there's more of them?"

"You do know that people who carry guns are more likely to be shot than people who don't carry guns."

"It's true," said Guin.

"Behyoo," squawked the parrot.

"I don't think those statistics include people who've had to fight off bloody Christmas elves," said Esther.

"Be-HY-oo!" said the parrot, loudly.

"What did it say?" said Newton.

"I think it was saying, 'Behind y—'" Esther looked back. Through the open doorway she saw a knife with a horn handle sliding through the gap between the body and lid of the vacuum cleaner. It flipped the catch aside and the top burst open. Dusty elves flopped out in varying states of alertness. The elf with the horn-handled knife was first to recover: it turned towards them. His companions seemed disorientated: they reeled and fell over as they emerged from the vacuum.

"Molotov cocktails," said Esther. Guin reacted fastest. She passed over one of the bottles as Esther fumbled for the lighter in her pocket. She flicked it once, twice and managed to set light to the torn-up tea towel with a shaking hand.

"Burn you pixie scumbags!" she howled and threw the bottle. It smashed into the hoover, but the spirits failed to ignite.

"Was that Malibu?" said Dave.

"Shut up."

The knife-wielding elf, soaked, made a show of licking its finger in a mocking display. Esther lit the remaining bottle's cloth and lobbed it at them.

It smashed with a satisfying and very final sound against the body of the hoover, but the flame did not take hold. Except one of the elves stamped its boots, which were definitely burning. It was hardly an impressive conflagration.

The elf laughed, a high and cruel giggle.

"I should have gone back for that shotgun," said Esther.

The gas explosion blew the four standing humans off their feet, and the front door entirely off its hinges. Elves, caught in its path, were hurled out of the door. One flew through an upstairs window on the opposite side of the street. The vacuum cleaner tumbled into the road. It would have crushed someone if it had landed on them.

Esther sat up and stretched her jaw, trying to shake off the high-pitched whine in her deafened ears. Shattered glass was everywhere. She found Newton and Guin laid out in the drifting snow, essentially unharmed but clearly shocked. As she pulled them up, Dave was beside her, helping. They scrabbled across to the far side of the road and huddled together.

"Are you all right?" Esther asked Newton, realising she couldn't hear her voice. He couldn't either. They all sat in dumbfounded silence and watched the house burn.

It was a few moments before any of them wanted to move. Esther looked at the others. Their faces all reflected the same exhausted shock as they crouched on the pavement.

Dave was the first to stagger to his feet. Esther could hear some of his words, which was excellent because she wasn't ready to be deaf, although it was good to be reminded what a blessing it really was to have all of her senses.

"We need to get the neighbours out, in case it spreads!" she was sure Dave was saying.

"Oh, God, yes!" Esther had been looking forward to putting this very much behind her, rather than continuing the nightmare, but she couldn't be selfish. Dave was right. "We'll do that and then get out of this place."

"Why didn't the neighbours hear all the screaming?" wondered Newton, his voice clearer. "Or notice the massive fire? Or the gas explosion that blew off the front of the house?"

He had a point.

There was a groaning sound from nearby. Mrs Scruples was lying on the pavement, her body twisted and her clothes shredded.

"Oh goodness me. Dave, we must help her!"

Dave started to run checks on Mrs Scruples' vital signs.

"There's a broken bench over there," said Guin, pointing at a high backed wooden seat. "That top part would work for carrying her, like a stretcher."

Esther dragged the broken furniture over. It must have been thrown out of the house by the gas explosion. "It's like an old pew. Look at the carving on it, beautiful piece."

"Careful lifting her onto it," said Dave, arranging them all around Mrs Scruples. "All together on my count. One, two, *three*."

He stamped out some scraps of smouldering curtain and used them to cover her against the falling snow and secure her onto the board. "Right, the adults will drag her along using the top corners, as if it's a sled."

"But the carvings will get scratched—" said Esther before stopping herself. "—Which is fine, obviously, given the circumstances."

***

# 47

Newton knocked on several nearby doors, but there was no response from any of them. An eerie stillness filled the town, compound by the still falling snow and his receding deafness. It felt like mufflers had been placed over the world, that they were now the only people in it.

"Which way should we go?" his mum asked, picking up her corner of Mrs Scruples' stretcher.

Dave looked across the marketplace, towards the hill which led down to the river and where they'd left the car. "The car is unusable."

"Is there another way out of town?" Newton asked.

Dave shook his head. "I don't know."

They walked slowly, the adults dragging the stretcher. The snow was slippery underfoot, yet somehow didn't make it any easier to drag the heavy board.

"It's really cold," said Guin, hugging herself.

"It's snow joke," said Newton, deadpan. "This weather, I mean."

Guin fixed Newton with a stare designed to shut him up, but he took it as encouragement. "I think it's settling. If you catch my drift," he said.

Guin sighed theatrically. "It's nice you're trying to make us all laugh, Newton—" she began.

She didn't even have a chance to reach the inevitable *but* before he responded with "I just want everyone to chill out." He grinned broadly. "Apart from Mrs Scruples, that is. She's out cold already."

"Poor taste, Newton," said his mum.

"Let's just keep walking," said Dave in a determinedly upbeat voice. "We'll get somewhere eventually, or get a phone signal at least."

It was hard going for the adults, even downhill. Newton wondered if they could lay Mrs Scruples flat, give her a hefty shove down the hill, and meet her at the bottom. But it was probably not a very charitable thought.

"What if there are more of them?" said Guin. "Elves. I mean, what if we didn't get them all?"

"You know, this whole thing might have escalated in our minds," Dave said, his words coming slowly, as if he was trying to shape his thoughts as he went. "I mean, is it possible we've just got ourselves a bit freaked out after a rough evening and not sleeping properly and everything?"

"Dad, you were there!"

"I know I was there."

"They're definitely real."

"Guin's right," said Esther carefully. "We can't wish them away. No matter how appalling they were and how far away from our normal lives this whole thing has been. There are more things in heaven and Earth than are dreamt of in your philosophy."

"Quoting Shakespeare does not make things true," said Dave.

"Well, I'm just glad we've seen the last of them."

"There's one over there," said Newton.

They all looked back to where he pointed. A small figure was just visible up an alley. It looked as though it was hard at work scooping something out of an indistinct shape on the ground. Faint gloopy noises reached them as they watched.

The elf looked up. The family instinctively held still against the shadows. The elf straightened and moved towards them, its hands stained with something that made them black in the dark. Esther judged it hadn't seen them.

"Come on, go. Go!" she said, sotto voce. They moved much more quickly. Newton didn't even glance back to see if the elf was following.

"Someone's coming," said Guin.

Newton looked ahead. "It's a person. An actual person."

"Please let it be someone with a working phone or a car," said Dave.

It was a man. He wobbled between the closed market stalls as though drunk.

They were in the thick of the market. At some time during the night it had lost its festive jollity and become cluttered and threatening. As if every rustic stall front concealed something dreadful. Newton saw the man wore a multi-coloured jacket and lime green trousers that put him in mind of a children's entertainer. It was unlikely he was out entertaining children at whatever time of the night it was now.

"He doesn't look right," said Guin.

"We shouldn't judge people," said Esther. "We have no idea what personal difficulties he might have..."

The man was close enough for them to see him clearly. Newton really didn't like the look of him. His face hung grey and slack; the face of a dead man. One who still walked – with an awkward gait.

"Hi there," said Dave and waved, almost dropping his corner of the stretcher in the process.

The man didn't respond.

Newton saw the man's jacket ripple and bulge. "His stomach..." Newton began to say and then a button came undone and a tiny head popped out, laughing.

"No..." Dave moaned.

"When I followed Elsa Frinton's footprints," said Guin, her voice low and distant, like she was recounting a dream, "I saw something on the wall. I thought it was a pink glove, like a human hand with no bones or meat inside it."

Elves burst forth from the man's stomach, leaping down onto the ground. As they left his body it collapsed, hollow.

"Back up, back up!" gasped Esther.

They started to drag the stretcher back the way they'd come. The elves were content to watch them with silent menace.

"And the stallholders at the market," said Guin. "They all moved oddly, didn't they? Like they were too tired and floppy to move properly. I guess a human suit is hard to steer."

The board bumped over hidden obstacles beneath the snow. Mrs Scruples groaned loudly.

"She's not dead. That's a positive," said Dave.

"Why am I tied down?" mumbled the old woman.

"There was an explosion," Newton told her helpfully. "Your house is no longer safe."

Mrs Scruples feebly tugged at the bonds tying her to the makeshift stretcher. "Kidnap!" she exclaimed, a loud bird-like squawk.

"Nobody's kidnapping you, Mrs Scruples," said Newton in his gentlest 'would anyone like a cup of tea' voice. "We're just trying to get you to safety. Just relax for now."

Mrs Scruples did not relax. "Let me go!" she shouted as she thrashed in place. "You've got no right to do this."

"Shush, everything will be fine," Newton urged her.

"Help me!"

"We are helping."

"Help me, little folk!"

The elves by the hollowed out human suit took this as their cue and began to follow.

"They're coming for us," said Esther, like there was any doubt.

"Here I am," called Mrs Scruples. "I told you I'd get them for you."

In silent agreement Dave and Esther let the stretcher drop. "We should put some distance between ourselves and these things," said Dave.

"Don't call them things," said Esther. "Could be considered racist."

Mrs Scruples dragged off the singed curtain remnants and staggered upright.

"You'd be better off if you stayed with us you know," Dave told her.

The look she shot back suggested she didn't agree.

The back of Newton's foot connected with something. It was a weight which held down a corner of tarpaulin covering one of the stalls. He picked it up, held it like a bowling ball, took aim, and lobbed it at the elves. Two of them were crushed into the deep snow as it rolled over them. The remaining elves hissed and began to run at them.

The fabric awning directly above Dave was heavily laden with snow. He punched the awning from below and sent a considerable pile of snow onto the nearest elves. They were instantly buried. "And go!" he yelled.

They ran.

"I'm coming, little ones!" yelled Mrs Scruples in the night. "You can rely on me!"

\*\*\*

# 48

Guin thought she heard the elves laughing. They were enjoying the chase. She glanced back: a lone elf was just a few paces behind.

They passed a chestnut stall; its brazier still radiated heat. Guin kicked it over. Hot pieces of charcoal rolled down the street, throwing off sparks. The elf stumbled and skipped over them, but continued its chase.

"This way!" Esther shouted. They twisted through the market and ducked down a side road while the elves were unsighted.

Mrs Scruples was still out there somewhere, calling to her 'little people'.

"Mad as a box of frogs," muttered Dave.

"Is that a clinical term?" asked Esther, nudging him in the ribs.

It was easier to move now they were out of the market and its clutter, but they were also very exposed. There was movement from some of the houses overlooking the street. Without looking too closely, Guin had the strong impression that elves were more or less everywhere. The ones chasing them were just a small sample of a whole townful of elves.

They were at the edge of the town square and there wasn't much more of the town beyond it. A steep hill rose up in front of them, its side thick with trees. The drystone wall and the church stood at the end of the road, but beyond that they'd be out in open countryside.

Guin didn't fancy their chances out in the woods, being pursued by a horde of murderous elves.

"Church?" suggested Dave.

"Really?" said Esther.

"Just as a place to lay low."

They moved together, up the road. Near the rear yard of a house, they skirted round a parked tractor. Guin stared at its convoluted shadows and recesses fearfully. A hundred elves could have hidden beneath it.

"Maybe there's keys in the cab," suggested Newton.

"Not enough room for us all," said Dave.

Guin knew how slowly tractors went. If they were to make any kind of a getaway, there was no point in choosing something that could be overtaken by an elf who wasn't even trying.

They crept quietly into the churchyard, the tree and snow covered slopes towered over the grey building. Esther got to the church first and tried the latch. It opened. They all piled inside and shut the door firmly behind them.

"I'll see if I can lock it," said Dave. "Try and find some lights."

Moments later the interior of the church was lit up. It appeared to be free of elves. Dave found a heavy iron key and locked the door. They got their breath back, sighing heavily with relief.

"Nice church," said Esther. "It's simple and functional. Nothing fancy or excessive."

"Suddenly an expert on churches, are we, mum?" said Newton.

"No elves," she added. "I especially like the fact there are no elves in here."

"Maybe the elves can't cross the threshold of a church," said Newton. "We should get some holy water and some crucifixes to defend ourselves."

Guin rolled her eyes. "Seriously? The elf crosses are the things that work against the elves. Holy water won't be any use at all."

"Can't hurt to try," said Newton, lifting the wooden lid on the font and dipping a finger into the dark interior. As he shook the water off he turned and pointed. "Stairs." A doorway led to a spiral stone staircase. "They'll lead to the bell tower. Maybe we could go up—"

"And ring the bells and see if someone comes to help us!" said his mum enthusiastically.

"Er, that," said Newton kindly. "Or I was just going to see if I could get a better phone signal high up."

"Yeah, yeah. That too," agreed Esther.

"Go with him," Dave told Guin.

"Why?"

"Safety in height. You know: like climbing trees to get away from bears."

"Bears can climb trees, dad. That's the one thing you shouldn't do when attacked by one."

"Fine," he said irritably. "Sharks then."

Guin could have pointed out how stupid that was too but simply went.

She ran up the stairs behind Newton. She didn't run far: physical exercise was not her friend. She was the pale and sickly looking girl in her class at school, a stereotype she was happy to live up to. After one circuit of the stairs, she resorted to walking. A dozen spirals later she reached a small square room with bell ropes hanging from holes in the ceiling. Newton flitted between the two small leaded windows, waving his phone about.

"Any luck?" asked Guin.

Newton gave her a terse, still look. "Maybe we will have to resort to fighting them off with holy water and crosses." He caught her expression. "We don't know those things aren't related to vampires or demons or something. They're ugly like demons, I mean those carvings on some of the pews downstairs even look a bit like them."

Guin pulled out the *Little Folk in European Folklore* book and sat with it, cross-legged on the floor, over a heating grill that was not entirely cold. There was a quote from Dr Epiphany Alexander on the subject of carvings that Newton needed to hear. Before she could locate it there was a loud braying din. Downstairs, the organ was being played, but not by anyone with training. Chilling, discordant notes echoed around the church.

\*\*\*

# 49

More than anything Dave wanted to protect his loved ones. The look of alarm on Esther's face as the church organ struck up was almost more than he could bear. He'd tried to deal with the situation in the best way he knew how: keep his head and deliver solutions to problems. But this was so far away from anything he'd ever experienced he was running out of ideas. They were trapped in an unfamiliar town, surrounded by an enemy that was not only ridiculously numerous, but also completely impossible for his brain to believe in.

"This is a classic villain scare tactic," he said, attempting to be reassuring. "Creepy organ music. I mean, doesn't it remind you of every horror film you ever saw?"

Esther wrinkled her nose. "Not sure about that. They normally at least do chords, don't they? That sounds like someone running up and down the keyboard."

Dave whirled. The church was essentially one huge open room. His original idea that they could lay low and get behind some cover seemed quite ridiculous now. "The kids!"

"We defend the stairs," said Esther. "Grab weapons."

"What?"

"When they show themselves we need to be ready to take them on."

Dave stepped up to the altar and grabbed a pair of candlesticks. Their weight felt good in his hands. Esther lifted a brass heating duct grille. It looked too heavy for her to carry, but that probably meant it had excellent elf-squashing potential.

Dave looked all around, wondering which direction the elves' attack would come from. The tuneless organ honking continued, but there was another sound. Almost like voices singing in a choir: a choir that tuned up by scratching their fingernails down a blackboard. Discordant, wordless and completely without a tune. The closest thing Dave could bring to mind was the noise he made as a child when working hard to irritate his family. It was optimistically known as 'the bagpipes', made by holding his nose, make a droning sound and making small rapid karate chops against his throat.

He spotted them, beyond the altar. Had they been in the choir stalls all along? They began climbing up and over the wooden seats, the grotesque carvings come to life.

Moments later the bells rang out. Even louder than the organ and almost as chaotic as the choir. Guin and Newton were giving it everything that they had, although they really didn't know what they were doing.

"Maybe someone will hear," said Esther optimistically.

Dave remembered bell ringers sometimes suffered serious injuries. If they forgot to let go of the rope, they could be whisked upwards at something like fifty miles an hour.

Elves came at them. Dave swung the candlesticks, one in each arm, and just for a moment he was Antonio Banderas wielding two pistols against Mexican drug peddlers with devastating style. There was a satisfying crunch and a lot of splatter as he made an elf sandwich with smeared elf filling.

"Consider that an exorcism," he said.

Esther had managed to pin one elf underneath her heavy iron grill. She jumped on it to get more momentum. Dave couldn't be sure from this distance, but it looked as though she'd created elf chips.

"Guin! Newton! Take care with those bells!" he called towards the bell tower.

Abruptly, he realised the bells had stopped. And so had the choir and organ.

"Guin! Newton!" Dave charged up the stairs. Esther close behind.

The bell-ringers' chamber was empty but for half a dozen swinging ropes.

"Guin! Newton! Where are you?" Dave turned in a circle as if he might have overlooked two children. "They must have just been in here."

One of the small leaded windows in the room was open, swinging in the wind and letting snow flutter in.

"It's not big enough," Esther murmured.

"If they were dragged through—" said Dave instantly wishing he hadn't.

There was scrap of fabric on the floor beneath the window, ripped from Newton's clothes.

Wordlessly they sprinted back downstairs, out the church's main door. There were no elves to be seen. They headed round to the outside of the bell tower and located the window. Footsteps in the snow indicated a great many elves had been here, and they had been dragging something with them. The prints headed up into the trees. It was wild and dark in there, the snow lying heavy and menacing.

"It looks steep and dangerous," said Dave.

Dave ran back into the church. Esther followed him. "I'm thinking a rope maybe, anything that could help us out in the woods."

"It's a church Dave, not *Go Outdoors*. What are we likely to find?"

Dave trotted to the base of the bell tower, looking around to see if there was any spare rope. A large box in the corner looked like a good prospect. He opened the lid and found a neatly coiled length of bell rope with a red, white and blue fluffy end.

"Good," he said lifting it onto his shoulder. "Candles! They could help us start a fire in a pinch."

Esther made a doubtful noise, but ran to the altar.

"I know it seems like overkill, but we run the risk of getting exposure out there in the open," Dave called.

"Yes! Yes!" Esther shouted back, knowing he was right but impatient to get on with it.

"Grab the cloth thing while you're there as well," he said.

Esther hesitated for a moment before she balled up the altar cloth with the candles.

They both sprinted for the door and went back round to the far side of the church.

"I'll tie the rope around both of our waists," said Dave. "We'll be able to move separately, but this snow is so deep I'm worried one of us might step into a gorge or off a cliff."

They started to trudge up the hill. The lights of Alvestowe disappeared as the concealing tree branches blocked out streetlights and the yellow light reflecting off the snow. Dave led the way, kicking the earth to find footholds among rocks and tree roots.

The going became tougher the deeper they went. The tree boughs sagged with snow and hung low to the ground. They had a choice of either crouching low to crawl through the pitch blackness beneath the trees, or stick to the more open areas where the snow came up past their knees and made walking extremely difficult.

"What about avalanches?" asked Esther.

Dave looked up at the snow. "It's a risk, but what choice do we have? The trees will help to break up any slippages, but let's hope that nothing happens to unsettle the snow."

He tried to recall what he knew of avalanches. Unfortunately, his only sources of information were James Bond movies and old disaster flicks.

"If there is an avalanche there's things you should do," he said.

"Like pee to see which way is up?" asked Esther.

"No, not that," said Dave. "If we get caught, we should try to swim uphill, face upwards."

"Swim?"

"Yeah, like our lives depended on it."

She held up a hand. Dave could barely see it in the darkness.

"What?"

"I heard elves laughing. Must mean we're on the right path."

He nodded, then thought she probably couldn't see him. "Yes, you're right."

"Let's go."

"Watch your rope," he said. "You're in danger of treading on the fluffy bit."

"Sally." She held up the furry striped end of the bell-rope. In the poor light, it wiggled like it had a life of its own. "This bit is called a sally."

"How do you know that?"

"I did a weekend heritage skills course," she said. He saw her shiver as the snow blew off the hill in savage gusts.

"I love you so much," he said and kissed her fiercely on the forehead.

"I know," she replied.

"And we'll get our kids back."

"I know."

From ahead, up the slope there was a sharp, loud noise.

"What was that?" Esther said.

"Sounded like a branch snapping."

"More like a Christmas cracker."

There followed a rapid report of dozens of bangs.

"A thousand Christmas crackers," added Esther.

There was another sound a more ominous one. A cracking sound which came from the earth itself. A rumble followed, felt as well as heard. It seemed to be growing louder.

"Oh no. Please, no." Dave turned to Esther.

"Just swim," said Esther. "I got it."

Dave felt out for a tree to shelter behind but his hands could find only wispy branches and snow.

Esther began to say something but her words were lost as the roar of the avalanche became the voice of an angry giant, punctuated by the crack of uprooted trees.

The ground bucked and tumbled. They were thrown off their feet. Dave could no longer see what Esther was doing. He couldn't see at all. When he should have been thinking clearly about what he needed to do to save their lives, he was consumed by two thoughts: that the furry bit of a bell-rope was called a sally, and he should have married Esther ages ago.

***

# 50

Guin shifted uncomfortably inside the sack the elves had stuffed her in. She constantly bounced against the sharp backs of the elves carrying her. She coughed, breathing in gulps of the foetid, stinking air inside the sack. She didn't like to imagine what this sack had been used for – rotten animal hides? Manky bales of hay? She decided, miserably, if she wasn't released soon, she'd either choke to death with a lung full of dust and dirt or contract plague.

She was dropped, suddenly and painfully, onto a hard surface. She cried out and heard a couple of elves tittering. "You'd better not be laughing at me!" she said. She held Wiry Harrison tightly in her hand and he gave her the courage to speak her mind.

Something gripped her through the sack material.

"Get off!" she shouted in alarm.

"It's me!" hissed Newton. "I'm in the sack next to you."

Guin considered this. "I repeat, 'Get off'. I did not sign up for this. Dad said—"

She was about to say he'd promised she wasn't going to share a bedroom with Newton, but thoughts of her dad cut her off. The last they'd seen of their parents was in the church, but they'd heard shouts on the hillside, and then there'd been the bangs and the rumble of an avalanche and...

"It's okay," said Newton, seemingly reading her mind. "I'm here."

She sniffed. "Is that meant to make me feel better?"

"I'll keep trying."

The floor beneath them suddenly shifted and rattled.

"Are we on a cart or something?" said Newton, a moment before Guin was going to suggest something similar.

"I don't know. Why haven't they killed us yet?"

"Let's be glad they haven't."

"But they will."

"But not yet," he said, like it mattered.

The cart – no, Guin thought it was a train: there was a click-clack noise below the creaks and rattles – carried them for several minutes. Guin occasionally felt the closeness of the forest trees or heard them scrape alongside. Then the surrounding noises changed. There was a closeness, a dull echo to things.

"I think we're inside somewhere," she whispered.

The train stopped abruptly and she nearly rolled on Wiry Harrison.

"We've stopped," said Newton unnecessarily.

Nothing happened for some minutes. Guin tried to find the opening in her sack but the elves had tied it tight. She'd probably have better luck trying to peel it apart at the seams.

Next to her, the gangly teenage boy was clucking and making weird sing-song noises. "That's it. That's it. That's right. I'm your friend."

"Are you trying to be comforting or creep me out?" asked Guin.

"I'm not talking to you," he said. "I mean, I am, but I was making noises to the— There's an animal here. I can feel its muzzle. Yes, there is. Yes, there is," he simpered to whatever he was talking to.

"Probably rats," said Guin miserably.

"It's a big animal," said Newton. "I don't think it's a horse."

Guin thought about what kind of animals elves would hang around with. "Maybe it's a reindeer," she suggested, not sure if she was being sarcastic.

"Are you a reindeer?" said Newton. "Yes, you are! Yes, you are, you lovely girl! Come snuffle me! Yes, you do, you – ow!"

"What?" said Guin.

"It bit me," said Newton indignantly.

Guin drew herself into a ball in the dark horrible confines. "Rats," she muttered. "It's rats and we're going to get the plague and die."

Newton jabbed her, possibly with an elbow. "You know this keeping our spirits up thing? It's a team effort, you know."

Footsteps approached. "*þáút ogrðu far í Gerd*," said an voice.

"What are they gibbering about?" muttered Newton.

Guin shushed him. "I'm trying to listen."

Several pairs of little hands were laid on them. Guin heard the *shing* of drawn blades before the sacks were slashed open with almost no regard for their contents. They were hauled out.

She coughed and sucked in fresh air – well, relatively fresh air. The air stank of damp and dirt with a pervasive underlying smell of something like petrol. They were in a cave of some sort. It was lit by row upon row of Christmas fairy lights, some old, some new, many of them broken, many of them fizzing and flickering like a fuse was about to blow. The lights were strung across ceilings, tacked to walls and wrapped round and round the dripping pipes that ran everywhere.

It took her a while to appreciate the scale of the place. Not just because of the gloom but because the size of it defied any rational expectations. The cave's sloping sides – she supposed it was big enough to be called a cavern really – rose up higher and higher until, at its conical top, there was a patch of dark grey which could possibly be the night sky of the world above. Along its sides and across its wide floor, elves in their dozens scurried and worked at distinct but disorganised work stations and storage areas.

She and Newton had been deposited alongside the train track. It was a ridiculously narrow and low train, little more than a children's theme park ride, with crude open top trucks behind a little pink locomotive that would have looked cute if it wasn't so wonky and rusted.

"Steam engines," said Newton. "Environmentally very unsound. Mum would have— Oh, my God!"

In a stall by the train line stood a reindeer – well, some sort of deer, or, some sort of hoofed ... some sort of quadruped. It definitely had four legs. Of that Guin could be confident. It had probably started out as a reindeer, or reindeer-shaped but...

It was a patchwork of fur and material that was not fur, wrapped around a body featuring a couple of very un-reindeery legs (one of which appeared to be elegantly carved from solid wood) and strange, very unhealthy looking lumps and bumps under the skin. Hide, cloth and patchwork flesh were held together with fine white stitching.

And the head... The skin was almost entirely bald. One of the antlers had been fixed in place with metal brackets and screws. The eyes were grey-green and shrunken, like ancient withered grapes. Its mouth was devoid of flesh, flat teeth champed and snapped against a jawline of exposed bone.

"It's a zomdeer," whispered Newton. "Frankenstein's reindeer," said Guin at the same time.

Whatever, it was a reindeer even Father Christmas would struggle to love.

***

# 51

The zomdeer or Frankenstein's reindeer or whatever it was, reared and bucked in its dirty little pen. Elves were unpacking bales, boxes and bags from the other trucks. Newton supposed they were meant to be important goods and materials for the elves but, for the most part, looked like the leanest pickings off a rubbish heap. Regardless, the elves' industry meant Newton and Guin were left standing alone for a while. Newton looked along the track they'd come down. There was a long high tunnel, but no suggestion of an exit apart from a quartet of elves standing on guard near the rear of the train, holding knives and larger billhook-type blades.

He looked down at Guin. Her pale little face looked even paler in this gloomy light. There was a concerned, distant look on her face. "Don't worry," he said, dropping into his default carer mode. "I'll look after you."

Guin looked at him. "What?"

"I said I'll look after you. Don't be afraid."

"I'm not afraid."

"Yeah," he said. "I'm just saying if—"

"Yes, but I'm not," she said with quiet certainty. "I was thinking, why do elves need reindeer?"

The patchwork reindeer thing rolled its shrivelled eyes and stamped its hoofs.

"Reindeer are cute," said Newton.

"That one isn't."

"We just haven't got to know her yet."

"Her?"

"Only female reindeer have antlers in winter."

"Those antlers are bolted on."

"We haven't got to know *it* yet," said Newton. Emboldened by his need to show Newton Woollby loved all animals, cute and ugly, he edged towards the reindeer. The creature blinked and angled its head as though trying to focus its clearly useless eyes on him.

"Hey, Blinky," he sang softly, holding out the flat of his hand to her muzzle as he slowly approached. "I could make friends with any of the horses at the stables," he told Guin.

"That is not a horse," said Guin. "It barely qualifies as an animal."

"She just needs to be shown a little love. Maybe she's feeling out of sorts. Hey, what do reindeer take when they've got a stomach ache."

"A joke? At this time?"

"Elk-a-seltzer!" Newton grinned.

Guin did not crack a smile, not even a fake one.

"You like my jokes," Newton simpered to Blinky. " You do, don't you? Don't you, you lovely little—"

The reindeer jerked forward and snapped at Newton's hand. He snatched it back barely in time before hard, yellow zombie teeth clacked together on the space where his fingers had just been.

"Bad reindeer!" he gasped in alarm. "Naughty Blinky!"

"I was saying—" said Guin, "—why do elves need reindeer? They're not native to this country and—"

Whatever Guin was about to say went unsaid as the nearest elf, having finished overseeing the unloading of the train, barked an order at them and waved his knife. *"Takka pokjót, ljóður mað!"* The elf gestured viciously at a bulging sack.

Newton looked at Guin, perplexed.

"I think he wants you to carry it," she said.

"You understand elf now?"

"I'm going by context." She pointed at the sack. *"Takka pokjót?"*

The elf waved its knife encouragingly.

Newton bent and tried lifting the sack. Whatever was in it was too heavy for him to lift. He grasped the wet corners and dragged it along, directed into the centre of the cavern by the elf.

The place definitely had the feel of a storage area. Add a forklift truck and some hard hats and it could be the distribution centre of a major company. Half-constructed (or possibly deconstructed) market stalls were leant together in one place. Piles of scrap wood – furniture and fencing – sat alongside far neater piles of freshly cut logs. A mountain of stollen, stacked like bricks, was positioned alongside a vat of sweets wrapped in colourful tissue. Shiny Christmas present boxes, red with gold ribbon, sat in a vast pile, waiting to receive their toys. A giant storage container, like a lorry container but on reinforced sledge runners, stood by the pile. On it, in wonky writing, someone had painted the words:

NORF AMERICA

Newton was curious, but was distracted by the strings upon strings of sausages hanging above them. "Hot dog sausages," he grunted as he heaved the sack along.

"Are you actually hungry?" said Guin.

"No, I'm... The elves run the market."

"Yeah," she said. "I don't get why. None of this makes sense."

"Not just me, then."

The elf barked at them.

"He wants you to leave it there," said Guin.

"Good." Newton let it drop and wondered when the feeling might return to his arms.

Elves – horrible sharp-faced elves, toddler-sized but as far from human as it was possible to be whilst still retaining all the standard features – gathered round Guin and Newton. They prodded and pushed the pair towards another tunnel leading out of the cavern.

"I think our dad and mum are alive," said Guin.

"That's the spirit," said Newton.

"No, I do. If they'd been dead, they'd have brought them here."

"Sure," he said, happy to say something that gave her hope.

Her hand gripped his. "Didn't you see?"

"What?"

She raised his hand. He looked at it. It was red with smears of blood.

"Your sack. It was that Duncan man's body."

Newton felt sick. In a frenzy he tried to brush the blood off on his jumper. But he was also thinking that maybe she was right. Maybe their folks were alive, somewhere.

\*\*\*

# 52

Dave had taken his own advice and thrashed around so he was facing uphill as the avalanche hit. As snow tumbled onto him in slabs and looser chunks, he'd tried to move upwards. It was a mostly hopeless task that was made even harder by no longer knowing which way was uphill after a few moments. A tree branch crashed down next to him and he held onto it, sliding along and hoping he was going the right way. After a few seconds all was silence. He could hear the distant echo of the avalanche, but he knew he was buried in the snow.

"Don't panic. Don't panic."

Dave's paramedic training had equipped him to keep his cool in extraordinary situations – although that was usually in the face of other people's imminent deaths, not his own. He'd tried to explain to Guin how her swimming lessons were giving her a similar skill. The breathing control she needed when she swam with her face in the water came from the same place. He firmly believed mastery over some of the body's basic functions was key.

Could he do it now? He made a conscious effort to slow his breathing. He knew his first instinct would be to pant wildly, but he needed to slow down his entire body to remain calm. It would also help him make the best use of his limited oxygen. He made a brief survey of his body. He didn't seem to be injured. His legs were both locked in place. His left arm was curled around his face, giving him space for the air he was so thankful for. He could flex his fingers slightly. His right arm was by his waist and a quick jiggle told him he had some movement.

Cautiously he moved it gently back and forth, fingers trying to pick up any useful information. He was careful not to make sudden movements, for fear of disturbing the air pocket around his face. His fingers pushed further, there was a rush of different sensations. He knew he was disoriented, but he really wanted to believe it was open air he could feel. Did he dare to push himself that way, knowing if he was wrong he might completely cut off his air supply by disturbing the snow? He had no real choice.

He pushed his arm as hard as he could, and then eased the arm protecting his face towards it. Snow fell into his face, filling his mouth. He pushed on, clinging to the belief that this was the way out.

Then he was through. His arm and shoulder were free. He was able to shove the snow off his face. He sucked in long, greedy breaths and shoved snow off the rest of him, grappling for the rope so he could find Esther.

She was nearby. If he didn't have the rope to follow he would have walked straight past her: underneath a large chunk of what looked like a fir tree. She only had a light covering of snow, but she was out cold, and there was a bruise across her face where the tree had struck her.

"Esther!" he cried, feeling for a pulse. She was alive. He scooped snow away from her and checked her breathing. She started to come round as he felt along her limbs.

"Mm, frisky," she said groggily.

"Bloody hell, Esther. We nearly died."

She sat slowly up. "Well," she said, "that might work out well for us. If the elves think they've killed us."

They stood and embraced, thigh deep in the snow. They were both shivering. Dave wasn't sure if it was shock, or the fact they were both wet and chilled to the bone.

"We have no idea what's happened to the kids," he said in a choked sob. "They could be anywhere. They might be de—"

"Shh, we must assume they are okay," she said. "And we're going to find them."

"Of course."

"We don't know how yet, but we will. I think we need to go back into town and start again."

It wasn't an appealing thought, but standing here in the snow was certain to render them both incapable of anything.

They wrapped their arms around each others' shoulders and walked slowly back the way they'd come.

***

# 53

Guin and Newton were herded and hurried along a narrow rock tunnel. The fairy lights along the walls were even more sparse and temperamental than the ones in the main cavern. They stumbled through patches of darkness between moments of rosy cheeriness.

The elf behind them screeched an order and they were diverted to one side and into a—

Guin blinked and looked about them.

Long, brightly painted workbenches were arranged in rows and columns. Twee little stools stood by the benches, along with neatly laid out sets of mallets, saws, gimlets, files, shears, paintbrushes and pots. From the rustic beams above hung boughs of holly, sprigs of mistletoe and metres and metres of festive paperchains. Against the far wall were a series of cutesy windows outside which the snow gathered thickly.

"It's Santa's workshop," she whispered. Except, she noticed on second glance, the paintwork on the benches was peeling, half the mallets were broken, the saws were either rusted or blunt, the holly was dead and black, the paperchains appeared to be made from ancient yellow newspaper, and the windows were painted on the cave wall. Not windows at all.

"What's going on?" said Newton.

An elf leapt onto the workbench in front of them. He – no, *she* – had the sharpest, pointiest features they'd yet seen on an elf. As though there had been a work related incident involving her face and a vice. A pair of half-moon spectacles balanced on the end of a long nose. A wooden ruler dangled dangerously in her hand.

"*Nei tala!*" she squawked.

"Sorry," said Newton. "We were just—"

"*Ekkla tala,* ya big lummox."

"Sorry. What?"

The elf lashed out with the ruler. It cracked sharply across Newton's shoulder.

"Ow! Okay, I—"

*Crack!*

"Oww! No, I get it. I—"

*Crack!*

Newton screwed up his face, held his yelp of pain in and nodded. Guin put a reassuring hand on his arm, and received a ruler whack to the knuckles from the elf. It was one of those terrible moments of pain that didn't initially hurt at all. Guin looked at her bloodless white hand in shock and knew – just knew – that in a five seconds it was going to hurt like hell.

... three, four, five...

Guin gritted her teeth and shoved her throbbing hand under her arm.

"*Svo*, mi'ducks, *ergi Gerd*," said the elf, strolling along the workbench. "*Þúert hértil aðna. Toy bygling.*" She swung round to indicate the entire workshop. "*Dúkir, lesnn, der Pooh ber.*"

Guin nodded, pretending/hoping she understood half of that. The elf, whose name was possibly Gerd, gestured to shelves and baskets of supplies on one side of the workshop.

"*Gerl semú vilen, ður rétt* Bobby Dazzler."

"Who's Bobby Dazzler?" said Newton.

*Crack!* Gerd's little ruler slapped across Newton's head. It was a surprise it didn't break, although Newton's mass of curly hair probably acted a bit like a protective cushion. A bit.

"*Þúátt sjöog fim mínútur. All hal góra skeggi.*" Gerd leapt away and scurried to a corner.

"What the hell—?" whispered Newton, rubbing his sore head.

"I thought it was obvious," said Guin.

The teenager looked at her blankly.

"She wants us to make toys. Wonderful toys. We've got *sjöog fim* minutes."

"How long's that?"

"Something-five minutes. I'm not sure."

"You are kidding me."

"Nope," said Guin. She began to explore the nearest workbench. "And I think we ought to do a good job of it too."

"Why?"

Guin held her arms out. "You see anyone else here?"

"So?"

"You think we're the first children they've ever kidnapped?"

"Um..."

"And do you think they just let the other ones go?"

Newton looked like he was thinking about it and didn't like what he was thinking. "Maybe we ought to make ourselves useful," he said eventually.

"I agree," said Guin.

\*\*\*

# 54

In a stiff drawer beneath a workbench, Newton found several crumpled and ripped instruction sheets for the construction of various toys. There were pictures, wildly unhelpful arrows and exclamation marks, and the limited written instructions were written in what looked like runes straight out of *The Lord of the Rings*.

"It's just like IKEA instructions," he said to Guin, cracking a smile to try to raise the mood.

They were alone in the workshop, but they were filled with a sense of being watched. The sounds of elves working, squabbling, ordering each other about and occasionally killing each other, echoed into the cave from afar, reducing individual sounds to a distorted ghostly murmur.

Guin decided it would be easiest to make cuddly toys from the large supplies of fabric in the corner of the room. Sewing was a more forgiving craft than carving or carpentry. That was when they discovered the big hoppers of material were in fact mostly full of discarded human clothing. Including children's.

"We need to show them we're useful," Newton repeated himself hollowly. He waved one of the printed patterns at Guin. "You want a pattern to follow?"

"I'm good," she said, rummaging through the materials she amassed. "I don't like instructions."

Newton nodded, picking out what looked like an easy pattern for a cloth rabbit. "Mum loves building IKEA flat pack furniture," he said.

"I think that's one of the reasons why dad likes her," said Guin.

Newton didn't particularly want to think about why Dave liked his mum. If he did it was too easy for his brain to drift into thoughts of their parents' love life. Through conversations with his mum (who had a tendency to overshare) he gathered even old people in their thirties and forties had something like a love life. He shuddered and tried to drive away the thoughts by busying himself with the rabbit pattern.

"I like the little bits you get in IKEA furniture," said Guin. She had cut out random shapes from a big dress with a floral pattern and was now fiddling with something else.

Newton saw that she had her little wire man on the bench in front of her. He realised her little robot toy made of spare nuts and bolts was probably still in the wooden box in the burning hotel. "What's his name?" he asked.

"Hmmm?" Guin saw him looking. "That's Wiry Harrison. He's my best one. This—" She put down a shiny crumpled thing she'd just made. It had four legs and a long neck. "This is Tinfoil Tavistock."

"A new Tinfoil Tavistock?"

She shook her head. "No. It's still Tinfoil Tavistock. Just cos I had to make her again, doesn't mean it's not her."

Newton wasn't sure that was true. You couldn't get a copy of a loved one or a best friend and it still be the same thing. He thought about Lily and knew that if she was ever replaced by a copy, *if* he ever got out of this place and returned to the stables, he wouldn't be able to accept a substitute. Even Yolanda... Yolanda was Yolanda and a rough approximation of her wouldn't be the same thing.

Newton and Guin worked side by side, he following the pattern step by step, she attacking cloth and cotton and buttons with seemingly no plan at all.

"Why do elves make toys?" he asked some minutes later.

"Is this the beginning of a joke?" said Guin.

"No," he said, wondering if it could be. "I mean it. Why do they make toys?"

"You mean, cos there's no Father Christmas to deliver?"

"Even if there was. Why would he do it? Why would they do it?"

"Because children love presents," she said.

Newton didn't think that was good enough. "Children love chocolate too. Doesn't mean that once a year a magical being comes into our houses and buries us under a mound of chocolate."

"The Easter Bunny," said Guin.

"You don't believe in the Easter Bunny do you?"

"I don't believe in Father Christmas, but we're having this conversation."

Up until a few hours ago, Newton would have agreed with her. Given what they'd experienced in the past hours, he was prepared to put what he did and didn't believe to one side.

"Picture it," he said. "There's this guy. Clearly he's fabulously wealthy because he can afford to build workshops and factories and stuff. And he decides to use that wealth to make toys and give them out to children across the world. What's his motivation?"

"Guilt," said Guin without hesitation. "Parents give their children stuff when they're feeling guilty."

"That's true," agreed Newton. He imagined the average teenager didn't get to enjoy the expensive hobby of horse-riding, and if his own father hadn't run out on them years ago, leaving his mum a sad and guilty mess, maybe he wouldn't either. It was another topic he didn't want to think on too deeply. "So, he's making up for his bad deeds of the past, huh?"

"Maybe he was a criminal," suggested Guin. "Or a soldier. Maybe he slaughtered hundreds of people in battle. That's why his clothes are all red."

"Good one," said Newton. "So he went from *slaying* people to *sleighing*. You know, on a sleigh with reindeer."

"Painful," said Guin.

"Needs work."

Guin sewed material together with enviable speed. "In fact," she said, "maybe Santa is Satan."

"Dyslexic Satan."

"Exactly. And this Father Christmas malarkey is him trying to make up for all the bad in the world. All of it."

"Another fine theory. Of course, mum says that Christmas encourages evil and greed. So really, if Santa is Satan then this is all just a ploy to create more greed and commercialism. Mum would say he's doing a really good job of it too."

Newton began to sew together the shapes he'd cut out. The material had caught in the shears and his rabbit toy was a bit jagged. But it still looked like a rabbit. Sort of. If given a range of animals to pick from, multiple choice style, people would identify it as a rabbit. As long as the options were sufficiently diverse. If the choices were 'rabbit', 'pointy guinea pig' and 'ill-favoured weasel' then it might be tougher.

"Do you think there is one?" he said.

"One what?" said Guin, who was embellishing the multiple ears (or was it arms?) on her creation with sequins.

"Father Christmas."

She looked about, thinking. "We'd have seen him already if he was here."

Newton nodded. It made sense.

"But," she added, "the thing that Gerd said: *'All hal góra skeggi.'*"

"What about it?"

"I think it translates as 'All hail the big beard.'"

***

# 55

Esther and Dave took care to be as quiet as they could, although Esther was convinced the chattering of her teeth was so loud the elves would be sure to hear it. The streets were silent and deserted as they walked in the shadows, keeping a careful watch. They passed a cookware shop, a pharmacy and a charity shop. Esther heard noises. Dave heard them too.

"What do you think's going on?" Esther whispered.

There was definitely fresh activity in the town centre. As they rounded a corner they could see that the marketplace had come to life once more. The jolly fairly lights and illuminations cast a warm glow over the dozens of elves congregating there.

"Look at all the stuff they're eating and drinking," murmured Dave. He sounded a touch envious. "It's some sort of party."

There were bottles of sticky liqueurs everywhere. Most of the elves were tucking into mince pies and candy canes as they jostled merrily around a central raised area.

"It's like a theatre show wrap party," said Esther. "All very self-congratulatory. And look!" She nudged Dave, nodding over to the left. Another human shape collapsed onto the floor as the elves climbed out to join the party. Esther recognised the human shell as a the stallholder who'd been selling nutcrackers earlier. She'd thought he had learning difficulties, instead, he'd had elves inside him all along.

"The last market day of the year," she said. "All the real humans are dead or have left. I bet the road into town is going to stay blocked now. Alvestowe belongs to the elves for Christmas."

"Do elves celebrate Christmas?" wondered Dave.

"Or do they have other plans?" she said darkly.

Esther crept forward but Dave held her back. "They'll see us for sure!"

"We'll never find the kids if we can't see what they're doing." She looked back along the row of shops. "The charity shop."

"Yes?"

"We need to get some dry clothes, right?"

"Yeah, but they're closed."

Esther sighed patiently. "Yes they are. I don't think that's our biggest problem right now. We need to get some dry clothes, and maybe, just maybe, we can dress ourselves in clothes that help us blend in a bit more."

"We're going to disguise ourselves as elves?"

"It sounds ridiculous when you say it like that."

Dave sighed. Esther handed him a soggy bundle: the altar cloth. He unwrapped it to find a heavy candlestick.

"We only wanted the candle!"

"It was jammed in and we were in a hurry," said Esther with a shrug.

Dave wrapped the candlestick back up in the altar cloth.

Esther reflected briefly on the ungodliness of using church equipment for breaking and entering as Dave smashed in one of the panes of glass on the door. He reached through and let them into the shop.

"At least it's a bit warmer in here," she said, looking around. "Right, now we need to find something we can work with. See if there's anything like make-up while I sort through the clothes."

Esther searched through the dark shop, among dead men's suits and out of season fashion items. She found a rummage box full of hats. She pulled out some stripy bobble hats.

Dave came back with a box. "This any good?"

"Yes, that's what we need." She pulled out some foundation. "Now, you know how the elves have all got really pale faces and red lips? Well that's what we need to have. Take this stuff and cover up your stubble as best you can. Then we'll put some lipstick on you."

"This feels so wrong," complained Dave as he dabbed on foundation while peering into a mirror.

"Oh, do you think we're guilty of cultural appropriation?" Esther said. It was something she worried about a lot, as it was a trap that was so easy to fall into. "I mean these elves are clearly authentic in a way that we could never—"

"I don't think we need to worry about that," said Dave. "Seriously."

"Well, all right then. We do need to practise talking like them."

"Do we? Can't we just keep our mouths shut?"

"No. Practise sounding a bit, er, Norwegian or something."

"I don't know what that sounds like. Can I do Swedish?"

"Sure."

"*Hurdy gurdy gur,*" said Dave to his reflection in the mirror.

"That sounds a bit racist to me," said Esther with a frown. "I'm not sure Swedish people even sound like that. Put these on."

Esther handed him a pair of stripy leggings. They were the right colours, like a candy cane, but she wasn't sure they were big enough for him.

They stripped down their outer layers. In the relative warmth of the shop, the snow that had found its way into every crevice of their clothes and bodies was rapidly melting.

Dave kicked aside his trousers and hauled the leggings up to his mid-thigh. "Not sure they're going to go any further."

"Give it a go," she said, "Go on, pull!"

Dave tugged and got them to his hips. The elastic gouged an uncompromising ring around his belly.

"Not bad," said Esther. "Go and find a big jumper to cover that up. Green, red or brown, and then a leather belt to go round your waist."

"This is absurd," moaned Dave, wandering away to find a jumper.

Esther had pulled on some stripy tights and a brown woollen dress herself. Now she had a slightly more tricky task to accomplish. She rummaged below the counter and found some sewing supplies. Finding a leather handbag in a fleshy pink shade and two pairs of ear warmers, she began to cut the handbag into sections,.

"Dave, would you be able to bend a wire coat hanger into a teardrop shape?" she asked.

"Er, sure." He twisted a coat hanger until it weakened enough for him to break off a length. He formed the shape Esther wanted.

"Excellent. Now do another three, please."

"Have we got time for this?" he said.

"We want to find our children, don't we?"

"I bet they're not doing bloody arts and crafts."

***

# 56

Guin finished her toy with time and materials to spare. She had constructed the plush toy as her whims and instincts dictated. As she sewed and stuffed and adorned, the name and character and back story of Starfish Eglantine came to life. Eglantine was a starfish out of her natural environment, trapped in a cold and hostile world, far from any friends and any help. But Eglantine was not afraid. Although her body was squishy and vulnerable, she had made her heart into a stone and refused to be frightened by the horrors around her.

Guin did not think she and Eglantine could be friends. Eglantine was too tough and embittered, but there was a grudging respect between Eglantine and Guin, between Eglantine and Wiry Harrison. Tinfoil Tavistock did not like Eglantine. The quadruped of indeterminate species was unnerved by the faceless creature's steely manner. But that was understandable: Tavistock was only a child.

Eglantine observed with cool approval as Guin used her spare time to surreptitiously gather supplies. The flexible lengths of wicker Guin had used for supporting Eglantine's arms could also be fashioned into serviceable elf crosses. Guin made four, held together with twists of wire, and pinned them to the inside of her top. She found three small blades and was wondering how she could conceal them in a roll of cloth when, from nowhere, the elf Gerd bounded onto the nearest workbench.

"*Hæltu!*" she screeched and pointed at Newton. "*Tími erk loð,* buggerlugs."

Newton dropped the ... thing he was making – a tuft of white stuffing still poking out of its rump – and stepped back from the bench.

Gerd strode up and down the bench, the curled toes of her tiny boots quivering with each step. She bent over Guin's creation, peered at it through her half-moon spectacles and then prodded and poked it.

"*Hver it það?*"

"It's a starfish," said Guin.

"*Starfiskur?*"

"A starfish."

"Star ... feeesh?"

Gerd turned it over, gave it an experimental bite like she was testing gold and then tossed it back down on the bench in a manner that was not entirely dismissive. She walked over to Newton's work. Guin knew it was meant to be a bunny rabbit. She'd seen the plans.

"*Hver it það?*"

"Um, it's a rabbit," said Newton nervously.

"*Du kani?*" Gerd picked it up, poked it and ripped off one of its eyes. "*Ger stykki rot.*" Gerd pinched and pulled and picked at the toy, all the while venting a litany of criticism which needed no translation.

"At least you can see it's a rabbit," Newton muttered. "It's not like it's some weird blob thing like that," he said, pointing at Guin's starfish.

"It's not a competition," said Guin.

"It probably is," said Newton, instantly adding, "But I'm glad you won. You've done really well."

As if to emphasise his words, Gerd picked up Guin's efforts and tucked it under her arm. Newton's work was kicked unceremoniously onto the floor. Newton automatically picked it up.

"Poor thing," he tutted.

"Sometimes," said Guin gently, "some animals are in just too much pain to let them go on living."

"What?"

"I'm just saying it might be kinder to let it die," she said.

"*Þú ud þú,*" snapped Gerd, gesturing for them to follow. "*Timi ger næxta verk!*"

"Time for the next test, I think," Guin translated.

Newton wasn't listening. "Kinder to let it die," he muttered. "Let the dog drown. All you want to do is kill things."

Outside in the cavern, they passed by the stall in which the mad-eyed zombie reindeer stood.

"You like my rabbit, don't you, Blinky?" Newton said, waggling his work at the undead creature. "You do, don't you?"

Blinky lunged forward. With yellow teeth he savagely ripped the toy from Newton's hand.

"I'm going to take that as a yes," he said, defensively.

\*\*\*

# 57

Gerd the overly critical elf stopped outside a door in the tunnel. This door was thick and looked like it had been repaired a number of times. She pulled it open with some effort and led the way inside. Newton had to bend to get through.

It was another workshop area, although not as gaily painted as the toy workshop. There were no fake painted windows on the walls, only intermittent scorch marks: little starbursts of sooty residue.

Newton looked at the tubs of knick-knacks and assorted junk: false teeth, car keys, teaspoons and the kinds of cheap Happy Meal toys even a charity shop would turn away. He looked at the lengths of cardboard tubing, the paper, the quills and the rolls of festive crepe paper.

"It's a Christmas cracker workshop," he said.

Gerd began to give a long speech of which Newton understood absolutely nothing, although mentions of '*jóli*' and '*sprenging bume*' and '*hæla fyni*' sounded like they ought to mean something.

"*Þúátt sjöog fim mínútur*," said Gerd.

"Something-five minutes, huh?" said Newton.

"*All hal góra skeggi*," said Gerd.

"*All hal góra skeggi*," Guin replied and the elf left them to it.

"Why do I feel we're being auditioned for jobs we don't want?" muttered Newton.

"Getting the job might be better than being rejected."

Newton went over to the piles of paper by the quill and inkwell: the joke writing station.

"Maybe," he chuckled, "I should write, 'Help! I'm trapped in a Christmas cracker—'" He tailed off, realising the cracker they'd opened at Mrs Scruples' dinner table, with that same lame joke, had come from this very workshop.

"She said they were locally sourced," said Guin, clearly thinking the same thing.

Newton shook his head. "The people of the town were in league with the elves."

"Or under occupation."

"I think we'd best get on with it," he said.

With little discussion, they decided upon a division of labour. Newton would do jokes. Guin would select toys to go inside the cracker and wrap them up.

"Snappers," said Newton.

"What?"

"The bit that goes bang." He looked round and saw a heavy chest of blackened wood beneath the heaviest concentration of scorch marks on the wall. Newton went to have a look. He lifted the weighty lid. Inside were not just strips of cracker explosives but several jars of interesting chemicals. And, by interesting, he meant dangerous-looking.

Avoiding the sticky gluey edges of the badly made cracker strips, Newton carefully lifted out a dusty jar with a faded label which was barely legible. "Silver nitrate," he said.

Guin had found an open book on the work surface nearby. "Silver nitrate, when combined with nitric acid and ethanol can form crystals of silver fulminate," she read. "Silver fulminate is explosive and very toxic."

Newton looked through the chest. Sure, there were bottles of nitric acid and ethanol too.

Guin continued reading. "Only very small quantities of silver fulminate should be prepared at once or else—"

"Else what?"

She shrugged. "The rest of the page has been burned away."

Newton looked. The hardback book was entitled *O-Level Chemistry for All Schools'*. It looked very old and, indeed, a whole corner of the book was nothing but blackened char.

"Yeah, let's be careful with this stuff then," he said, leaving the jars well alone. "Maybe if we need to go all *A-Team* later, we can use it for something."

"What's an *A-Team*?" asked Guin.

Newton wasn't sure. "It's something my mum says when she tries to make things out of stuff not meant for that purpose. I think it's from an old film, starring that guy from *Taken*. You know, the guy who has a 'very particular set of skills.'"

"Sort of like *Bob the Builder*," said Guin.

"Possibly," said Newton. "But with more explosions."

\*\*\*

# 58

In the charity shop, Dave grabbed more coat hangers while Esther set to work with a needle and thread. She covered the teardrop shapes with the flesh-coloured leather and sewed them onto the ear warmers. She popped the finished article onto her head, covered it with a bobble hat and looked in the mirror, turning her head to view the effect.

"Elf ears. Very good!" said Dave.

"Let's do yours now."

They both paraded their finished outfits up and down. Dave grinned. "These stupid leggings are really uncomfortable, but I think we make pretty good elves, all told. Let's go and see what they're up to!"

"There's just one small thing that we need to fix," said Esther.

Dave gave her a questioning look. She beckoned him over and plucked a pair of lightweight shoes from a rack. She used the scissors to cut away the back of the shoe and then applied it just above his knee. With the needle and thread she sewed it onto the leggings.

"In case you hadn't noticed, we're way too tall to be elves," she said.

"Wait – we're going to shuffle around on our knees?" Dave asked.

Esther nodded, her head bent in concentration. She fixed the other shoe and gave Dave's legs a critical stare. "Go, on, see how it looks."

Dave got down onto his knees and moved about. He tried shuffling at first, then experimented with lifting his knees to make the walking more realistic. It looked very uncomfortable.

"I wouldn't worry too much about technique," said Esther tactfully. "I'm hoping we won't come under too much scrutiny. Let me fix my own shoes and we'll be ready to go."

A few minutes later they made their way carefully out of the shop, using their hands to brush the broken glass out of the way as they shuffled out onto the street.

"*Hurdy, gurdy, gur,*" murmured Dave.

Esther tutted, falling silent as they drew in closer to where all the elves seemed to be congregating. She trawled her memory for the elf language that Guin seemed to have picked up so quickly.

"*Ek man, dum de dum … svín,*" she tried.

What did it mean? She couldn't remember. She had to confess Dave's elf speech might be just as effective. She pulled up short. That was a really racist thing to think! Was she a racist?

"Dave, am I a racist?" she asked quietly.

"You refuse to eat in Italian restaurants," he said.

"That's because it's just pasta and pizza," she said. "Any idiot can cook that. I don't hate Italians."

"We're going out for pizza when we get out of here then," he said, as they approached the square.

The party was in full swing. There was scratchy music coming from somewhere, like the sound of an orchestra composed entirely of broken violins. Elves were swigging drinks from little cups and shoving cakes and sweets into their mouths.

"I feel ill just watching. Everything they're eating is at least ninety percent sugar," Esther said.

"Shhh."

They sauntered in, on their knees, trying to stick to the gloomier areas and nodding at elves who looked their way.

"*Hurdy gurd,*" nodded Dave.

"*Svin svin ekki mek,*" said Esther.

Esther thought it would have been nice to believe their disguises were amazing. It was more likely the elves were too drunk, or that now they were off-duty, they didn't give a toss about human interlopers.

Dave squeezed her hand. "Look," he whispered. "The stage."

An elf walked to the front of the raised area and raised his hands for silence. He started to speak in the strange elvish language, and Esther listened hard, trying to discern any meaning. She almost convinced herself tiny fragments were English-like, if someone spoke English with Dave's weird *hurdy gurdy* accent.

"Enemy? Is he talking about an enemy?" she whispered to Dave.

Dave gave her a blank look.

A cheer went up from the crowd; Esther and Dave joined in. Everyone raised their snacks and drinks in an obvious toast to something. Esther didn't have a cup so raised an invisible one instead.

The elf reached into a leather bag that hung by his waist. He pulled out a big folded sheet of paper.

"I've seen those plans before," said Dave.

"What?" said Esther.

"Catheter had them."

The elf on the stage ripped the plans in half to raucous applause. He threw them to the floor and stamped on them.

Dave and Esther looked at each other.

"We need them," said Dave.

"Right."

The elf on the stage hadn't finished. He fetched something else out of his bag. It looked like a wisp of sheep's wool. He cradled it reverentially in his hand before holding it up for all to see. There were *oohs* and *aahs* from the crowd. He then used something from a small jar to apply the thing to his chin. He strode from side to side of the stage, sticking out his chin so that everyone could see.

From the crowd, some of the elves started chanting. "*All hal góra skeggi. All hal góra skeggi.*"

Esther really didn't think a stick-on beard was a good look, but she reminded herself she wasn't one to body shame someone for their choice of facial hair.

Dave nudged her and nodded to the left of the stage. Another elf was climbing up, although it clearly wasn't easy, given the extent of his injuries. He had clearly suffered extensive burns: his clothes hung off his livid body in singed rags. What was not clear was how he'd come by the other injuries. It looked very much as if half of him had been crushed: one limp arm dragged behind, like an empty flap of skin.

"Bacraut," whispered Dave. "We put him in a trouser press."

Esther thought she saw one of the nearby elves give Dave a sharp look. She elbowed him and munched down on a candy cane, trying hard to fit in.

Back on the stage, Bacraut approached the elf with the beard. There was clearly some sort of disagreement in their brief exchange, but Bacraut didn't look very threatening with his injuries. Beardie laughed at him and turned away, still proudly displaying the beard to the crowd. Bacraut growled and used his good hand to pull a huge knife from a sheath.

Bacraut lunged forward and stabbed Beardie repeatedly in the back. Once on the ground, Bacraut turned Beardie over by kicking his twitching body. He slashed at the exposed belly. He pulled out lengths of intestine, held them up and yelled something at the crowd that clearly conveyed the message the young pretender was no longer in a position to usurp authority.

"Trouble in elf-town," muttered Dave.

Bacraut put the knife away. He bent down to pluck the wispy beard off the face of the dead elf and stuck it onto his own face. As he did so, the injured Bacraut seemed to straighten and find new energy from this symbol of power on his face. The crowd erupted in applause, having held its collective breath while the drama played out.

Bacraut waved to the crowd, basking in the adoration, or fear; Esther really wasn't sure which. After a few moments, Bacraut clapped his hands and a box was brought on stage by two helper elves. It was a sturdy red cardboard box, bound in gold ribbon. The helpers placed it before Bacraut.

He spoke to the assembled crowd. Esther understood almost nothing, although his affected and exaggerated manner suggested he was acting something out. Bacraut gave a big tired stretch as he talked to the elves and rubbed his eyes as though he had just awoken. He strolled over to the box, expressed pretend surprise and pulled on the ribbon.

A hush had fallen over the audience.

Bacraut lifted the lid away and feigned delight at whatever was supposed to be inside. He pretended to lift something out, something heavy and wriggling. He beamed at it and held it close, suddenly gasping in horror as the imaginary thing began to choke him.

"He's quite the actor," Esther whispered to Dave, then uttered a small "*Ow!*" as someone trod on her lower leg.

She looked back. An elf, crowding forward, had trodden on her trailing lower legs. Esther muttered a wordless "Don't worry, no harm done." The elf was a millisecond away from nodding and moving on when the creature realised elves didn't have extra bits of leg trailing behind them.

"*Erir du footurna?*" it said.

"Er, Dave," muttered Esther.

Dave turned, saw and, making matters much worse, leapt to his feet. The look of horror on his face an instant later, in other circumstances, would have been comical.

Dave tried to laugh. "Oh, look," he said. "I appear to have suddenly grown taller."

He grabbed Esther's hand and they ran for it. They kicked, flailed and knocked over elves as they went. Their stitched on shoes flapped at their knees as they ran. As they knocked elves into each other, fights broke out. Elfin alcohol had definitely been consumed in volumes throughout the celebration.

Esther tried to snatch some of the plans off the floor. An elf, its eyes full of malicious intent, leapt at her, scrabbled, missed and then latched onto her arm with its teeth. Esther howled at the pain, shook the elf off viciously and ran to catch up with Dave.

"Tree!" panted Dave, grabbing an armful of prickly branches on the massive Christmas tree in the centre of the square. Esther joined him, pulling with all of her might. Together they toppled it onto the elves who were chasing them, rather than fighting each other. It bought them a few precious seconds, but they were definitely not out of danger. There was a pair of elves, sprinting around the edges of the tree, who would easily catch them in no time.

Dave lifted a mead barrel from a stall and bowled it at the pursuing elves. It caught on the kerb and glanced slightly off-course, taking down one of them. The other elf skipped free. Dave grabbed a second barrel and raised it.

Esther glanced at the elf. She wasn't sure, but it looked just like the one who had bitten her. Well, they all looked the same really—

"Oh, God, I *am* a racist!" she said. With an anger that was divided equally between the elves and her own preconceptions, she helped Dave slam the barrel down on the elf, crushing it so completely that when liquid seeped out, Esther didn't for a second imagine it was just mead.

"Come on!" Dave took her hand and they ran.

Esther ran on feet that felt suddenly sluggish. She registered Dave was talking to her. His words were fading in and out.

"Dave, I feel a bit funny."

"What?"

She tried to make the words fit the light-headed detachment she was experiencing. "Woozy, a bit dreamy."

The chaos in the market was fading behind them. Everything was fading.

Esther stumbled. The snow was powdery soft beneath her feet. It looked surprisingly inviting. "Maybe a nap would help."

"No, no," he said and held her upright. "Back to the shop, it's just over there. We can hole up for a few minutes. Stay with me, Esther."

***

# 59

Gerd came to inspect the crackers Newton and Guin had made. She was not alone.

The two elves with her didn't exactly look older or more senior than her – all the elves looked like underfed children, albeit ones who had undergone some ill-advised cheek-lift and eye-tightening plastic surgery from a doctor with very poor Google reviews. However, there was something in their stiff posture and pompous manner that marked them out as higher up the chain of command than Gerd. One even had a wisp of white beard on his chin.

As the elves approached, Newton stepped back respectfully, hands behind his back. Guin wondered if this was because Newton had watched a lot of bake off TV shows and knew how the contestants acted when the judges walked back in, or because his hands were covered in a sticky fluffy mass of crepe paper and glue that no amount of picking could shift.

Gerd and the elders regarded the five crackers critically. Guin listened attentively. She was tired and frightened (she recognised this and had confided as much in Wiry Harrison) but she was picking up snippets of the elves' language each time she heard them.

The elders prodded and closely regarded the crackers before pulling them. The first one exploded with far too big a bang, making Guin's ears ring, setting fire to the paper wrapping and knocking the spectacles off Gerd's head.

"*Ut mikið!*" she yelled. "*Ut mikið*, yer daft ha'peth!"

The children cowered. Newton positioned himself protectively in front of Guin, which she found both comforting and irritating.

The other four crackers didn't crack quite so catastrophically and the three judges peered critically over the contents. In the search for knick-knacks to go inside the crackers, the barrels of odds and ends had offered Guin slim pickings. She suspected their contents came from the pockets and bags of all the humans the elves had kidnapped over the years, and the good stuff was long gone. The four toys were the knob of a car gearstick, a golf ball on which Guin had drawn a smiley face, a broken pencil, and fish cut out from an old sweet wrapper, stuffed into an envelope and optimistically labelled *Fortune-telling fish*.

Gerd took it out of its envelope and stared at it furiously.

"You put it in your hand," Guin explained "How it moves tells you what your future holds."

Gerd laid it flat in the palm of her tiny hand. The fish did nothing.

"It's sleeping at the moment," said Guin.

Gerd spat in contempt. One of the elders pulled out a joke Newton had written.

"*Hver* did *góð kong* Wenceslas...?"

"Good King Wenceslas," said Newton helpfully.

The elder tried again. "How did *góð kong* Wenceslas like his pizza?"

The other elder shrugged. "*Eg na ekki. Hver ði góður kong Wenceslas els og pizza?*"

The first peered at the answer. "Deep pan, crisp and even."

The elves did not laugh. Newton gave them a deliberate and pathetically fake laugh. "Oh, that's a good one. That one will have the family rolling on the floor."

Embarrassed for him, Guin felt compelled to join in. "Oh, yeah. Really good."

The elder swept the crackers onto the floor dismissively.

"You should read the others," said Newton, his voice wobbling with nerves. "The one about baby Jesus's weight is a killer."

The elves shouted and argued amongst themselves. They were talking too quick for Guin to follow, but she imagined they were arguing whether to kill the pair of them or keep them as slaves. Guin should have been terrified, maybe her overtired mind had reached peak scaredness and had no more fear to give. She found her attention drawn to the beard of the shouting elder. His chin glistened wetly: glue. The beard was stuck on, like a theatre performers. That was interesting.

The argument was coming to some sort of heated conclusion but Guin could not work out which viewpoint was winning. An elder whipped out a curvy knife and bounded over to Newton and Guin. She dropped to her knees and bowed her head.

"*All hal góra skeggi*," she said.

She didn't die so that was something. She reached up and pulled Newton down beside her. *"All hal góra skeggi,"* she repeated for him.

"Er, yes," Newton trembled. *"All hal—"*

*"—Góra skeggi."*

"Yes. That."

Moments passed. The ringing in Guin's ears from the first cracker explosion filled the silence. Still they did not die. There was the soft padding sound of the elders leaving the room and then Gerd shouted for them to get up and follow her.

Guin and Newton were herded out, down the corridor and out to a recess in the large central cavern. With threats and the application of many granny knots, Gerd tied them with frayed rope to a thick pipe running up the wall before leaving them there. The ground was covered with hay and muck and soft rotting material.

"What was all that about?" said Newton.

"I think we passed the audition," said Guin. She considered the filthy floor, and the weariness filling her body. "I don't want to sit on this."

Newton crouched down. "Come sit on my knee if you like."

Guin gave him a long look. "Doesn't matter how you say that, it sounds creepy."

"I'm just trying to be a good stepbrother."

"You're not my stepbrother yet."

He took a deep breath, like he was trying to quell an unpleasant feeling. "We will get out of here. We will find my mum and your dad. We'll run away – maybe take Blinky with us—"

"We're not taking the zombie reindeer."

"Zombies deserve love too."

"Not happening, Newton," she said.

"We'll all run away. Mum and dad will get married. It'll be a lovely wedding and embarrassing as hell, and then we'll all live in a big house together – with separate bedrooms at opposite ends of the house, don't worry – and we'll be able to happily ignore each other for ever after. What do you say?"

Guin waggled a finger in her ear. "Didn't hear any of that. I think that cracker explosion has affected my hearing."

"It'll wear off soon."

"I went deaf for a whole term when I was seven," she said.

"Did you?"

"Pardon?"

He raised an eyebrow. "Was that a joke?"

"Pardon?" she said and against her better judgement and mood, found herself smiling a fraction.

"*Snakkur!*" said Gerd, returning with two large and dirty bowls. She presented one to Newton and the other to Guin. The two bowls were not the same. Newton's contained several steaming hotdog sausages. Guin's was filled with something dark green and damp. It looked like the seaweed starter from a Chinese restaurant soaked in a layer of misty gravy.

"What's this?" she said. "*Hver it það?* I have allergies you know."

Gerd ignored her and walked off.

"You can have one of my sausages if you like," said Newton.

She shook her head. "I didn't like the one I had in the market. It tasted funny."

Newton munched on a sausage. "They don't quite taste like any normal meat," he conceded. "But that's hotdogs for you, right?"

Guin pinched up a fragment of the soggy green stuff and sniffed it. She couldn't smell it above the overwhelming oily petrol scent in the air. She looked at the pipe they were tied to and, cautiously, wiped at a droplet that had trickled from a leaky joint.

"Petrol," she said.

"Or something like it," said Newton. "They're pumping a lot of it through here. Your dad would have a health and safety fit about it."

Guin tried some of the food. It tasted a bit like cabbage, a bit like snot and a bit like leather but mostly it tasted like grass.

"Why give us different food?" she wondered. Not knowing the answer to her own question, added, "Did you see that the elf's beard was glued on?"

"Glued on?"

"Like he's pretending to be Santa. And this 'All hail the big beard' stuff. It's like..." Guin hummed. She half-remembered something she'd read in a book once about islanders in the Pacific or somewhere who had seen white people – probably Americans – come along with their planes and their equipment. And how the white people had radioed down planes and supplies of food and such from the sky. So when the white people had gone, the islanders thought if they made pretend radio sets from bamboo stalks and coconut shells, the gods would send down food from the sky because that's how the world appeared to work. She only half-remembered it, and it was probably from a book written by a white person – probably an American – so it probably wasn't true anyway, but still…

"You think these elves actually have a plan?" she said. "Or are they just—"

"Going through the motions?" said Newton, starting on his third sausage.

Guin squatted down, rested the food bowl on her knees and pulled out the copy of *Little Folk in European Folklore* by Dr Alexander and turned to the last page she had been reading. She had just reached a section further detailing fairy children and changelings, and decided to read it while eating. Dr Alexander subscribed to the view that the idea of changelings – faeries put in the place of elf-stolen babies – was used in past times to explain why some children were born with disabilities, or autism. Guin wondered, not for the first time, if her dad should get her tested for autism. Her dad had already told her quite clearly he did not believe she had autism, although Gun was certain if they got her tested, and she tried really hard, she could get a diagnosis. The section on changelings was long (and included such pointlessly difficult words as 'victualise', 'cerebrate' and 'kineticism') but the food was quite unappetising, so Guin reached the end of the section just as she finished eating.

At that moment, there was a shout from outside in the cavern. It was human, and familiar sounding.

"I am coming! There is no need to hold my hand, little man. I don't know where you have been and there is far too much touching for my liking these days. We wouldn't have half the problems in the world today if people would just keep their hands to themselves."

It was Mrs Scruples, the hotel woman. She was walking into the cavern, surrounded by a large number of elves.

"She's still alive," said Newton, surprised.

"Doesn't deserve to be," said Guin.

The elves were shaking snow off themselves and had clearly just come in from outside. There was a wild, unhappy energy about them, like they were angry about something. There was one with a stuck-on white beard at the head of the group. His clothes were ragged and burned and smeared with blood.

"I think there's been trouble in town," said Guin.

"That's Baccarat or Backrub or something," said Newton, nodding towards the white bearded one. "Your dad and me stuck him in a trouser press."

"No wonder he's angry," said Guin.

***

# 60

Dave elbowed open the door of the charity shop, led Esther inside and sat her on the floor out of sight of anyone looking through the window.

"Tell me how you feel funny, Esther," he said.

"Just want to sleep," she murmured.

"No, Esther, you need to stay awake. It's really important."

"It might be where it bit me."

"What?" He looked her over, saw the tear on her sleeve and pulled it up. There was a shallow cut, little more than a row of teeth marks that had barely broken the skin.

Dave leaned forward, sniffing. "Fruity breath."

"S'my new nickname?" she mumbled.

"It seems as though you might have excessively high blood sugar."

"Candy canes," said Esther and then giggled.

Dave had his first aid pack with him and he checked the contents. There was nothing for hyperglycaemia.

"I won't be a minute," he whispered in her ear. "There's a pharmacy next door. I need to see if I can get in there. Jesus, Esther, please hang on in there."

She was barely responsive.

He went to the back door of the charity shop. There was a key inside the lock. He opened the door and eased himself partially through, taking a good look around before committing himself to going fully outside. He was in a yard, with bins, and a gate at the far end. The next door along had to belong to the pharmacy. He tried the door, naturally it was locked. A brief search of the yard revealed a half-brick being used as a gate stop. He took off his elf top, muffled the brick in it, and punched in the glass of the door.

He slipped inside the pharmacy and looked around for their refrigerator. A few minutes later he had several bottles of insulin, a blood test meter, some hypodermic needles and syringes. He slipped back through the yard and into the charity shop.

He ran a blood test on a drop of blood from her thumb, to see if his suspicions were correct. They were: her blood sugar was dangerously high. He loaded up a syringe with insulin, pulled down the waistband of her trousers a little and injected into her buttock.

***

# 61

Mrs Scruples, all the while talking on such diverse subjects as how draughty the cave was, what the elves could be doing to make the place more homely, and how prudent she was to have insured her now demolished home for more than it was worth, was manhandled (or elf-handled, Newton thought) into the centre of the cavern and onto a raised area.

"Yes, yes, my wee folk," she said. "This is all well and good, but where is my husband?"

There was something entrancing about the way the elves slowly circled the raised area in unison. Newton recalled watching a David Attenborough documentary in which a pod of dolphins circled round a mass of fishes, herding them into a tighter and tighter ball in preparation for the kill. Even the soft and silky tones of Sir David couldn't disguise the menace in the dolphins' orchestrated actions. Newton saw the spoons – bent, battered, blunt and rusted spoons – the elves carried. He had initially assumed it was dinnertime for everyone in the cavern; now he was not so certain.

He chewed on the last of his hotdogs as the inevitable slowly unfolded.

"I have been a good and faithful servant," Mrs Scruples was telling the elves. "I have kept your secrets and provided you with the ... materials you needed for your work. And, yes, though I do say so myself, I believe I have helped you better yourselves. Although I can see more than a few of you still need to learn how to use a handkerchief and— *Ah!*"

The "*Ah!*" was at the sight of a man strolling into the cavern from a tunnel entrance. He was old, red-faced, with a straggly silver comb-over and mutton chop whiskers. He wore a tweedy suit over a bright yellow waistcoat. He looked like an extra from a non-specific period drama, a mild-mannered middle class chap who ought to have a name like 'Cholmondeley-Warner' or 'Rutherkins' but was, of course, the much-mentioned and absentee Mr Scruples.

"Donald! Donald!" called Mrs Scruples. It wasn't the heartfelt call of a wife to her one true love. It was more the sound of a mistress calling her dog to heel. "Donald! Stand up straight and greet me!"

Donald wasn't standing up straight. He moved with a strange rolling gait, his arms flapping with a fluid motion, like he was walking in time to a mellow reggae tune only he could hear. There was also a slack look on his face.

"Is he drunk?" whispered Newton.

"No," said Guin.

"He looks like he's had a stroke."

"No, not that either," she said.

"What's the matter with him?" said Mrs Scruples. "Donald! Wake up, man. Look at me."

Mrs Scruples' head turned towards her, and kept turning. Ninety degrees, a hundred and eighty, further—

"Donald!"

The old man's head wobbled and popped off, dropping to the floor with the lower half of an elf poking out through his neck.

"Bloody hell," whispered Newton.

Mr Scruples came apart entirely. Torso and legs parted company; buttons and zips opened and at least five elves jumped out of the artfully reconstructed Donald Scruples.

"It's a suit," said Newton.

"Not quite," said Guin.

"Where's the real Mr Scruples?"

"You're looking at him."

In the central area, Mrs Scruples was doing a fine impression of Edvard Munch's *Scream*. "Donald! Donald! Get up! Don't do this!"

The elves thought it was all hilarious. They continued to circle Mrs Scruples, gradually drawing closer. Some waved their handkerchiefs at her mockingly; far more were waving their spoons.

"Are they going to eat her?" said Newton. Even at a distance he could see the wide-eyed shock on Mrs Scruples' face. She turned and saw Newton and Guin, peering out of their alcove cell.

"Them!" she screeched. "Take them! They'd make far better material. Much more elastic skin. Oil of Olay can only do so much. You don't want me. You don't want me!"

"I think I know what's going to happen," said Newton.

Guin tutted. "Took your time, didn't you?"

"You shouldn't look," he said. But it was too late.

The beardy elf, Bacraut, leapt at the old woman, aiming at her midriff with his spoon. It wasn't a sharp spoon but an edge doesn't need to be sharp if it's directed with sufficient force. Mrs Scruples didn't manage a scream, producing a wounded, worn out sigh: the kind of noise a dying sofa would make if sofas could scream or, indeed, die.

Thankfully (for Newton at least), Mrs Scruples was swiftly hidden from view by the tide of elves pouring on to stick the spoon in. "That's horrible," he said.

Guin was looking at the workstations around the cavern. "I don't think it's over yet," she said slowly

Elves were rushing over with big copper pots balanced on their heads. Out of the scrum of spoon-wielding elves, gobbets of red wet flesh were passed and dumped into the pots.

"Thought they tasted funny," said Guin.

"Hmmm?"

She pointed. At the butchering elves. At the metal pots. At a crank-handled mincing machine in a work station. At the strings and strings of sausages hanging overhead. She looked meaningfully at Newton's empty bowl.

"Oh, God," he murmured and put his hand to his mouth. He didn't feel sick. He felt disgusted, but he didn't feel physically sick. He should have done, shouldn't he? But he didn't. He found himself wondering if this made him a bad person.

***

# 62

Esther blinked and looked up at Dave.

"You're coming round," he said. He pricked her thumb.

*"Ow!"*

"Just running another blood test.". The tester beeped and Dave nodded with evident relief.

"How are you feeling?" he asked, rubbing her hand.

"Pretty good," she said. "That was ... weird." Her fingers explored the dressing that now adorned her arm.

"It certainly was," said Dave. "Candy Cane Venom."

"Hmmm?"

"Those elves seem to run on pure sugar. One bite sent you into hyperglycaemic shock."

"Like diabetes?"

"Right. One to be avoided, definitely. These little bastards are toxic in more ways than one."

"Yes" said Esther. "What are they doing?"

Dave rolled his eyes. "Wish I knew. I had to drag you out of sight of the window. They were marching around with flaming torches. I mean, where do they even get flaming torches from? It's gone properly medieval out there."

Esther raised herself up cautiously. They were behind the counter of the charity shop. She risked a peek over the top. Dave was right: outside elves were everywhere.

She sat up uncomfortably, wondering what she was leaning against. It was a stack of ancient board games and jigsaws. She remembered they were in a charity shop. "We must put something in the till as a thank you," she said.

"Sure, maybe."

"And, I got some of those papers, the ones they ripped up in the square."

She pulled them from a pocket. It was dark behind the counter, so she pushed them carefully along the floor until they were out of the shadow. She and Dave stayed back out of sight, trying to see what they were looking at.

Dave gave a grunt of recognition at the heading. "Catheter Holdings. Duncan Catheter was doing some kind of local land deal. Brownfield site."

"Doesn't look very brownfield to me," said Esther. "See where it is?"

Dave failed to make out any hint of a location.

"It's that area at the back of the church. It's mostly steep and inaccessible, but there's part of it that looks flat. He was going to build houses there."

"Makes sense," said Dave. He could see there were numerous house-shaped boxes drawn around an access road. "What are those circles?"

Esther shuffled forward. "It says they're sinkholes. Sinkholes? Wow. And what's that?"

Dave peered closer. "Playground and recreation park."

"Built over a sinkhole? The man was a complete monster!"

"He's dead, remember."

"I used the past tense."

Dave tapped the map in thought. "So, the elves were pretty pleased this isn't going ahead now—"

"Way ahead of you," said Esther. "That's got to be where their hideout is."

Dave nodded. "Where we need to go and look for the kids."

Esther got up from the floor, clearly as pleased as Dave to have a sense of purpose. "Yes, but how? We can't just walk up there and hope they won't notice us. We don't stand any kind of chance in a full-on fight against hundreds of elves."

Dave started to pace the floor, but realised that would draw the attention of the elves. He squatted again. "There was a tractor."

"Sorry?"

"A tractor, on the road not far from the church."

"Yeah! " grinned Esther. "Turn it into an assault vehicle and squash and barge our way into their bloody grotto."

"Squashing and barging are good," said Dave, pleased to see life and energy come back to her. "Assuming the tractor can climb that gradient."

"Assuming one of us can drive the thing."

"How hard can it be? It's just a big car, isn't it?"

Esther didn't look so sure. "I spent one summer helping out on a collective farm in Cuba. I sat up in the tractor once. It didn't look like just driving a car."

"That's probably just Cuban tractors," said Dave. "Come on, it's going to work. We're going to squash them and barge them. We're going to annihilate the buggers."

"Vaporise them," said Esther.

"Well, that would be nice."

"I've got an idea for the headlights."

She dragged some of the supplies she'd used earlier onto the floor and picked up the scissors. "We haven't got time to do the whole *A-Team* thing and transform the tractor into an armoured vehicle, but if I put a mask around the headlights so they shine in the shape of an elf cross, maybe it will fry some of the little shitbags."

"Elf lasers! You work on that, I'm going to see if we can rig up some stabby things. I did see a broken coat rack near the bins. It would be quite dangerous if you fell on it."

"If it's got heavy bits with nails sticking out then it sounds brilliant," said Esther without looking up. "Look in the kitchen area for knives as well."

"Cool." Dave said. "And there's this pole thing for opening the skylight in here as well."

"Bring it all," said Esther.

***

# 63

The hollowing out and sausagifying of Mrs Scruples occupied many of the elves for quite some time. They took obvious glee in the task.

Guin used her own time wisely, reading from the academic book of elf stuff and discussing what she read with Wiry Harrison and Tinfoil Tavistock to make sure they understood completely. Perhaps, at some point, the book would save their lives. Newton sat close by, knees drawn up to his chin, eyes raised and muttering to himself. Guin wondered if he'd gone mad. There was a thing, years and years ago, like probably in Victorian times, when all the cows in England went mad because they'd been given bits of dead cow to eat. Maybe Newton had caught Mad People Disease. Whatever it was, it was distracting her from her reading.

"What are you doing?" she asked.

"Counting sausages," he said, gazing at the ceiling of the cavern.

"Okay," she said. "Why?"

"They've made at least a hundred sausages so far."

"From one old lady?"

"I know. I counted. And up there." He pointed at the links of stored sausages, loops upon loops of them.

"And then there's all the sausages already eaten at the market," Guin added helpfully. "Those are just the leftover ones."

Guin considered the tonnes of sausages. She had no intention of counting them, but it was clear the elves must have been processing people on an industrial scale. "I think these elves are part of the Wild Hunt," she said.

"You mentioned them before, at dinner."

"Maybe these ones got lost, or decided to set up a base. A sort of non-moving hunt."

"Get the people to come to them. Draw them in with a cheesy Christmas market?"

A great shout went up from the elves in the centre of the cavern. Guin raised herself as high as possible to see what was going on. One elf was holding something white and long aloft.

"That's a leg bone," said Guin, in a matter-of-fact manner she wouldn't have expected of herself when seeing a leg bone of the recently deceased.

"They seem very excited about it," said Newton.

As one elf held it out, another placed a plastic ruler against it. Whatever the result, it was a source of much delight. The chief elf, Bacraut, snatched it up, and like a marching band majorette swung it about as he led them all out of the cavern.

Soon after, the elves came for Guin and Newton again. Guin noted that Gerd was especially keen to see if Guin had finished her food. Pleased that she had, the elves untied them, using teeth to pull apart the worst granny knots, and led them away.

"More tests?" said Newton.

"*Nei tala!*" shouted Gerd. Newton wisely shut up.

They were drawn deeper into the tunnels. The darkness grew about them and they were suddenly pressed in among countless elves heading in the same direction. The air became close and foetid.

"Smells like the stables," whispered Newton. A moment later they passed by a side opening onto a deep, well-lit cave, lined with animal stalls.

"More reindeer?" said Guin.

"*Nei tala!*" shrieked Gerd from somewhere close.

The massed elves erupted into a hall which nearly rivalled the great storage cavern in size. It appeared the elves had put more effort into this part of their lair than any other. Guin concluded the elves had a construction philosophy which generally blended great skill with a blasé attitude, like an order of genius artisans and craftspeople who had become extremely lazy. Their workshops, their machines, even their stitched together reindeer all had flashes of technical brilliance but were, for the most part, run down and falling apart.

This hall was quite different. The floor was polished to a marble shine. The arches were carved with geometric precision. Pillars, decorated with red and white candy cane spirals were brilliant and immaculate. The pointy-eared elves behaved accordingly and stood in neat rows, while Bacraut with the white glued-on beard took up his knife and waved it over the elves.

The elves sang. They sang well. They sang like mice on helium, but their voices were high and pure. "*Hriupp all chiand nin og tu þei pokðið.*"

Gerd prodded Newton and Guin.

"Singing practice," said Guin. "We're expected to join in."

"But we don't know the words."

"*Stihem ina sac þeiog sjúút litun,*" sang the elves. Guin was just about able to join in.

Newton stumbled and failed. He tried to just mouth long.

"You have to try," Guin whispered.

Newton was just about to point out he was trying when the knife flew out of Bacraut's hand and speared an elf on the front row.

"*Hriupp all chiand n-i-i-n!*" he yelled at the quite dead elf. "*Chiand n-i-i-i-n!*"

Guin used the pause to quickly try to teach Newton. "*Hriupp all chiand nin og tu þei pokðið,*" she whispered.

"Rip all Channing, octopus potted," he said.

"*Stihem ina sac þeiog sjúút litun*"

"Stick'em in a sack, bog shut lantern."

"*Ripeir blocks táí hádífa.*"

"Rip her blocks to Halifax."

"*Ráupp meðó fu og fið.*"

"Wrap my tofu in figs. Got it."

When Bacraut took up a fresh knife for his new baton, Newton was ready to join in. Five repetitions later and he was really getting into the swing of it. Gerd watched him shrewdly throughout but did not complain and, more importantly, no one else got a knife through the chest.

As the practice came to an end, and most of the elves dispersed back to wherever they'd come from, Newton bent to whisper to Guin. "Maybe I can learn elvish after all. Making toys and crackers, singing songs about, whatever, sparkles and raindrops and living in a magical winter wonderland."

"No," she said. "That song wasn't about sparkles or unicorns—"

"I didn't say unicorns."

"I think it was about what elves like to do to children."

"Give them presents?"

"The bit which actually translates as 'Stick 'em in a sack'...?"

"Yeah?"

"It was the nicest bit of the song."

Guin looked around. At the far end of the hall was a raised dais with a huge shape – a statue or a space rocket or a tree or something – hidden beneath a red velvety cloth. Two elves, with Mrs Scruples' leg bone between them, scuttled under the cloth and started banging and thumping about.

"Thing I want to know is," said Guin, "if they're practising songs and making Christmas presents and crackers and stuff, what are they doing it for?"

Newton shrugged. "Maybe the unveiling of their Christmas tree composed entirely of human bones." He nodded at the shrouded shape.

"Be serious," said Newton.

"I dunno. Christmas Day?"

Guin gave him her best serious look, the kind she used on stupid teachers and idiot school children who wouldn't let her join their gangs. "Do you want this lot to be in charge of Christmas Day?"

Newton looked worried for a moment, which Guin judged to be the correct response.

***

# 64

While Esther cut out her elf cross headlight covers, Dave manufactured the world's first industrial elf-stabbing tractor fender from a clothes rail and a dozen bent coat hangers.

When they judged they were finished, they made their way cautiously out of the shop. The street was quiet. It looked as though the search for them had moved off elsewhere.

They crept on, away from the town centre and down the narrow lane leading between the houses and up to the church. Dave struggled to carry all of his metal elf-destroying kit without making too much noise, but they made it to the tractor. It was bigger than Dave remembered, which was good.

Esther crouched to look underneath. "Checking for elves," she said.

He was about to make light of it, but he would have done the same. The damned creatures secreted themselves in every hidey-hole, enough to make a man paranoid. He instinctively looking up and scanned the rooftop in the houses that crowded on either side of the lane.

"Let's do this," he said, fastening his clothes-rail-elf-destroyer to the front of the tractor with the remaining coat hangers. Twisting the thick wire was really hard on his fingers, but it was worth the discomfort. He climbed up into the open cab and stashed the weaponised window pole. He added to his weapon supply with some edging bricks that had surrounded a nearby garden. A well-aimed brick could come in handy.

Esther fixed her elf cross stencils onto the headlights. Dave looked around the cab, wondering how the lights turned on. Come to that, he wondered how the tractor actually started. He looked down at the controls and tried to relate them to what he knew about driving.

"There's two gear sticks!" he hissed to Esther.

"Pallets!" hissed Esther in reply.

He frowned. She pointed to an alleyway across the road where there was a pile of empty pallets. "We can use them to protect the cab."

Dave jumped down to fetch them. They were surprisingly heavy and he had to take them back to the tractor individually. By the time he had four of them lashed into place over the front and side windows with baling twine, it felt more secure.

"It's going to be a bit tricky to see where we're going," he said as Esther climbed up to join him. "But I reckon we can manage

She peered forward. "We can do this," she said. "Right, let's fire her up."

"Oh yes, about that," said Dave. "I'm not sure how—" The engine roared into life, cutting off his words.

Esther grinned at him. "Collective farm in Cuba. Off we go!"

Standing in the cab behind his amazing and resourceful girlfriend, Dave picked up the pole in one hand and a brick in the other. Esther had to turn the tractor so they were facing the right way. He could tell it wasn't easy to manoeuvre in a tight space, but Esther managed it with a combination of dextrous handling and crushing everything in her path.

"It's like *Mad Max*, isn't it?" he said, grinning despite himself.

"If *Mad Max* was a Christmas movie."

"True."

"And set in rural northern England."

"Yes."

"It's more *Wallace and Gromit* than *Mad Max* really."

"Possibly."

***

# 65

From choir practice in the great hall, Newton and Guin were shuttled to their next task: reindeer. Newton wasn't sure how he felt about that.

On the one hand: reindeer! Furry, soft-nosed quadrupeds in need of the kind of love he was eager to dish out.

On the other: the reindeer in the cavern of animal pens were all like Blinky: partially decomposed, partially reconstructed; patched together from old reindeer or bits of animals that clearly weren't reindeer.

Still ... reindeer! Ugly or not, these were innocent creatures a lad like Newton was born to care for. Yes, they were a bit bitey. Yes, they looked like they favoured human flesh over grasses and moss, but that wasn't their fault, was it?

A new energy had overtaken the elf cavern since the bizarre excitement with Mrs Scruples' leg bone. Elves ran back and forth, carrying things. Bells, big and small, rang continuously, echoing along the tunnels like large scale tinnitus. Even in the reindeer cavern, elves were hurrying about, checking harnesses and reindeer against clipboards.

Gerd led Guin and Newton up one side of the pen and down the other, chanting a long list as they went. *"Hér er Bitður, Barari, Hlager og Gouper..."*

"There's got to be hundreds here," Guin whispered.

"I know," said Newton. After realising most of the creatures would try to bite off his fingers if he stroked them, he was making sure to give every one of them a cheery wave and some direct eye contact to show he was friendly.

*"Stoker, Kicgut, Gunch-munða og boriða..."* said Gerd.

"Why would anyone need this many reindeer?" wondered Guin.

Newton tried not to dwell on that because he knew full well in colder northern climates reindeer were providers of meat, hide, and more besides. Anyway, the obvious answer was the elves needed several teams of reindeer to pull several sleighs. If there were presents to be delivered, in all directions, the elves would need dozens of sleighs. Maybe even hundreds.

"*Meiuða og Daugum*," said Gerd with some finality. "*Nú, ður þúað læröll nöfra.*"

"*Læröll nöfra?*" asked Guin.

"*Ga, þúað læröll nöfra*, ya mithering get!" said Gerd angrily and stomped off.

"All their names," said Guin. "We have to learn them."

Newton sighed. "This is like the worst episode of *The Apprentice* ever."

"Except in the real one, Lord Sugar doesn't kill you if you fail your task."

They began another circuit of the hall and tried to recall some of the names. Newton found he remembered more than a few. Although their rotting faces and hides, stitched together with the same white thread, made them a little harder to love, it did make the reindeer that bit more memorable.

"That's Graumper and Scromdir, and I think that's bultaða..."

He remembered he had his phone with him. Although there was still no signal, he could use its camera to take photos of the creatures as they went. Several recoiled angrily from the flash, so he turned it off.

"We need to think about our escape plan," said Guin.

Newton looked round nervously. "We don't want to anger them."

"They are going to kill us if we just stay here."

"Me perhaps," said Newton. "You definitely won the toy challenge, and the singing competition." He sniffed. "And that's a good thing. You deserve to win."

"Jeez!" said Guin. "What do you call those people who just want to die for a cause?"

Newton frowned. "Martyrs?"

"Yeah, that's you. Is it your life's goal to die for me?"

"Not exactly."

"No?" It sure sounds like it. If you want to be helpful, how about growing a spine for me. Let's get out of this place together."

It was a hurtful remark. Newton could have cried. He moved on rapidly and took pictures of *Gunch-munða* and *boriða* and ... one he couldn't remember the name of.

"I made some elf crosses," said Guin. "Stuffed them up my top."

"Clever," said Newton, trying to sound positive, even if Guin's martyr comment still stung.

"I thought we could maybe make a bomb or some grenades from that cracker explosive."

"Dangerous," he said, "but definitely doable."

He wandered on. He flicked back through the phone's images, trying to remember names. He flicked back too far and came to the pictures of Lily he'd taken at the stables the morning before. His Lily.

"I do want to get out of here," he said to Guin, earnestly. "I really do."

"Good," she said.

A thought occurred to him and he chuckled. "You know that old joke? How does an elephant get down from a tree?"

"No," she said, clearly meaning "No, I don't, and I don't want to."

He was going to tell her anyway. "It sits on a leaf and waits until autumn."

"That's not even practical," said Guin.

He tutted and shook his head. "How do you escape from Santa's grotto? Climb into a sack and wait until Christmas."

Her eyebrows rose like she was at least thinking about it. Her expression suddenly changed and she flapped her hands at him to pay attention.

"*Læröll nöfra*," said Gerd sternly, appearing behind them.

"The names," said Newton. "Sure."

Together, they walked round the pens, pointing out various chomping, stomping undead reindeer and they certainly did their best to name all of them.

"That one's Hlager and that's *Gouper*..."

"That's Scromdir and bultaða..."

"Bitber and Paugir and ... Yongari?"

"And Dasher? And Dancer?"

"Sprongler or something?"

"Comet, Vixen, Cupid..."

"Rudolph?"

"Bifur, Bofur, Bombur..."

"Sleepy, Dopey, Sneezy, Grumpy..."

"Posh-deer, Scary-deer, Sporty-deer..."

"Kicgut! That one's Kicgut!"

There were occasional grudging nods from Gerd as they got some right. Out of the dozens in the cave, Newton estimated they got maybe one in four, which he considered pretty good going. Gerd was clearly less impressed.

Newton came to the last of them that he remembered. "And this one's Sleipnir— *Ow!*"

He had not been paying attention and the reindeer nipped his outheld fingers. When Newton checked, although he still had five fingers on that hand, the reindeer had ripped skin and flesh off his fingertips. Newton hissed and shoved his hand under his arm, dancing around to drive away the pain.

Gerd, who in another life could have been happy as a sadistic PE teacher, watched him with obvious glee. In the pen, bitey old Sleipnir was leaping with similar amusement, high-kicking leaps like a pronking antelope.

Gerd directed them back to their recess cell where they were tied up with ropes that were old and rotten, but coiled around their wrists again and again until they were solid as handcuffs.

Elves appeared with yet more bowls of food, even though it couldn't have been more than an hour since they'd last been fed. Sausages again for Newton; green mush for Guin.

Sucking on his wounded fingers, Newton contemplated the steaming sausages. How many different townsfolk had gone into each of those sausages? Were they a tasteful blend of butchers, bakers and candlestick-makers? Or was *this* sausage made from mature middle-aged school teacher and *this* one from fresh locally-sourced youngsters? And would he be able to tell the difference?

Guin tucked into her own food.

"You like that stuff?" asked Newton.

"I'm hungry," she mumbled.

He looked at the green mass in her bowl. "I think that might be reindeer moss."

"You mean the kind of moss reindeer would eat?"

Newton, who had seen a survival programme about arctic adventures, made a doubtful noise. "It's moss than the reindeers have already eaten. You know: pre-processed."

Guin stared at him, her cheeks bulging. She gave the matter some silent thought and then shrugged and carried on eating.

"Why have they given us different food?" said Newton.

"I think—" said Guin, then didn't say what she was thinking.

"You think they're fattening me up?" he said.

Guin was silent for a while. "You going to eat your sausages?" she said eventually.

"Er, no. Human flesh isn't my thing." He sucked at the cuts across his fingers. "Apart from my own. I think that's acceptable. Hey, did you hear the one about the two cannibals who were eating a clown? One turned to the other and said, 'Do you think this tastes funny?'"

After a long pause, Guin said, "That's actually a funny joke."

"You didn't laugh."

"Maybe I'm not in a laughing mood. That reindeer liked human flesh, didn't it?"

"I did notice."

"And did you see what happened when it bit you?"

"The jumping. Yeah. I don't believe animals are capable of evil, but I'd prepared to say that reindeer was a bit of git."

"It wasn't jumping."

"It was. I saw."

"You didn't see clearly enough." As the girl ate, she scooched round on crossed legs and fixed him with her pale eyes. "It had all four feet off the ground."

"That's pretty much the dictionary definition of jumping," said Newton. "I'm doing my GCSEs this year. I think I know what words mean."

"Don't be arrogant," she said. "I mean its feet were all floating off the ground."

"What? As in flying?"

"You don't believe me? We're in a cave, surrounded by Christmas elves and there's reindeer, and you don't think they're flying reindeer?"

Newton was about to object, about to say it just didn't obey the laws of physics. Then he heard his mum's voice – well, not her voice as such, but her manner and her views. Notions about the universe being far more complex than even scientists understood; about how perhaps homeopathy and crystal healing and angel therapy might really work in some instances. The kind of things his mum might say after a couple of glasses of wine or a visit to a psychic fair at the local community centre. She'd probably end up saying things like "It's only called the *theory* of evolution" or "No one knows how bumble bees fly" and Newton would grit his teeth, smile politely and put on an episode of *Planet Earth* to calm her down.

"Flying reindeer," he said neutrally. "Who get excited by human blood."

"Maybe."

Newton looked at her. "You know your ears...?"

"I believe so."

"Did they always have those pointy bits on the top?"

Guin reached up and felt her ears. They weren't exactly pointing, but at the top of each there was a pronounced fold that looked sort of pointy. It certainly looked pointier than when he'd first met her.

Guin felt the ridges of her ears, frowning. She stood and looked down at herself, tugging at the waist of her trousers and the rumpled folds around her ankles. "Am I getting shorter?"

She looked at the bowl in her hands and carefully put it down, like it was the most dangerous thing in the world. "We need to escape," she said.

"I agree," he replied.

She reached under her top and pulled out her fairy folklore book, two elf crosses, and a roll of cloth. "Hold onto that," she said, passing him a cross.

She unrolled the cloth on the floor and revealed three scalpel-like blades. "Stole these from the toy workshop," she said, passing one to Newton. She used another to start slicing at her own bonds.

"We will get into trouble," Newton said automatically.

"We're already in trouble.".

"We need an escape plan."

"Like you said, climb in a sack and wait till Christmas."

"I was joking," said Newton.

"Or, to put it another way, climb in a train truck and wait till it leaves. I've heard it go in and out at least twice while we've been here."

Newton gave this some thought and put renewed effort into cutting his ropes.

***

# 66

Guin and Newton's escape plan was simple but it still took time. The ropes tying them were worn, but there were a lot of them. Guin was sensible enough to not want to hurriedly saw at her bonds and end up sticking a blade in her ulnar artery. Her dad had told her enough paramedic horror stories about sliced wrists to give her something of a complex. In the past, she'd just stared at her white wrists and the pumping artery she knew was just beneath the surface and thought (not for the first time) that the human body was stupidly fragile and badly designed.

Also, the elves did not leave them entirely unguarded. Gerd swung by a couple of times, once to just shout at them, and the second to check they had eaten their food. Newton had concealed the sausages in his pockets so he could show an empty bowl. When Gerd demanded to see Guin's bowl, she pantomimed eating handfuls of the stuff.

She very much wanted to ask if the reindeer moss was magically turning her into an elf. She didn't, because the question sounded stupid in her head. And because she feared the answer would be yes. And, if the answer *was* yes, were all the elves children who had somehow 'passed the test'? There was a line she'd read in poor dead Elsa Frinton's book about what happened to people who were foolish enough to eat food while visiting the Lands of Faerie. Guin didn't think a stinking cave underneath an English town counted as the Lands of Faerie, but they were here, and they'd eaten. And although Wiry Harrison, Tinfoil Tavistock and the sharp blade she held concealed in her hand gave her the courage to act bravely, she really, really wanted to be out of here and miles away with her dad (and, yes, with Esther and Newton too, if that made everyone happy).

Gerd wandered off, satisfied Guin was being a good little elf and eating up. With the new urgency in the elves' work, Newton and Guin were no longer being supervised so closely. It was as good a time as any to escape.

"She'll probably be back with some more soon," said Guin. "We need to hurry."

There was the dull slap of heavy ropes falling to the ground. "Done," said Newton, massaging his wrist. "Can I help you with yours?"

"I'm fine," said Guin, irritated the older boy felt the need to assist.

It took her several more minutes to cut through her ropes.

"I can help," he said.

"I'm fine!"

"We need to hurry."

"I'm just trying to avoid cutting myself. Did you know, your artery can pump out blood at the rate of five litres a minute?"

"I did not know that," admitted Newton. "Not sure I wanted to."

"So be patient." The last threads came away. "Let's go." She saw the nervous look on Newton's face. "You want to see your girlfriend again, right?"

"My girlfriend?"

"Lily?"

"No. Lily's not— Who told you...?"

Guin tutted. "Come on!"

They carried elf crosses and knives. Although Newton was a big lumbering ox of a boy, they could stay close to the wall and the shadowy areas least lit by the dim fairy lights. From their recess cell, the main cavern was directly ahead, full of noise and industry echoing up to the chimney-like opening high above. Off to the left was a long tunnel, leading past piles of stored goods and mounds of rubbish, past Blinky the reindeer's stall and alongside the elves' little steam train.

"Hello, girl," Newton whispered to the reindeer as they passed.

The nightmare creature still had Newton's misshapen rabbit toy clenched in its mouth. Strands of stuffing hung from the gaps between its teeth. It sniffed at them and stamped its feet excitedly.

"That thing's as daft as you are," said Guin.

They crept on, along the low line of rotten little train trucks. Blinky grunted and huffed at them as they went.

"Couldn't we just carry on walking to the exit?" said Newton.

Guin looked along the tunnel and the fading string of lights. She listened hard, tried to pick out what sounds were coming from that direction. "You don't think there'll be guards at the exit?"

"Probably."

There were bundles of sack cloth in the nearest cart. Newton boosted Guin over the lip and followed. They burrowed under the sacks and tried to make themselves as small as possible, which wasn't all that small in Newton's case.

Guin lay in the dark fusty folds and closed her eyes. She willed herself to be still and at one with the sacks. Tiny. Invisible. In a sudden panic, she wondered if the act of willing herself to be small and unnoticeable was aiding the elves' magic. So she willed herself to be a perfectly ordinary girl-sized person who happened to be well-hid under the sacks.

She heard the plaintive grunts of the zombie reindeer. Something had clearly got her excited. There were raised elf voices and the crack of wood.

"*Er skeypis! Reindýrn hef skarpa!*"

The reindeer had scarpered?

There was a clattering next to their little truck and then a yell of pain from Newton. "*Ow! Ow!* What are you doing that for?"

The elvish yells were closer.

"*Ow!* Okay! Okay!" called Newton.

They'd been discovered. Guin sat up. Newton was standing up in the truck, trying to fend off Zomdeer Blinky who was biting and snapping at his clothes. More than a dozen elves were gathered round, weapons drawn.

"*All hal góra skeggi?*" said Guin.

\*\*\*

# 67

As Esther drove the tractor up the steep slope at the back of the church she worried that it might simply slide backwards or tip over. She kept those thoughts to herself and put her faith in the tractor's tyres and pulling power.

She kept the revs high and refused to let the machine stall. The tractor ran roughshod over the snow, its massive tyres gripping well. Branches as thick as her arm scraped against the bonnet and cab, dislodging the snow lying heavily along them. Any branch that could not bend and yield snapped. The pallet over the window turned out to be an effective and necessary shield against the debris.

"That's where we got buried!" Esther shouted back to Dave over the scraping and clattering and snapping.

"What?"

"That's where we— Never mind! Where are we? On the map! The map!"

Dave leaned forward with the remnants of Duncan Catheter's plan in his hands.

"I think the ground should level out shortly," he said.

Sure enough, the tractor bumped over a ledge and they were able to make out a sizeable plateau. Esther tried to match up the narrow view she had between the slats of the pallet with what she recalled of Duncan Catheter's plans.

"There were going to be houses over there," said Dave, waving to the left. "And over there as well. That part in the middle is where the sinkholes are marked."

"Then that's where we need to look."

"Do you know what sinkholes look like?" said Dave.

"No," admitted Esther after a moment's thought. "Not really. Holes, I suppose."

"Are they big enough for a tractor to fall down?"

Esther peered forward, almost wishing she hadn't applied her elf-cross silhouette shapes to the lights, since they cut down so much on the light they cast. "No idea. We'll take it really slowly from this point."

They edged forward.

Dave clutched her elbow. "Elf at one o'clock," he whispered.

Esther steered towards it, wanting to see if the light would have any effect. The elf was lit up by the blurry image of an elf cross. It blinked against the light, then raised its weapon and charged, curly-toed shoes running crisply over the deep snow's surface.

"It's not working," said Dave. He struggled to get his elf-poking stick out.

"It's too blurry," said Esther. "It just needs to find its focal length."

As the elf and tractor closed, a perfectly-formed elf cross focused in the middle of the elf's chest. It howled in pain and clutched itself, staggering.

"What's that smell?" Esther said.

"I think it's burning elf flesh."

"Cool," she said, adding remorsefully, "Jesus, Dave, what's wrong with me? I enjoyed hurting that elf. I *enjoyed* it!"

"You should, because we're one step closer to rescuing the kids. You're focused on the end game and that's what it's all about."

They trundled on, over the prostrate body of the elf with a smouldering chest.

They both leaned forward to see through the gaps in the pallet. Esther wondered why the tree coverage was so thin here, speculating if Duncan Catheter had sent in a chainsaw team to pre-empt the planning process. She found herself getting angry at him, as she always did at selfish developers. It was probably pointless, as he was already dead, but he represented the evil scourge of deforestation across the globe. She nurtured the anger in order to focus her new-found murderous instincts as she had a feeling that she'd be needing them.

"Can you see that dark area over by the hillside?" whispered Dave.

Esther could see what he meant. At the edge of the plateau, the ground rose steeply again. Mostly it was covered with snow, but there was some sort of shadow close to the ground. Esther steered towards it. As they drew nearer it was clear this sinkhole was more like a tunnel descending into the hillside.

"We going in?" asked Dave. "Only I'm not sure the tractor will fit."

"Look on the ground," said Esther, carefully ignoring his concerns. "It looks like train tracks. This is definitely where we need to be looking." She turned the tractor in a wide arc to get a run up to the tunnel.

"The tractor's too big," said Dave.

"Men are awful judges of size," said Esther and accelerated hard.

"You're not thinking—?"

"Just hang on, my love!"

"I honestly don't think there's much to hang—"

"Brace yourself!" Esther yelled as they approached at top tractor speed.

Dave ducked down behind the seat and wrapped his arm around both the seat and Esther as the tractor smashed into the gap. The tunnel was far wider and taller than it looked: the opening made smaller with wood panels and piled up debris. The cover shattered as the tractor ploughed through. Something caught on the tractor roof and it was wrenched off. The tractor bucked severely, but they were inside. As Esther peeked up, she could see the train tracks up ahead. They plunged on.

\*\*\*

# 68

At spear and knife point, Newton and Guin were forced out of the truck. One of the elves barked something that sounded very much like an accusation.

"This isn't what it looks like," said Newton, knowing full well it was exactly what it looked like. He couldn't tell if the elves believed or even understood him. Their sharp little faces were screwed up in unreadable anger and Newton was somewhat distracted by Blinky, who continued to nip at him, especially around his trouser pockets.

"What do you want, girl?" he asked, batting her away while trying to stroke her mangy muzzle. He felt in his pockets and found the sausages he'd hidden there.

"*Dreda ster kindi!*" snapped one elf.

"Don't kill him!" said Guin. "*Emeið og him!*" She held up her elf-cross to ward them off, immediately dropping it. She clutched her hand, shocked. "It burned me!"

Newton's heart pounded in his chest. She *was* being turned into an elf! Elf-crosses were now effective against her. And he, clearly not elf material, was surplus to requirements.

Even as he acknowledged the truth, he pulled a sausage from his pocket it and fed it to Blinky to keep her happy. The hungry undead reindeer wolfed it down.

An elf came forward, pushing Guin aside in order to get to Newton.

"Wait!" she shouted. "*Bædu!*" She took out a tiny object. It was one of her little homemade toys. "This is Wiry Harrison!"

"*Viry* Harrison?" said the elf.

Guin placed the little wire man on the floor, straightening the sword made from twists of wire in his hand. "Wiry Harrison is a fierce warrior."

The elves stared at the two-inch figure.

"He is brave and dependable and would kill every one of you to protect me."

"Ooh," said one of the elves.

"He's never been defeated in combat."

An elf carefully got on its hands and knees to inspect the still and silent warrior. Newton watched with bated breath.

"Get out your elf cross," Guin whispered to him.

"Then what?" Newton whispered back.

"No idea."

The elves chatted among themselves, clearly torn between wariness of the miniscule foe, and understandable derision at what was clearly a little figurine made of wire. Blinky had finished her sausage. She nudged Newton for another, making snotty, phlegm-like marks on his sleeve. He hoped it was phlegm and not zombie brain juices.

"Okay, girl," he said, fumbling for sausage and elf-cross simultaneously. At the same time he realised Blinky's hoofs were not on the ground. They were pawing the air, inches above the ground.

"You're flying!" he said. He remembered the effect his blood had on the bity reindeer – and these sausages were made primarily of unfortunate locals...

Newton's next course of action seemed obvious. He shoved a sausage in the reindeer's mouth and grabbed Guin, swinging her onto the reindeer's back. She yelped in surprise.

The elves hissed, probably guessing he was kidnapping their latest recruit. Newton warded them off with his elf-cross; long enough for him to feed Blinky a third sausage and leap astride the creature's back. Blinky's body was a mass of knobbly bones wrapped in a thin hide and painful to sit on.

"Yah! Fly, Blinky!" he urged.

***

# 69

Dave was worried the tunnel, though surprisingly wide by British standards, might get narrower up ahead and the tractor would get jammed. Esther kept up a steady speed, planning to smash through any minor constrictions as she bumped along the train track.

"I can see light," said Esther. "Up ahead. Arm yourself."

Dave didn't need telling twice. He had a pile of bricks at the ready, and the pole ready to go. "What's your plan when we get there?" he asked.

She shrugged. "Crush as many elves with brute force as I can and fry a few with the lights for good measure. You stop them getting into the cab and we'll see if we can spot the kids."

Dave didn't like to point out that the cab was a thing of the past. They were sitting in a vehicle that was very much an open-top model.

They emerged into a huge cavern. Esther had to swerve off the train track, as there was a train already parked on it.

"Holy hell, what's going on?" said Dave.

"I would say," said Esther, steering towards a crowd of elves and making sure both elf cross lights and elf-stabbing fender were lined up, "that the kids are attempting to escape on a flying reindeer while these elves try to stop them."

"Not just me, then."

A number of elves were already noisily smouldering from the lights, along with screams from those who had been impaled on the stabbing fender. Too late Dave realised there was a fatal design flaw with his stabby fender: once it had a full complement of impaled elves, it became harmless.

An elf stood ahead of them, fearlessly taking aim with a catapult. He scored a direct hit on one headlight, then re-loaded and took out the other.

"Bugger!" said Dave. "All we can do now is run them over. Crush them with the tyres!"

Esther did her best, doing tight figures of eight (or as tight as she could accomplish with a vehicle designed to have an entire field for manoeuvring), but the elves were too numerous. Dave threw bricks at any in range, but even a direct strike was more of a deterrent than a fatal blow. The elves had been initially worried, then simply distracted; now they looked as if they were enjoying the sport.

***

## 70

At three sausages' worth of power, Blinky was soon hovering with her hoofs at elf head height. As she bucked and galloped against the air, all three moved off at something like strolling speed. The elves stabbed at Newton's dangling legs so he hoisted them up out of the way.

"Is this your escape plan?" yelled Guin behind him. "We can run faster than this!"

Newton felt her disappointment burn deep inside him. He dug his raised heels in. "Come on, Blinky!" he urged. "You can do it."

He had pictured them soaring up, circling towards the large chimney opening in the cavern's apex, and out into cool, crisp night-time freedom. Instead they were just ambling along, six feet off the ground, with as much excitement and urgency as a toddler's coin-operated animal ride.

"They stamped on Wiry Harrison!" exclaimed Guin.

Newton leaned forward. Awkwardly he fed the fourth and final sausage into Blinky's gnashing teeth.

"Fare thee well, fallen warrior," said Guin softly.

"What?" Newton called back.

"Nothing," sniffed Guin.

Even with four sausages, Blinky didn't seem to have much lift.

"Maybe they take a while to kick in," Newton wondered out loud, but he didn't think that was it. Sleipnir had been given instant lift from just a nibble of his fingertips. Volume-wise that was nothing compared to four briny hotdogs. Maybe that was the problem: blood and sausages were not the same.

Fearing for his fingers and hoping he wasn't wrong, Newton leaned forward and presented his already injured index finger to Blinky.

The sudden bite made him yelp. He yanked his hand back, but Blinky had already gotten a good taste. There were smears of blood across her muzzle.

"Blinky ... the red-nosed reindeer," Newton whimpered as he bunched his hand up in pain.

It was enough. With a wriggle and a shiver, Blinky leapt. Guin held onto Newton; Newton grabbed the reindeer's one good antler with his one good hand.

They were ten feet off the ground and rising. Below them elves shouted and shrieked. A spear flew past them, wobbling and warbling like a startled bird.

"It's working!" yelled Guin.

"Never doubted it!" Newton yelled back. "What in—?"

Looking down across the cavern, he saw a whole bunch of elves gathered around what appeared to be some sort of open-top jeep. Newton realised it was, in fact, a tractor with its top half sheared off. In the remnants of the cab were two figures, fighting off elves with bricks and a window pole.

"Mum! Dave!"

***

# 71

Dave glanced up to see how Guin and Newton were getting on, hoping they'd long gone. To his horror they were flying down, presumably to help. He could clearly see the terse and uncompromising looks on Guin's and Newton's faces.

"No!" he yelled at them. "Away! Away!" He waved furiously. "Let the dog drown! Let the dog drown!"

"What's the matter?" asked Esther, who couldn't afford to take her eyes off what she was doing.

"The kids," said Dave.

She glanced up for a split second. "What's the plan?"

Guin was leaning over and making upswept hooking gestures with her arm, like she wanted them to prepare to be airlifted out.

"I think we're beyond plans," said Dave hollowly.

"We can leave the tractor making a nuisance of itself," said Esther. She pushed the steering wheel onto a hard lock and put Dave's pole through it to hold it in place. "Brick!"

After a moment he caught on and jammed one of the bricks onto the accelerator.

"That reindeer's coming in fast," she said. "You think we can grab it?"

"Is that reindeer even real?" muttered Dave. The creature looked like a bad animatronic, or as though someone had dipped a real reindeer in paint stripper and then tried to mend the damage using the remains of a rotten sofa.

"You need to recalibrate your beliefs, dear," said Esther. She hurled the last of the bricks and then the two of them reached out for the reindeer as it flew overhead. They grabbed a leg each. Dave was yanked off his feet and hugged the thin leg close.

"Hold on!" shouted someone.

Dave held tight. In his spinning vision, he caught a glimpse of Guin's leg against the creature's flank. He'd found her. They were back together for however long.

The reindeer wobbled with the extra weight and dipped towards the ground.

"This leg's got woodworm!" said Esther.

For a moment Dave didn't grasp what she meant, but a crunching sound from above was a dead giveaway. Esther fell. She slid into a wall and to the ground. The reindeer tipped. Dave tumbled to the ground, landed on his feet by pure luck, hit the ground, and rolled against the side of the train tracks.

He looked up, hoping to see Guin and Newton flying far away. Instead he saw a distressed, three-legged reindeer completely out of kilter, flying in rapidly-decreasing circles towards the far side of the cavern and out of sight among the storage areas and workstations. Elves ran in pursuit.

Dave looked round for Esther. She stood some distance off, by the wall she'd hit. In her hand was the remains of the zombie reindeer's woodworm-riddled leg. She stood tall wielding it like a club, snarling at the elves to back off. She lunged forward and whacked one of them into the middle distance.

She turned to the tightening circle. "Come on then! Who's next?" She smacked another one just for kicks. "Dave! Get the kids!"

Dave scuttled off, keeping low, heading in the direction he'd seen the reindeer and children take.

***

## 72

Esther was backed up against the wall with only a reindeer leg to defend herself. She held it like a rounders bat, since that was the one sport Esther had excelled at as a child. She channelled years of practice into swing after swing as elves tried ducking below her guard with their nasty little blades. She didn't know their language, but she made her meaning very clear.

"Come on you elfy bastards!"

She thought she heard Newton's voice in the distance, saying something like "Actually they look pretty unelfy to me", but it was just her imagination.

However, her arms were going to tire soon. Weekly Zumba sessions at the local community centre and Pilates in the park had helped her maintain a decent level of fitness, but there was only so much elf-whacking one could do. Eventually, one of them would slip past her guard, or find a way to sneak up on her.

The thought made her look around and check the spaces beyond her peripheral vision. A string of fairy lights looped across the cavern wall just above her head, disappearing into a hole off to her left. An elf was crawling hand over hand along the lights to get to her.

Grunting like a tennis pro, she swung the wooden leg and mashed the sneaky sod against the wall. The creature gave a satisfyingly pathetic, *"Urk!"* and dropped to the ground.

But as she brought her weapon down, the inevitable happened. The rotten leg broke away completely, leaving her holding a ragged stump. She held it in a threatening pose and moved away from what was left of the group. There were only a few, but she was very aware her small piece of wood was no match for their knives. Even so, she couldn't let that affect her positive mental attitude. Esther was a doer, and she knew the value of keeping busy.

She scanned the cavern, looking for escape routes, any answer to her predicament. There were boxes everywhere, to contents of which might have been useful, there was no time to check them out. Then she remembered the hole in the cavern wall off to her left.

It was like a duct. She'd probably fit inside. And a stack of boxes provided a handy staircase up to it. She peered in and decided to commit to the full Bruce Willis. She was going into the ducts.

She hurled her useless reindeer remnant at the nearest elf, pointed and yelled, "Look! It's Father Christmas!", and ran for the boxes. They creaked under her feet but did not break. The elves, momentarily distracted by the possible appearance of old St Nick, were hot in pursuit.

Esther leapt into the duct, hands and knees coming down on a dusty and greasy surface. She turned, kicking the nearest pursuer in the face, tumbling the sharp-faced fiend off the box pyramid.

She kicked out several more times until she was able to reach down and grab the topmost box. She feared it might be too heavy to lift, but from great desperation came great energy. She pulled it up and into the duct behind her. It didn't exactly wedge into the space, but it filled it sufficiently to slow any elves that might get past the missing top box-step.

She twisted the obstruction, jamming it more thoroughly, before starting to crawl away. Her hands and knees squidged on the greasy metal floor.

"Bruce Willis never got this dirty," she said to herself. *Die Hard* was another Christmas movie that had lied to her.

\*\*\*

# 73

As elves ran by, Dave kept still. He had managed to escape them by rolling underneath the train and lying between the rails. He knew he couldn't stay there: he needed to locate Guin and Newton. Also, he didn't want to be bacon-sliced and mushed if the train moved off. Playing on train tracks was a big no-no. As a paramedic he'd seen the evidence with his own eyes.

Thoughts of medical matters made him check for his first aid kit. It was attached to his belt, with dressing, antiseptics and a dozen insulin shots inside it. He'd probably need those again before the night was through.

He wriggled along the track as far as he dared, then rolled off, looking around to see where he was. It was darker here, but he could make out a side cavern up ahead. He couldn't be far from where Guin and Esther's boy had crash-landed. They might have gone to hide in there.

He crawled forward on his belly, keeping to the shadows. When he made it round a corner, he stood, carefully. The side cavern's roof was lower and it stretched deep into the hillside. Boxes – Christmas boxes, shiny and tied with ribbon – were stacked in rows, extending as far back as he could see.

Now he came to think about it, the entire hill had to be hollow. How could Catheter have imagined it would be safe to build houses here, when the whole place was riddled with caves?

"Guin!" he stage whispered. "You here? Newton! Guin!"

***

# 74

When she fell from the doomed reindeer, Guin landed heavily on her backside, jarring her spine and knocking all sensation from her bum . She immediately leapt up and ran for cover. While Newton yelped over in one direction, and his mum could be heard shouting aggressively from another, Guin did her best to shake off her own pursuers.

In her pocket, Tinfoil Tavistock heartily approved. The juvenile quadruped pointed out it was like that old joke about running away from a bear. She didn't need to be able to run faster than the bear; she just needed to be faster than the other people the bear was chasing.

Guin would have argued she wasn't abandoning Newton or the others, rather she was regrouping and preparing to lead the retaliation. Or she would have done, if she hadn't been sprinting for her life: dodging and weaving around piles of boxes to shake off the main crowd of pursuers. As she ran into a familiar side tunnel, she could hear the shouts of outrage fading into the distance.

She recognised the first door she came to. It was the toy workshop. She slipped inside, grateful the place was empty, and bolted the door behind her.

As she got her breath back, she took Tinfoil Tavistock out of her pocket so she could explain clearly how and why, despite the fact she appeared to be selfishly fleeing for her life, she was actually making a tactical decision.

Tavistock – oh, so simplistic Tavistock – said it was not okay to leave loved ones behind, even if one of them was a bumbling and annoying teenage boy. Guin was swift to explain the situation was far more complex than that, and she didn't expect someone like Tavistock to understand.

On the workbench, Starfish Eglantine, the plush toy she'd created earlier in the night regarded her with its many eyes as though to say, "Oh, yeah?"

Guin tutted. She didn't like it when her imaginary friends ganged up on her.

***

# 75

Through various twists and turns, jumping at sudden sounds and occasionally cowering for his life, Newton eventually found himself in a corner of the reindeer cave. He hunkered out of sight while elves busied themselves, taking Scromdir and Bitber and Dancer and Rudolph and whatever their names were out of their pens to be harnessed up.

Over the crackly tannoy, an elf announced something. Newton did not speak elf apart from the universal greeting *"All hal góra skeggi!"* and he didn't plan on learning any. However, the words coming over the tannoy had a clipped and measured rhythm, a sort of "The rebel base will be in range in ten minutes" kind of cadence. Something was very much afoot.

Two elves entered, herding limping Blinky between them. They were arguing. From his hiding position by a vacant reindeer stall, Newton could see much gesturing towards Blinky's missing leg. Blinky did not seem to be in much discomfort from the lack of a leg. She looked from elf to elf as they bickered, and then she ate one of their hats.

The elf shrieked in frustration, grabbed its half-eaten hat from her mouth and stomped away. The other, having won the argument but not gained much from it, irritably led the hobbling reindeer past the hidden Newton, through an opening, and returned, moments later, Blinky-less.

Newton had a mental image of what he needed to do. The simple version was find his mum, Guin and Dave and get the hell out of elf-central, in that order. A priority list based on personal familiarity, some deep-rooted chivalric sexism (that he really didn't feel comfortable with) and a nameless thing he saw as a sort of Newton Woollby Personal Vulnerability Scale. However, the list wasn't a simple line. Newton's complex and over-thought mental image took into account what he imagined other people's priorities would be. He was probably near the top of his mum's, possibly on a par with and in danger of being over-taken by Dave (which he stiffly thought was all fine and proper). Dave's would have Guin and Esther vying for top spot. Guin's... Well, Guin's priorities were unclear.

Newton wouldn't have gone so far as to call her selfish but she certainly wasn't the kind of girl ruled by big-hearted selflessness. So Newton's priority list was an odd sort of web in which he featured at the bottom because, well, it was his duty to put others first, but in which he was also raised up by his mum's love for him. One in which Guin was generally of middling importance, but given a super boost by Dave's affections for his daughter and the simple fact she was a child. All of them bumped and bumbled around in the web.

Animals did not figure in that particular web. Newton loved animals, generally more than he did most people, but they didn't appear in this current real-time crisis priority web. Blinky's fate was notionally unimportant. Blinky was not in the web; she was off to one side. Separated. With a big fluffy cloud drawn around her in pen. And little stars, or possibly rainbows, in highlighter.

Blinky was unimportant, but Newton needed to know what had happened to her.

With elves focused on getting nearly a hundred zombie reindeer into harnessed teams, it was easy for him to slip out of his position and into the side tunnel Blinky had been taken down. The tunnel ran for some distance, alongside various thick pipes that stank of petrol, before it came out in a poorly lit service chamber.

Blinky was tied up beside a pit. She three-leggedly hobbled round to face Newton. He charitably decided the wild look on her face was a greeting between old friends.

"I wondered what they'd done to you." He reached out with gentle hands. Blinky – playful as ever – tried to rip off his fingers. She missed as she over-balanced and stumbled on her three legs.

"I think," said Newton. "we might need to change your name. Should it be Limpy or Wonky?"

***

# 76

Esther quickly discovered a way of moving through the small tunnel vents, a sort of bent-kneed frog-like super-crouch that allowed her to scuttle along efficiently. She'd also discovered a small string of battery-powered fairy lights which she'd wrapped around her head for light. She must have looked like a weird halo-wearing frog-saint or the world's cheapest R2-D2 fancy dress effort.

Within minutes of entering the vent tunnels, she realised there was a complex warren of them. They looped between the main caverns, doing their own thing in between. She got the hang of navigating them by looking out for the fairy lights. Where there was a direct passage between the larger caverns there was very often a string of lights she could follow.

As she approached an opening into a larger cavern, she smeared dirt onto her face for camouflage. She leaned out to see what was happening. Despite having humans running willy-nilly through their nest, the elves seemed mostly focused on their work. In the biggest cavern Esther had yet seen, a large-scale operation was underway. It wasn't just large: it was colossal.

There were lots of shipping containers. Except they had been crudely fashioned into open-top containers. All of them had sled-like runners welded to their sides, but were presently being transported along the elf's miniature railway line, on relatively tiny carriage beds hidden beneath the containers' bulk. The place was clearly the hub of whatever was being planned, a focus of operations. The containers were being lashed together with some sort of enormous harness. It appeared to be made from metal, wood, leather and various other materials. Esther was well-acquainted with upcycling and re-use. It looked very much as if someone had taken fence posts, traffic lights and every imaginable type of street furniture, and fashioned them together to make a wonky shell to connect all the sled-containers. It gave the entire thing the look of a colossal segmented insect: a centipede in plate armour.

Together, the train of containers formed a single sleigh, a giant parody of Father Christmas's sleigh at that.

The armoured sheets along its sides had been indifferently painted in red, and fashioned into a wonky scalloped shape. At the front of the massive vehicle (which was at least a hundred feet long) was a place for the driver to sit: a scrolled front end twenty feet high. All of these facets were clues to the enormous vehicle's cultural origins, but the monstrous thing had as much in common with the traditional Santa's sleigh as ... a wooden sailing boat with a ten-storey Caribbean cruise liner. No – it was like comparing a sailing boat to a giant cruise liner that had sunk in a storm, been raised up again, and repaired by medieval blacksmiths who had no notion of boat design. It was a gigantic travesty of a sleigh, a bloated and unnatural tumour-growth copy.

Esther wanted to think this industrial monstrosity was a solid metaphor of what had happened to Christmas in this age of selfish commercialism, but witty socio-political metaphors weren't going to help rescue the family.

One thing that did puzzle her about the sleigh was how on earth the elves expected it to move. True, it currently sat on rails, but the railway line was miniscule, monorail thin compared to its bulk, and there was no engine at the front. There were stubby metal wings on the side, and four great barrels that might have once been aeroplane turbines, although it was hard to tell beneath the mass of fuel pipes and brackets covering them. At the back was another cluster of cylinders, salvaged perhaps from jet planes, or some dodgy space programme. Even with the mass of engine parts. Esther could not believe they alone could give the vehicle sufficient lift. They looked like they would drag it down with their weight, not move it along.

If this was supposed to be Father Christmas's vehicle then it would traditionally be pulled by reindeer. She thought about the sorry specimen Guin and Newton had ridden on. It would take hundreds of those creatures to move the thing.

Shaking her head at the insanity of the elves' endeavour, she backed along the duct, and down one of the narrower spurs of pipe. Through a grille in the floor she saw she was over a corridor tunnel, and a quieter one at that. She couldn't spend the rest of her life crawling around like a wise-cracking, folliclychallenged New York detective. At some point, she'd have to get out, arm herself, find her family and maybe sabotage an elf sleigh along the way. Plus, Pilates or no Pilates, this sort of undignified crouch was starting to do her back in. She lifted away the grille, poked her head out to check the coast was clear, and wriggled through feet first.

Only superficially gouging her ribs on the narrow opening, she dropped to the ground. No elves in sight.

She moved swiftly along the corridor. Some of the doors she passed were marked with signs hinting at what lay on the other side. Many were scrawled with Nordic runes of some sort, and she sort of wished she could spend time studying the language and culture of these ancient peoples. Only sort of, because mostly she wanted to smash their faces in for what they had done to her little family, or would-be family. Some doors also featured little wood and pokerwork symbols. She found one marked with a crossed hammer and saw: a workshop of some sort surely. Workshops equalled tools. Tools equalled weapons.

Esther tried the door. It appeared to be locked. She rattled the handle to make sure.

***

# 77

The door to the toy workshop rattled and shook.

Guin made sure the bolts were securely in place. The door rattled a second time. She listened out for sounds of elf chatter, for indications they were going to try and break in or raise the alarm. She heard nothing. There was silence.

On the bench, Starfish Eglantine regarded her haughtily. *You are running away*, said Eglantine.

"I'm not running away," Guin told her.

*You're a coward.*

"It's okay to be a coward," she said. "Being scared is normal. People who are scared and run away are the ones who survive. My dad told me that."

*I'm scared all the time*, said Tavistock.

"And I've got to look after Tavistock here," said Guin.

*Tavistock is just a piece of screwed up tinfoil*, said Eglantine.

*I am*, agreed Tavistock.

*You are trapped in a dangerous place*, said Eglantine. *You've got nowhere to run away to.*

Guin pulled a face. "Yes, but—"

*But?* said Eglantine.

"What can I do? There's hundreds of them and only one of me."

There was a voice over the echoing and crackling public address system. *"Taskepta stelör bairnsk að hefjá fifttán mínútur."*

"Project something-something in something minutes?" said Guin.

*They're up to something*, said Eglantine. *These elves have a plan.*

"What plan?"

*What would your plan be if you were stuck somewhere alien, where you were surrounded by hostile idiots and with no friends?*

Guin thought. She didn't have to think much. It was a fair description of every day she had to spend at school. Tinfoil Tavistock didn't have to think much either.

*Hide*, said Tavistock without hesitation.

"I'd make my own friends," said Guin, looking at Tavistock.

*I don't think these elves are planning on hiding for much longer,* said Eglantine. *Do you?*

Guin thought about the things in the elf lair that just hadn't made sense. The on-going preparations, the piles of present-like boxes, the vast number of reindeer in the pens. Were the elves planning on launching their own Christmas mission, to visit all the children in the world?

Were the elves going out on a colossal diplomatic mission to make friends?

*What do you think?* said Eglantine.

***

# 78

"You are a good girl, aren't you?" said Newton as he cautiously petted Wonky Blinky.

Newton peered down into the pit. It was several metres across but it was hard to tell how deep it was, it being almost filled to the lip by reindeer parts. Severed legs and decapitated heads nestled among less identifiable chunks of flesh, organs and hide.

"Oh, heck," Newton whispered.

Much of the reindeer mix was still, very much as diced deer ought to be, but throughout the pile various bits of undead reindeer wiggled and crawled. Mouths moved, hoofs kicked, flanks rippled, and a length of severed reindeer spine was trying to crawl out of the pit. Newton could feel his knees weakening and the vomit rising in his throat.

"Okay, man, don't go to pieces," he said, turning to Blinky to see if she appreciated this grim quip.

Blinky's reaction was unclear. However Newton did see an elf fast approaching him across the cavern from a stout door he had not previously seen it guarding. It ran at him, waving a flinty-tipped spear and yelling something unintelligible that Newton severely doubted was, "Here! I would like to present you with a gift of this lovely spear! Can we be friends?"

Newton tripped in surprise, spinning away from the pit edge and avoided a skewering. He found himself grabbing the spear shaft and, with no real effort on his part, flipping the elf up into the air like a pole-vaulter. The elf-guard came down, squealing, into the pit of reindeer bits. The elf yelled. A reindeer spine wrapped itself around him. A nearby head, sensing food, bit down on the elf's arm. The elf screamed for a second, then something powerful from beneath the surface layer latched onto it and dragged it down, silencing it utterly.

"Nasty." Newton turned to Blinky. "They weren't planning on recycling you in there, were they?"

Blinky affectionately tried to bite off Newton's face.

"Well, I won't let them, old girl," he said. "I think you should come with me."

He crouched at the pit edge and, avoiding a very active loop of undead intestine, reached down and snagged up a leg. It kicked and jerked in his hand and generally tried to pull his arm from its socket.

"There," he grunted, standing up. "This will—"

He was holding a hind leg. Blinky was missing a foreleg. A left foreleg.

"Hang on."

Newton crouched again and fished around. He narrowly avoided the snapping teeth of a severed head, but did come up with a left foreleg.

"Let's try this." He positioned the leg against Blinky, regarding it critically. "It's a bit long but it will definitely do."

Blinky's various body parts were stitched together with a wiry white thread. Newton looked around. If this was the location of the pit of body parts then...

"Ah." The door that the now deceased elf had been guarding across the cavern had a letterbox opening in it. Threaded through was a length of white material.

"Potentially promising. *Ow!*" Blinky bit him on the shoulder. "Knock that off. I'm going to get some thread and sew your new leg on, you ungrateful creature. Maybe I'll – *stop it!* – get a nose bag and put it over your face, Hannibal Lector-style." With a tut and an eye roll for Blinky, he went to get thread.

"Best foot forward," he said to her, waving the wriggling limb.

Newton had revised his plan: get some thread, sew on Blinky's leg, find mum, Guin and Dave (in whatever order the complex web of his priorities deemed appropriate) and then get the hell out of Christmas town.

As he neared the door, he saw that there was a pair of scissors hanging on a chain next to the door. The white threads poking through the letterbox opening were soft to the touch, slightly greasy, like—

"Is this hair?"

\*\*\*

# 79

The elvish voice was making another announcement over the PA. Guin wished she understood the language of the elves a little better.

*You will soon enough,* said Eglantine.

The starfish was right. Guin was certain some horrible, possibly irreversible transformation had come over her. She felt the tops of her ears, which were well on the way to becoming properly pointed elf-ears.

"Is that how they 'make' friends?" she mused unpleasantly.

Tinfoil Tavistock made it quite clear that she didn't want Guin to turn into an elf. Guin agreed. Bullied and rejected at school or not, she preferred to stay as a girl.

Then she had an idea.

If she was undergoing some sort of elf transformation, surely she could use it to her advantage? Guin ran to the bins full of clothing remnants and found a red jumper sleeve that, with minor alterations, would make a passable elf hat. She tied off the cuff end, turned it into a floppy pom-pom with some pinking shears and pulled the hat down on her head, making sure she pushed her hair out of sight.

She allowed her ears to pop out, fairly sure she made a passable elf at a glance. She rootled through the clothing bins to find the gaudiest, elfiest clothes she could, slipping on some children's leggings and a stupid little jacket.

*Going to try and escape in disguise?* said Eglantine dismissively.

"I'm not going to try to escape," said Guin. "Not without my family."

Eglantine scoffed.

"Watch," said Guin.

If she was to help the family she needed to be more than just a decent elf facsimile. She needed to become a bona fide elf, preferably one that was respected. Guin was convinced the beard was a symbol of power amongst the elves, so she searched for something beardy. She went to the toy-making workshop, striding purposefully and hoping that Gerd wouldn't be there. Her disguise certainly wouldn't fool anyone who had seen her up close.

She searched through the supplies. They'd used some sort of stuffing when they made their toy creations. It wasn't the normal, snowy-white kapok you'd get from a craft supplier: something much smellier and organic-looking. It had probably been recycled from past victims. Guin reckoned she could tease beard-like strands from it. She sorted out the best bits, along with some glue to stick them onto her chin.

She wished she had a mirror to check how she looked, but elves didn't seem to be big on personal grooming. Instead she decided to practise her strutting. If she was to be an important elf she needed to master the art of posturing like the most arrogant of them.

She marched from one side of the workshop to the other, realising there was a problem. Every self-important dictator that she'd ever seen on the news combined their strutting with a narrative of some sort. While her elf language skills were improving all the time, she was not up to delivering a villainous monologue.

She tried again. She marched across the workshop making expansive gestures, punctuating her movements with the occasional *"Pah!"* and other dismissive non-words. It was probably as good as it was going to get. She shoved Elsa Frinton's *Little Folk in European Folklore* book under her shirt for safekeeping and made to leave.

As she unbolted the door ready to put her elf impersonation skills to the test, Eglantine said she wasn't going to fool anyone.

"At least, I'm doing something," she told the starfish. "I'm going to get my family and, if I can, stop those elves from doing ... whatever it is they're doing."

Eglantine sneered, pointing out she was almost certainly doomed to fail.

"I don't need that kind of negativity," said Guin.

In Guin's pocket, Tinfoil Tavistock did some little quadruped cheerleading and threw in some bold, *Go, Guin!*s to boot.

"Okay, a bit too much positivity," said Guin and stepped outside.

***

# 80

Dave crept through the hall of Christmas presents. "Guin?" he hissed. "Guin? Are you here? It's me!"

He paused. Adding "It's me!" to the end of a sentence really added nothing. He gave up on the whisper-shouts and explored the room silently.

Between the stacks of Christmas presents were various workbenches, equipped with the means to make ... he dreaded to think. There were boxes of eyes and ears on the bench. Human eyes and human ears. They weren't real, but they were unpleasantly soft and malleable. Behind a bench was a massive roller dispenser on which hung a huge roll of peachy-pink material. He reached out and tugged on it. It was like sheets of skin. Artificial skin, he hoped. On the rear wall drooping faces sagged from hooks.

"Okay, you're creepy."

He picked one up, unable to help himself. It was like a peeled baby face. What was it made from? If the elves had a 3D printer that built models from stuff out of a waste food bin, they would look like this. It even smelled rotten, glistening with a sweaty sheen. Dave wondered if they were hung up to dry. He remembered the elf-baby thing that had surprised him in the market. He dropped the face and wiped his hands in disgust.

Components and materials to make little people.

There was a shout from the hall entrance. A team of elves had entered but were not looking his way. One of them gestured to a wheeled pallet laden with boxes. Together, the elves wheeled it away.

Lots of little boxes. Weird human body parts.

"Yeah, this ain't normal," Dave said, adding it to the long list of not normal things he'd encountered in the last twenty-four hours.

He turned to the nearest stack of boxes and pulled down a Christmassy one. It was heavy, with an uneven weight. He'd seen one just like it earlier, but couldn't recall where. He put it on the workbench, untied the bow (feeling momentarily guilty because it was only Christmas Eve morning and not the right time to open a present) and lifted away the snug cardboard lid.

He pushed aside the shredded paper cushioning the contents. He gasped at the face staring up at him. It was a reasonable copy of a human baby's face, but looked as though someone had taken it out of the mould before it was properly set. The features sagged and oozed in a flesh-coloured nightmare. Lips melted to the left while the nose was oddly flattened and twisted. It was the eyes that held his attention, though. Cold, dead eyes that blended the hollow emptiness of a doll with the soul-sucking malice of the elves themselves. He reached out a trembling hand and moved more of the packaging. It wasn't just a face, there was a body attached.

It was a toy baby. A toy baby made from badly formed mush.

"You're enough to give any child nightmares, mate," muttered Dave.

From nowhere, he remembered something Newton had said back in the hotel room, when the elves had first attacked. He had been babbling nervously about the elves in the market and said something about the baby Jesus in the town nativity open and close its eyes.

"You one of them dolls that can open and close its eyes, eh?" said Dave.

Then he recalled where he'd seen a box like this before. Bacraut had brought one onto the stage in the market square, before performing his elaborate mime for the amusement of his underlings.

The baby in the box blinked at Dave and grinned.

Dave dropped the box with a scream.

***

# 81

The workshop marked with the hammer and saw sign was locked but, a few doors down, Esther found something just as interesting. It was a workshop, filled with benches and masses of papery and sparkly materials, and a pervasive sooty aroma. They looked as though they were to make Christmas crackers. A small piece of paper caught her eye and she picked it up. It was a cracker joke. Her breath hitched as she recognised Newton's handwriting.

*How did Good King Wenceslas like his pizza?*

She didn't even need to read the punchline. She put it aside with a sigh and wondered if he'd been here recently. Surely, he would be writing jokes only if someone had forced him to.

"Or maybe not," she said. She knew her boy.

She moved along the bench and found the tattered remains of a textbook. She read it with interest, as it seemed to contain incomplete instructions for some sort of rudimentary explosive. She opened a chest and hit pay dirt.

"Well hello, silver nitrate!" she said, holding up a jar. "And nitric acid, and ethanol. I wonder what I'm supposed to do with you." She put the jars down onto the bench and stared at the book. It did not contain any helpful hints.

"I suppose," she said thoughtfully, "there's only a small number of ways to combine three substances. Maybe this is one of those times when I just need to wing it."

She dragged a stool across and took an empty dish down from a shelf. "Let's try."

\*\*\*

## 82

Guin heard a sharp crack of an explosion from the direction of the workshops, but she didn't break her stride.

The workshop elf, Gerd, appeared through a doorway, looking stricken, and headed towards the noise. Guin put her hands on her hips and made the angriest non-verbal noise she could manage. She stuck out her chin and tried to convey as much meaning as she could with her harrumph of disgust. Something like *"Why are you running round like an idiot just because there's explosions and bangs going on?"*

Gerd muttered an elvish apology and rushed away. Guin was pleased. If she could fool Gerd (even though she was clearly panicking), she could probably fool the other elves.

She moved on, wanting to find the epicentre of the activity. She needed an audience for her new role. *"All hal góra skeggi,"* she said to herself.

The next cavern was a small one, with tunnels leading away in several different directions. It seemed to be some sort of junction-cavern. At its centre was an elf in brown overalls, distributing clipboards to a queue of workers.

Guin decided if she was to work her way up the food chain she should take on this supervisor. She marched up to the head of the queue and pushed aside the elf who was next in line. She pointed at her beard with meaning; the elf drifted away without a word. She faced the supervisor and stared hard at him. She brought a hand up and stroked her beard in an ostentatious way. He cringed and dropped to his knees, cowering in subservience.

*"All hal góra skeggi,"* Guin said quietly.

*"All hal góra skeggi,"* shouted the supervisor elf, and all of the elves in the queue, really putting their hearts into it: with raised-arm salutes and small whoops of enthusiasm.

Guin knew that she couldn't leave it there. She faced all of them and raised her arms above her head. *"All hal góra skeggi!"* she shouted.

They replied again, hollering as loudly as they could, punching the air in excitement. Guin recognised the sentiment: in her mind hearing the chant *"fight, fight, fight,"* that could sometimes be heard in an unsupervised playground. She felt mounting dread: clearly she had issued some sort of bid for supremacy.

And she realised the bid for supremacy was not between her and the supervisor elf . She heard the crowd muttering *"Bacraut!, Bacraut!"* The chief elf himself was approaching!

She held her head high and maintained an attitude of mute superiority. Her fingers found Tinfoil Tavistock in her pocket. Tavistock believed in her.

***

# 83

The doll was alive! The baby with the ugly melted face packed in shredded paper in a Christmas box on a pile of similar boxes was very much alive!

When Dave dropped the box the baby thing had rolled out. It certainly was no human baby, and not just because of its hideous face. Its limbs were too spindly, its manner too co-ordinated. Human babies, dolls or real, did not hiss and try to claw people to death.

It charged at Dave with sinister nimbleness. Dave tried to shoo it away with his foot, but the thing was determined.

"Nice baby, nice baby," Dave whimpered. "Go to sleep. It's beddy-byes."

He tried, for no sane reason, to recall any lullabies he once knew. It had been years since he had needed to use any. What he really needed was a weapon, and there were none to hand.

He threw a box of eyes at the creature as he backed away. The baby thing slipped and slid on them momentarily. Dave threw a bunch of ears at it. They had even less effect.

He was about to pull down sheet after sheet of rolled skin, with the vague plan of wrapping the thing in it until was immobile, but the opportunity passed. The baby thing latched onto his lower leg and began to climb.

Dave swatted at it. The thing bit his finger. He snatched his hand away, and the face came with it. "Oh, God!" he burbled.

Beneath the baby face was an elf, a small one, but a vile ugly hate-filled elf nonetheless. It licked his blood from its lips and, discarding its encumbering nappy, resumed its climb. It had bitten him, and Dave knew what effect an elf bite had had on Esther. In fact, he could feel (assuming it wasn't just panic setting in) wooziness already coming over him.

With one hand on the elf's forehead to keep it back, Dave fished for his first aid kit with the other. The zip sprang open and the contents began slipping out. Dave managed to grab a prepped insulin syringe and, with a medical negligence that would have got him fired from his day job, jabbed it in his own thigh.

Pulling it out, the next course of action seemed natural. He was being climbed by a malevolent pixie, and he had a sharp object in his free hand. He stabbed the elf in the arm.

Afterwards, Dave could only assume the elf had a bad reaction to the insulin. If the bite of an elf induced a dangerous sugar-rush, perhaps their own blood sugar levels were entirely different to humans. The elf dropped immediately from Dave's leg and began dancing on the floor in squealing circles. It's arm fizzed and melted like chocolate on a hot windowsill. It barely had time to notice the loss of its limb before the remnants of the insulin reached the rest of its body. It sagged, its legs gave way. Its horrified face sank into the sticky cavity of its collapsing body. Finally it pooled on the floor in a brown-pink puddle, like a gallon of toffee sauce. The smell reminded Dave of the lingering smell from an empty tin of car sweets.

"Sweet mother of—"

Dave checked his first aid kit and the items he had dropped on the floor. He had five full doses of insulin left. Just a droplet had utterly splaticated that one. That was the good news.

It was a reasonable assumption each of the boxes contained an elf-baby, and each pile contained hundreds of boxes. That was the bad news.

And the piles... The elves had been carting them out for some time, taking them somewhere to be loaded and shipped out. Thousands of elf-babies being sent out into the world, but for what reason?

A word rose in his mind, something Guin had mentioned at the dinner table last night: changelings.

"Oh, crap."

\*\*\*

# 84

Bacraut the elf stood in front of Guin. *"Eretta el fáskorun?"* he scoffed. *"Gekki ség haf besta skeggi?"*

Guin knew her best bet was to keep her mouth shut and try to assert her dominance with body language. She had the advantage of being taller than Bacraut, so she sneered down her nose at him and thrust her beard right in his face, drawing imaginary circles in the air with her chin and jabbing it for emphasis.

He spluttered with annoyance. His tiny fists balled at his sides as he unleashed a stream of abuse. Guin had a pretty good handle on the language of the elves, but this rapid-fire profanity would have been recognisable in any language.

Guin cast her mind across the kind of coolness she had never possessed or craved, but had often observed. The kind of dismissive sass American pop stars could channel so well. She pursed her lips and conjured the nonsense phrases in her mind, letting her eyebrows and head-waggles do the talking.

*Don't mess with me sugar.*

*Talk to the beard.*

*Put a ring on it.*

It seemed to be working. Bacraut was definitely losing his composure. He visibly quivered with rage. He closed his eyes for a moment; when he opened them again he looked more focussed. He strutted up and down, with some beard moves of his own. He tried the head-waggle, but it didn't really work for him. Guin wondered if elves had a different sort of neck joint to humans. He was a good beard-jabber though. He worked up a rhythm and created a kind of duck-walking dance move, his chin leading the way like an exotic bird. Guin thought back to the ancient pop videos her dad liked to watch and realised that Bacraut was moving like Mick Jagger.

When it was time for Guin to move, she had a new idea. This time her entire display was based around her beard remaining still while her head and the rest of her body moved around it. These moves owed more to Loony Tunes cartoons than pop videos, but she was certain she pulled it off. Her chin remained stationary while her body scooted off to the sides, kicking and hip-swaying to an unmistakeable rhythm. Her face was inscrutable while her body did the work.

The circle of elves shrieked with delight.

Bacraut was clearly outclassed. He seemed to be out of ideas. He reverted to the angry screaming again, making the other elves shrink away in fear. Then he stood upright, a thought coming to him. He faced Guin with a look of blazing malevolence. He stood tall and wound his finger into his beard, corkscrewing it right in and then tugging sharply. The challenge was clear: whose beard could withstand being pulled?

Guin wasn't happy at this. She had no idea whether Bacraut's beard was real or not, and even if it wasn't, there was a good chance his was stuck on more securely, or he wouldn't have suggested it. She was prepared to fake a small tug at her own beard, but she had a pretty good idea of what would follow. The next step would be pulling each other's beards, or inviting someone else to do so. She needed to de-rail this train of thought before it went any further.

Several ideas collided in her mind. The elves clearly held the beard in great esteem. Christmas seemed to be their life, or religion, or whatever. It was the power of Santa that she was essentially evoking.

She took a step back from Bacraut. She positioned herself so that she faced both him and the audience for maximum impact. She glared around to be certain she had their full attention, then raised her voice as loud and deep as it would go.

"HO! HO! HO!" she yelled.

The reaction was immediate. Bacraut shrank away. The other elves piled onto him, sensing his weakness. He disappeared from view, although there were gloopy thwacking noises that suggested he might be suffering. Guin strode away, keen to move while she had the upper hand. Several elves ran after her, bowing in a subservient manner. They beckoned eagerly to her. She inclined her head in agreement and left the cavern, following their lead.

***

# 85

Newton tugged at the wisps of hair in the letterbox opening and they came through with ease. Like the allure of a loose scab, or the visible edge of a roll of sticky tape, Newton felt an urge to pull further. As he did so, he thought he heard a voice from within. It wasn't an elf voice. It was deep and full-bodied, even if it was muffled.

"Hello?" he said. "Is anyone in there?"

The voice responded, although he couldn't make out what it was saying.

Newton thought about the deep voice, and the hair, and the fact there was an elf guarding the door. Even though he had a list of things to do, with stitching Blinky's leg back on at the top and get the hell out of Christmas town at the bottom, he decided to open the door and see exactly who was inside.

The door was unlocked. Behind it... Behind it was a doorway-filling wall of hair. It was white, tinged with grease and age to the faintest of yellows. It sat in clouds and bundles, looping round and round in swirls.

"Hello?" called Newton.

"O-o-o-h," said a deep voice, the "Oh" rising like a folk singer about to burst into song, or a bad actor about to launch into a Shakespearean soliloquy. "Oh, dost mine ears hear the voice of an Englishman?"

Newton tried to push into the mass of hair. He couldn't part it. It was all bound and knotted together. He picked up the scissors hanging on the chain outside the door, but they wouldn't reach. A sharp tug ripped the chain in two. Newton cut his way in like a jungle explorer, except this jungle was hair and he was using scissors instead of a machete.

"Are you all right?" he said. "I'm Newton."

"Would you, sir, happen to have about you such a thing as a cup of mead?" called the man.

"I don't, sorry. Dave – that's my mum's boyfriend – he bought some at the fair yesterday but I don't know where that's gone. I think it got burned up, or the elves destroyed it."

The voice began to wail, in a manly baritone. "Oh, those cursed creatures!" The wailing sounded well-rehearsed, as though more a matter of habit than genuine emotion. "I did my best, young sir. I did my best."

"I'm sure you did," said Newton, not certain at all what he was on about.

He snipped his way the direction of the voice. The towering walls of hair sprang back into position behind him. There was little danger of being crushed or suffocated by the hair, it being light and airy in nature; but if he lost the scissors or got himself turned around too much, there was a danger of getting irretrievably entangled.

"I did try to divert their maleficent manner in productive habits," said the voice.

"Uh-huh."

"The devil makes work for idle hands, he does."

"Does he?"

"He does."

"O-o-o-h, those elves, with naught to occupy them but whimsy and fairy-wine, would cause all manner of trouble across the land. Spoiling milk, upsetting livestock, ruining the lives of finer folk than I." He sobbed momentarily. "I was such a wicked man. I deserved it. I deserve it all."

"Hang in there," said Newton. "I'm nearly with you."

"There's no saving me. I am grievously wounded."

"You're hurt? It's okay. Dave's a paramedic – Dave, the one with the mead. He can help you."

"Perhaps with a splash of amber sweetness for a doomed man. I did my best to turn the elves from their given natures. I set them to crafts and construction. I ordered them to bring materials to our dank grotto – not this place, far to the north, in the high reaches, as far from the cities of man as I could take them – and set them to carving and sewing and crafting toys."

"Sort of like rehabilitation therapy?" Newton was getting the craziest idea of who this chap was. Or at least who he thought he was.

"Rehabilitation? To restore? To give purpose? Yes! Yes! But their inclination towards evil was so strong, as foul and as wicked as mine own weaknesses. They would have us all go out on wild hunts, to snare the unwary, to steal infants. What could I do but go along, to steer their path, to divert their eyes? Did you say you had a cup of mead, fine sir?"

"Dave might," repeated Newton. "Probably not."

"I was so thirsty. But no matter how much I drink I am not satisfied. I said as much to my huntsman. 'Bring me a drink, man!' I demanded but he had none and then—" He sobbed once more. "I demanded a drink, saying I would be willing to go to hell to fetch a cup. O-o-o-h, is this now mine own private hell?"

"Dando!" exclaimed Newton.

"What?" said the man (who must be only a foot or two away now, Newton thought). "Oh, yes. That was me. At least, I thought it was me."

Newton snipped through the final inches, thinking furiously. Guin had mentioned Dando and the Wild Hunt: one of the stories in that book she'd picked up. But this man's tale, of elves and grottos and crafting toys... Had he really set up the Santa Claus racket to get the elves to do something other than terrorising the countryside. And why were they here? Had Santa/Dando been drunk at the wheel – that is, the reins – of his sleigh?

"Begging your pardon," said Newton. "You must be quite, well, old."

"I am but a shadow of the man I once was," said Santa-Dando. "But I am whole, cursedly so."

The tips of the scissor scraped against stone. Newton pushed aside the curtains of hair in front of him. There was nothing but bare stone wall.

"Er, Mr Dando, sir?"

"Yes?" said the voice, a little off to the right.

Newton moved along the wall in that direction. He passed a door, not the door he had entered by. Further along from it was a set of shelves. "Mr Dando?"

"Yes?"

Newton looked along the shelves and saw Dando. To say he had the face of an old man would be to understate the matter and do a disservice to old men generally. Nor was his the face of a corpse. There was life in those cheeks, a light in those rheumy eyes. He had a full white beard, a Father Christmas beard. (Of course he did: he *was* Father Christmas). It was that beard which had grown and grown and filled this room. Newton found himself pondering how many centuries would have to pass to grow as much beard as this.

The years had not been kind, but it was clear some supernatural power kept the man alive. This Santa character (Newton had no idea if the Dando myth was medieval or older) must be a least several centuries old, if not longer. Only strange elven magic could explain that. But more significantly, only magic could account for the fact that whilst this beardy man had a wizened and ancient head, he had no body at all.

No wonder the man was thirsty. Any liquid that passed his lips would be instantly trickling over the shelf.

***

# 86

Esther tried not to think about how hot and tight the skin on her face was. She knew she'd lost her eyebrows in the last blast she'd created. She'd also had to put out several small fires in her hair and clothing. Nonetheless it was a positive result. She'd definitely got the proportions right; the charred chemistry textbook concurred. Keeping the whole thing stable and stopping it going off prematurely was the key.

She needed to keep the ethanol away from the other chemicals until she wanted the whole lot to blow up. A further search around the workbench revealed that bomb-making wasn't the primary function of this cracker laboratory, so there were no useful containers to safely stop the chemicals from mixing until she was ready. Esther devised a slightly dubious contraption where the ethanol was held in test tubes suspended with string above a box containing the other components. All she had to do was keep it upright and not allow it to be jostled – even slightly – and all would be well.

To disguise the box and give it a bit more rigidity, she wrapped it in red crepe paper and tied it securely with a green tartan ribbon. The bomb was going on that mockery of a sleigh. Not only would that put paid to the elves' inexplicable plans, it would surely create enough of a distraction for her and her family to escape.

Slowly, watchfully, she exited the workshop, and with an awkwardness that only holding a box full of high explosives could generate, she climbed back into the vent system.

Once she was back in the tunnel, she adapted her previous method of moving around: carefully lifting and repositioning the box in front of her. If she moved too quickly, the test tubes clinked against each other, making her cringe. If one drop fell from a test tube she suspected it would set off the whole thing. She was under no illusions that, in a confined space like the tunnel, the blast would kill her. She moved on through the tunnels, towards the cavern containing Santa's sleigh.

***

# 87

Newton tried to keep his cool while talking to Father Christmas's disembodied head. "It's an honour to meet you, sir," he said.

The cloudy eyes blinked. "O-o-o-h, dost mine ears hear the voice of an Englishman?"

"Er, yes, it's me, Newton," he said, presenting himself into Santa's field of vision.

Santa struggled to focus on him. "Would you, sir, happen to have about you such a thing as a cup of mead?"

Right, thought Newton. Either Santa was drunk (how much alcohol would it take to get a disembodied head drunk?) or was suffering with dementia (deeply understandable given his age and circumstances) or the magic keeping him alive didn't extend to giving him much brainpower.

"You're looking well, sir," said Newton kindly.

Santa humphed. "It's my fine beard. Like Samson of old, it's the source of my power."

"*All hal góra skeggi*," Newton muttered.

"Indeed." Santa sniffled. "Those wicked *wicked* creatures. They would rarely do what I told them."

"No elf-discipline," said Newton. He couldn't help himself.

"They gave me life without end in punishment for my godless ways and my beard – my beautiful beard – can you see it?"

Newton turned to survey a room full of beard. "Yes, I believe I can. You could keep a wigmaker in business for years with all this."

"This beard gives their reindeer the power of flight."

Newton nodded, seeing some weird stupid logic in that.

"And each year, long after I had given up on mending their wicked ways, they forced me into the sleigh, to take the reins. And then, one year, I decided I had had enough. I determined to crash the sleigh, kill myself and all those vile things." The wrinkled face frowned, adding more wrinkles. "I wonder if I would have succeeded."

Newton made a face. "It's ... it's hard to say."

"Tell me, young sir, did you say you had a cup of mead?"

Newton was about to answer, politely and patiently, when he heard a rattle at the nearest door. He pulled back into the mass of hair. It closed about and concealed him. Through the fog of hair, he could see the shadows of elves enter the room.

"*Tími tila far a reð, Dando*," said one.

"O-o-o-o-h, please. Not again!" pleaded Santa.

There was the *shing* of heavy scissors and the thump of a heavy object rolling off a shelf.

"How will I even reach the reins!" wailed Santa.

The door closed and Newton was alone. He tries to assimilate all he had heard and learned. He was in a room of magic beard hair; hair that granted reindeer the power of flight. Madness though it undoubtedly was, that didn't mean it wasn't true.

"Maybe I could build myself a hairyplane," he smirked, but jokes weren't as good when there was no one to groan at them.

He gathered up armfuls of the stuff, cut it away with the scissors, stuffed it up his jumper for safekeeping and went back to find Blinky.

***

# 88

As carefully as she had climbed into the air duct, Esther descended into the vast sleigh cavern. Beyond its front end she saw the tunnel continued. Was that the track leading out into the entrance cavern, and the broad tunnel along which they'd driven the tractor? Had the sun risen outside in the world beyond? Was it now Christmas Eve morning?

If the elves were planning on launching this thing, then there was still a full day until Christmas Eve itself, and the traditional time for Father Christmas to be about his rounds. She chided herself, reminding herself to think more globally. If it was Christmas Eve morning here then it was only a few short hours until Christmas Day on the far side of the world. If the elves were going to be all logical and begin their insane Christmas flight near the international date line and all those lovely Pacific islands, then launch was surely imminent.

Another elvish message over the tannoy cemented the idea in her mind.

Once at ground level, she saw a niche in the rocks where an elderly elf sat at a desk, covered in pieces of paper, some sort of antique adding machine, and things that looked like abacuses. Other elves rushed in and out of this alcove, apparently acting on instructions. Esther crept closer. There were numerous drawings of sleigh sections, and map fragments showing the destination for each one. Badly-spelled labels like *Yoorope* and *Sentrul Asha* were scrawled onto some of the shipping containers, so there was clearly a plan for the intended journey. It looked as though this was the logistics planner.

"*Mora oilía tað ber auxleg oilíu,*" barked the elderly elf to a minion, stabbing a paper. It was marked up with *Fool to cross Persifik*.

Esther had seen enough. Sabotaging the sleigh looked like the ideal plan. If she fastened the bomb somewhere near the middle, then hopefully it would take out the whole thing when the chemicals mixed. Which they would if the ride was sufficiently bumpy.

She moved carefully through the cavern. There was lots of cover, but she couldn't afford any sudden movements while she carried the bomb. She made it to the edge of the sleigh and ducked under a runner. She was directly underneath the long vehicle. The heavy containers really did sit on flatbed railway trucks which were really too small for such bulk. She imagined if the elves could manage to haul, or rocket-propel this thing out beyond the extent of their narrow railway, they were hoping it would slide on runners and leave the trucks behind. She couldn't picture it ending as anything other than a horrible train wreck.

Once underneath, she was able to move almost invisibly along its full length in the gloomy tunnel created by the raised containers overhead. The underside stank of the fuel pooling on the floor.

Judging herself to be near the centre, she squeezed upwards between linked containers, climbing up the mesh of piping and rope and chains (and what was this white thready stuff running over everything like cobwebs?). It was tricky to keep her footing, and not a little claustrophobic, but she persevered. She looked around for a good place to stash the bomb but ultimately decided the best place to hide a gift-shaped bomb was among the gift boxes filling the containers. Even if hers did have a tartan bow that marked it out as different from all the others. She laid the box on the top of the nearest pile and made her way back down, relieved not to have to carry the bomb any more.

***

# 89

Guin's elf deputies delivered obsequious commentary as they ushered her, their new leader, into the grand hall where Newton and she had been forced to participate in elf chorus practice. Now the elves were in full choral mode: a high-pitched and full-throated celebration.

As she proceeded down the central aisle between candy-cane striped pillars, the voices rose higher in pomp and joy. Guin felt a momentary thrill run through her before realising the songs and the adoration were not specifically for her.

At the far end of the hall, elves worked beneath the cloth covered shape on the dais.

Guin's underlings chattered enthusiastically. She picked up snippets of words but they spoke too fast for her to fully grasp. Something was done. Something was ready. Pieces were ... in place?

The choir's song spun to a dizzying finale and the red velvet cloth was ripped away.

"Oh," she said, surprised.

"Oh," she said, bewildered.

"Oh, my," she said, frankly disgusted and more than a little afraid.

It was Father Christmas, but nothing like the department store Santas most people would expect. No twinkly-eyed old gentleman with a luxuriant beard, a red suit with soft fur cuffs and gloves. No shiny boots and belt with brass clasps. No jolly floppy hat with a white pom-pom.

This Father Christmas was as tall as a house. Yes, there were boots, great conical hoofs of wood and rotting leather, reinforced to take the weight of the whole. Yes there was a belt, several belts in fact. The torso, bigger than a minibus, had been strapped round and round with rope and leather, all over a frame that was a patchwork of – was that skin? Was that animal hide? Whatever it was, it looked something like the patterning on a

Friesian cow and a lot like the aftermath of a messy surgical procedure. Yes, there was a suit, but where the suit ended and the man began was hard to tell. And as for the head. It was a normal-sized human one, the head of a tired and wizened old man, lashed into place with ribbon and thread. With a pathetic threadbare hat stuck on top. The whole thing had been assembled, reassembled and patched to the point where it looked like a bad art project left out to rot.

Three thoughts fought for dominance in Guin's mind. The first was the view she had expressed to Newton earlier: that a Tinfoil Tavistock, remade from new materials, was still Tinfoil Tavistock. That the materials did not make the individual.

The second thought was about those islanders who believed if they could build their own make-believe radio sets from coconuts and bamboo, they could call down aeroplanes full of cargo and food. The elves had rebuilt their own Santa Claus, much bigger than before (because bigger was better, obviously) and now in their ridiculous, spiteful, stupid hearts believed what they had made was as good as the original.

The third thought, simplest of all, was this was a giant zombie Father Christmas, or more properly, a giant Frankenstein's monster of a Father Christmas. Had the bones or body parts of the horrible Mrs Scruples provided the last components?

As she looked at Santa's head, strangely out of proportion with the rest of the thing, it swivelled to meet her gaze. The eyes were clouded and vacant. She realised the head had turned because there was a pair of elves on Santa's shoulders working his neck joint. They manoeuvred a complex set of wires like master puppeteers. Guin guessed the rest of Santa was animated in the same way, so she stepped clear as the huge figure lurched towards the entrance.

Guin hurried after, overtaking the Santa as it moved between caverns, cheered on by rapturous elves. Guin didn't miss a beat. She waved to the crowd, proudly stepping ahead, as if this was all her doing and she expected the gratitude of the masses for her efforts. The elves loved it. They made enthusiastic whooping noises as she thrust her beard forward and Santa followed, very slowly.

***

# 90

"There!" Newton proudly snapped the final piece of thread. Blinky showed her appreciation by trying to bite his face off.

Sewing her leg back on had been easier than Newton expected. It was clear the zombie reindeer had very little in the way of pain receptors. Also, Santa's magic beard hair almost leaped at the chance to re-stitch the tripedal creature back together. Newton was sure his mother would have approved of his handiwork, keeping any quibbles about the quality of his stitching to herself.

He stood from his task. Blinky flexed her leg.

"Now, we rescue everybody else," Newton said, having no idea how to do it.

There was sound of movement: mass movement from the reindeer cavern along the tunnel.

"Sounds like everyone's on the move," said Newton. "Let's mingle."

# 91

Dave peered out between a gap in the crates and stared at the sleigh. He had followed a consignment of boxed up fake baby elves from one part of the elf complex to here. Babies in boxes, boxes on pallets, and now pallets in open top shipping containers on the back of a sleigh.

He crouched on the damp floor and hid behind some unused wooden packing crates

This was on a scale he just couldn't wrap his head around. He thought he glimpsed parts of an aeroplane built into the thing. Something about a long grey part of the frame reminded him of an F-15 fighter jet. And those turbines under the stubby wings must surely have been cannibalised from a downed RAF plane. It was horribly non-aerodynamic, and the tubing and pipes feeding those massive engines must had added several tonnes to the weight. How on earth was it going to get airborne? He dismissed the technical challenge with a heartfelt sigh. That sort of thinking belonged to yesterday, when the world was sane. Right now, he didn't need to know how this monstrous sleigh was going to get airborne, just accept that it would. The elves had constructed a work of magical engineering madness. Clearly they had been planning this for a long time.

The cavern stank of grease and oil and— Dave dabbed and sniffed at the puddle at his feet. "Hell," he whispered.

The whole place was awash with aviation fuel, or something. The cavern was a monumental fire risk.

There was movement by a side entrance.

A delegate of important looking elves came into the cavern. The foremost one, with a luxuriant beard, waved imperiously at the gathered crowds. Dave thought if he dropped a lit match in this place, he'd be able to take out the majority of the elves and their upper echelons in one act. He'd also be condemning himself to a fiery death in the process.

Those thoughts were pushed out of his mind by the arrival of Father Christmas: a homemade giant on ponderously slow legs. It moved into the cavern like a Day of the Dead carnival monstrosity, a next level Wicker Man.

That thing deserved to burn, he thought.

***

# 92

As Esther crept away from the sleigh she made a wide detour around the busiest area. Some sort of enormous figure was being led across the cavern and onto the sleigh. With a jolt she realised it was a Father Christmas.

It reminded her of the worst examples of fairground artwork. Fibre-glass models of clowns, horses and cartoon characters that were supposed to add a sense of fun to the rides, but invariably made them sinister and creepy. Its body was as big as some of the shipping containers, and the tiny head at the top swivelled and stared in a way that was deeply disturbing. An elf swung round the front of Santa's head on a rope. It looked as if were attending to some last-minute maintenance, whether mechanical or cosmetic was difficult to tell.

At least that would hold everyone's attention while Esther made her exit, but she was keen to see what was going on. She circled round the sleigh to take a look.

A team of reindeer – God, it must have been a hundred-strong at least! – was being led up to the front of the sleigh and harnessed up. Two abreast, with a shaft and leather tackle binding them to the monstrous vehicle. Esther felt a momentary pang of self-recrimination as she thought what Newton would say about her blowing up the sleigh with reindeer attached to it.

But they weren't even real-life reindeer, she immediately countered. And Newton wasn't here to see it. Except he was! She caught a glimpse of his curly mop of hair among the many reindeer.

"What are you playing at?" she whispered desperately.

\*\*\*

# 93

Guin was still trying to process the sight of Santa's sleigh. It was incomprehensibly huge.

Of course, she thought, a massive Santa required a massive sleigh. Like everything else the elves had in this place, it was an unsettling parody of a sleigh. Its enormous size; the badly-executed mess of its construction.

While the puppeteered Santa was steered to the front of the sleigh and lowered onto his seat, the elves nearest to her ran through an itinerary for the sleigh's upcoming journey. Maps detailing a route across the world were passed around. Guin was sure the maps weren't quite right. Was Japan actually that shape? And was Australia really that close to India?

An elf pointed at containers and then the corresponding locations on the map. *"Þal turt superlegt?"*

*"Superlegt,"* Guin agreed.

She became aware of a small scuffle amongst the massive herd of reindeer and turned to one of the elves, an arrogant, questioning look on her face. It scuttled off to investigate.

It was then she saw a figure by a stack of packing crates by the wall. Her dad! She almost yelled out in delight. He was doing a bad job of hiding but none of the elves had spotted him yet. She gave him a surreptitious waist-high wave.

\*\*\*

# 94

Dave gasped when he realised his own daughter was the head elf. He was gripped by a terrible fear. She had placed herself among those creatures! Simultaneously he was filled with a chest-swilling pride that Guin was keeping her cool while the elves literally bowed down before her and obeyed her every command. She was smart, and far more adaptable than he'd given her credit for: fitting in as if she'd been born to it.

Seeing she had his attention, she made a number of subtle gestures. She pointed at herself and the sleigh and made a swooshing fly-away motion.

Dave nodded.

He didn't exactly approve of taking a ride on that thing. Elf-Airways looked like they had a horribly slapdash approach to vehicle maintenance and air safety. He looked around, saw all the elves were principally occupied with either the Father Christmas creature, the reindeer or the packing of yet more shipping containers, and dashed across the cavern floor to the sleigh. He slipped between two container crates (nearly tripping over some of the cable mesh binding the whole thing together in the process) and climbed on board in the shadow of a patched up jet engine.

***

# 95

Guin watched her dad break from cover and head for the sleigh. She would have watched him longer, but a band of elves was marching back from the ranks of reindeer. Newton was held between them. One held a knife to his throat, or would have done if it was tall enough. It actually held a knife to his kidneys.

"*Hanst mið reindýrum,*" an elf said.

Guin nodded, understanding.

"Guin!" said Newton, recognising her. "It's me!"

*Hanður að die!*" asked another elf.

"What happened to you? Did they turn you into an elf?"

Guin wished the boy would shut up. She stayed in character.

An elf made a slicing motion with its knife. "*Drepan staba nú!*"

Guin nodded in full agreement and held out her hand for the knife.

"*Mi—*" She tried to order in her mind what little she knew of the elf language. "*Mi slautra him-ni myssjálf.*" She sneered at Newton and indicated the elves should hand over the prisoner to her.

"Please don't," said Newton. "Guin. It's me. You're Guin, remember?"

She gestured for the elves to put him on board. When one of them queried her, she scowled at him and made a surprisingly effective finger-walking pantomime to suggest she was going to throw him overboard once they were airborne.

The elves cackled.

"No, please," said Newton. "You shouldn't have eaten all that reindeer moss! You don't know what it's done to you!"

She gestured for the elves to take him away. Newton kicked and wriggled.

"There's no point struggling," she squeaked in her best attempt at an elf attempting English. "We are going to *sleigh* you."

Newton looked at her. She gave him the smallest wink. The teenager's eyes lit up. He still struggled, but now it was an act. He allowed himself to be dragged up a ladder and onto the sleigh's steering platform.

\*\*\*

# 96

Esther was having trouble processing what she was seeing.

Dave had just scurried into the rear section of the sleigh. Further ahead, though mostly out of sight, she had seen her son taken at knife-point onto the front of the sleigh and (although it had taken her long enough to realise it) the bearded elf with him was little Guin.

Her family, through accident rather than design, were now all aboard the sleigh. All of them, all in one place and with the means of escape. Which was brilliant, except for the fact Esther had just planted a bomb on the sleigh.

What was she to do now? Could she get her family off, or could she remove the bomb before it departed? Both options were fraught with risk. Esther couldn't face the idea of choosing the wrong one. She sighed: the only thing to do was to get back on the sleigh and get to the bomb as quickly as she could. If she disassembled it, at least she could buy some more time.

She climbed under the rear of the vehicle, picking her way carefully along the length of the sleigh.

\*\*\*

# 97

From atop the sleigh Guin spotted Esther and smiled. They were all here, so if she could get the sleigh to fly them out of here, all would be well. Once they were outside, they could dump the sleigh and put a stop to the elves' stupidity.

Santa was now front and centre of the sleigh. The cockpit area was a gigantic bench in front of a foot well as deep as she was tall. Fat reins of woven white fibres ran hundreds of metres from the lead reindeers to the lip of the sleigh. The reins were clamped into Santa's meaty hands. Arranged on what could only be called the dashboard were numerous buttons, levers and dials. They had clearly been ripped from other machines and welded or taped into place. They must, she assumed, link to the wires and tubes to the engines further back on the vehicle.

High above, the zombie Santa's jaw worked up and down as if it had just remembered how to chew.

Next to Guin, bound and guarded by elves, Newton murmured, "It's Dando, the man taken by the elves and the Wild Hunt."

Santa's eyes rolled, and as much as a decapitated head could strain, his head strained. "Would any of you good sirs happen to have about you a cup of mead?" it asked hoarsely.

An elf up on the shoulder of the meat puppet slapped the head to shut it up.

Guin decided the head was just freaky. Tinfoil Tavistock gently reminded her that she shouldn't be hasty to judge others. She turned her attention to her elves and indicated that they should leave now.

They consulted each other in alarm. "*Þaðer mora ah lada!*" one argued.

She made a dramatic slamming gesture to show that she was not waiting for anything else to be loaded. "*Við* – um, go? – *fara nún!*"

She expanded on it with wild circles she hoped expressed the near-impossible task of going around the entire earth in the course of one night. They elves bowed and withdrew, shouting that they should finish up to the loading teams.

She whispered aside to Newton. "You think you can steer this sleigh?"

"What?" he whispered back.

She was about to discreetly suggest driving a sleigh must be quite like riding horses when there was a shout from behind. Bacraut was approaching across the cavern floor. He was in bad shape. The beating he had received following her leadership challenge had left him bruised and limping. His wounds were the sticky red of cranberry sauce.

He yelled at her almost incoherently. She thought it was just a matter of revenge but then she realised he was pointing towards the back of the sleigh.

"*Ik móðer!*" he yelled. "*Ik móðer en á sleð!*"

Guin realised Esther had been spotted. Bacraut and the elves on the floor raced towards the sleigh.

"We've got to go!" yelled Guin.

"What?" said Newton.

She pulled at his bonds and freed his arms. "Fly!"

\*\*\*

# 98

Newton grabbed the reins. They were crazy heavy but Newton was able to lift one and send a small ripple down it to the front reindeer.

"Go!" he yelled. "Mush! Yah!"

Ahead, reindeer shifted listlessly. The front-most one walked a little.

An elf, seeing what he was up to leapt down from the giant Santa body. Guin intercepted the elf and grabbed it, diverting its trajectory so that it pitched over the side of the sleigh.

"Go!" she yelled.

Newton was gripped with a mad and sudden notion. The reins were made of Father Christmas beard. It was the hair that gave the reindeer the power of flight, yet it was human blood that had propelled Blinky upwards. Life blood and magic hair.

He picked up a dropped elf blade, stabbed his own hand (perhaps more enthusiastically than necessary) and smeared the blood on the reins, shaking them again.

"Ya! Onward Blinky!" he yelled. "On Scromdir and Bultaða! On Sleipnir and Kicgut! Hlager and Paugir and, er, Dancer and Prancer and ... all of yous! Mush!"

The power of Santa's magic flowed down the ropes. The reindeer moved. The sleigh jolted, sluggishly resisted and then, with a massive Titanic hitting the iceberg groan, began to move forward.

***

# 99

It was disconcerting to be beneath the sleigh as it started to move. Chains clanked and twisted. The container above Esther's head moaned like it was full of ghosts. The flatbed truck next to her struggled: over-burdened wheels turning and grinding on the rails.

She did not want to be here when the sleigh built up speed. The bomb could explode at any moment. She needed to get to it as quickly as possible, or get herself and the three surviving humans in this town as far away from it as possible.

She ran forward to the next intersection between sledge carriages and began to climb.

\*\*\*

# 100

From his position high up on the front of the sleigh, Newton could see the confusion among the elves in the cavern. The sleigh was hauling out: many of the elves cheered. Hats were whipped off and either waved or tossed in the air.

Elsewhere, urged on by the hobbling Bacraut, other elves were running to the vehicle, clambering up onto its side.

Amid this confusion, other elves just focused on their jobs. Cargo-loaders attempted to thrust last minute parcels on board. Reindeer handlers encouraged their beasts forward. Santa puppeteers puppeted.

"We've got to go faster!" said Guin. "They're going to catch us. Isn't there a whip?"

Newton looked at her horrified. "Whip them? I'd never use a whip on Lily."

She looked back at him with equal horror. "Who uses a whip on their girlfriend?"

"Lily's my horse!"

Guin frowned. "You said she had an Instagram account."

Even in the panic of escape, Newton felt it vital he fish out his phone and flick to the app. "Horses can have Instagram! Look at her!"

He was struck once more by the thought that, unless they did something about this current situation, not only would his family, old and new, be dead, but he would never see Lily again. Nor Yolanda who worked at the farm.

He scanned the instruments before him. There were any number of switches and toggles. It would be dangerous if he just flicked some at random.

But there were four in a row marked *TURBINS*. One to four. That seemed promising. He flicked them all. Far, far back something started to whine. Emboldened, he saw another labelled *AFTABURNA*. He flicked that too.

\*\*\*

263

## 101

A light appeared in the jet cylinder directly in front of Dave's face. A slow, lazy, stupid part of his brain thought it was a pretty light; a nice orange glow. Fortunately, a quicker and cleverer part of his brain leapt in and made him slip into the gap between cargo containers before the jet roared into life, sending out a super-heated column of air. A third part of his brain, quick but perhaps too busy scoffing at the first part of his brain, made him grab onto some support before the container accelerated.

There was loud and screeching and shunting as the train, originally pulled by reindeer at the front, was now being pushed by jets from the rear. The whole vehicle accelerated beyond walking speed into a respectable run. If it didn't tear itself apart on take-off, it might actually get up to flying speed. Dave wasn't sure how he felt about flying speed.

He climbed between rattling carriages and crested the top of the foremost container.

Ahead, the leading edge was heading towards a tunnel that was just tall enough and wide enough to let the vehicle through without decapitating Father Christmas or ripping off the bolted on additions to the side of the craft. He looked back. His heart leapt as he saw Esther awkwardly making her way across the tops of the container vehicles.

"Christ," he whispered, seeing her pick a way over piles of elf-baby boxes. She might as well be trying to tiptoe across the eggs of velociraptors, or aliens, or whatever horror they best equated to. Eggs that were absolutely ready to hatch.

There was a shout behind him: a half-second warning of attack. He whirled, immediately leapt upon by a trio of elves. As they grabbed him, he lost his footing. All four of them fell through the ropes and webbing between carriages. Dave snagged on a rope, stopping his fall. Two of the elves clung on. The third fell onto the rails and with a thump was gone from sight.

"Get off me, you idiots," yelled Dave as though it might have some effect. "It's dangerous to mess about on trains."

One elf, fallen against a chain in an awkward position, was fighting to free his knife. The other was attempting to throttle Dave with hands too small for the job. Dave's groping fingers found one of his insulin syringes. He stabbed the would-be throttler. Jabbering in panic as it started to melt, the creature fell away. The remaining elf had finally drawn its knife. It swung at Dave.

He booted it hard. It nearly flew out of the side of the gap but clung onto Dave's shoe.

He angled his leg round. Without proper consideration for his foot, he presented the dangling elf to the roaring jet flame. For an instant, its lower half was alight, like a marshmallow over a campfire. Then it was gone, whipped away by the jet's power, leaving Dave with a smoking hot foot.

\*\*\*

## 102

Watching the elves trying to storm the accelerating sleigh, Guin saw a bundle of fire fly out from the vehicle's side some distance back. Was that an elf?

The moment it touched the ground, flames sprang up around it. The floor all across the cavern had smelled sort of petrol-y. Now it didn't just burn;:it exploded.

Elves that had been cheering and waving their hats were now running and bursting into flame. Guin's attention flicked to all manner of pipes and barrels around the cavern. If the fire reached any fuel containers, either in the cavern or worse, on board the sleigh—

"Faster!" she yelled to Newton.

"We are!" he shouted back.

There was a sucking *whoop* of air as they plunged into the tunnel. The yellow glow of the blazing cavern was replaced by the gloom and streams of fairy lights in the tunnel. Enclosed, the clatter of undead reindeer hoofs and the rattle of the godawful sleigh on its tracks were amplified.

"—meant to be a silent night!" Newton shouted.

Guin didn't hear the beginning of that joke. She assumed it wouldn't have been worth the bother.

"I'm going to find our parents!" She climbed up past Father Christmas and into the gap, no more than three or four feet high, between the top of the sleigh and the rock roof.

Towards the rear, the fire was an orange halo, making a silhouette of the train. It sort of looked like it was chasing them.

\*\*\*

# 103

The fire was chasing them, Esther noted. The exploding fireball that had taken out the cavern was now racing to overtake the sleigh. Boxes in the rearmost container were steaming as the pursuing flames cooked them.

Wherever the bomb was (she was sure it was much further forward) it was too late to look for it.

She staggered forward and leaped the gap between the carriages and threw herself down just as the last portions of the train plunged into the tunnel. She didn't pause to collect herself. She didn't wait. She crawled forward over a sea of uneven cardboard boxes as fast as she could.

As she reached the front of the next carriage, something reared up through the gap. She punched it in the face as it stabbed her in the shoulder.

"Ow!" said Dave with feeling.

"Ow!" she replied. She looked at her shoulder. In the light from passing fairy lights, she could see there was a syringe stuck in it. Dave was suddenly contrite and pulled it out.

"Ow!" she said again.

"It's okay," he said. "It's only insulin."

"That wasn't the problem," she said, kissing him fiercely because it seemed absolutely the right thing to do. "Why insulin?" she said.

"It makes the elves go squish."

"Is that a medical term?"

They looked at each other.

"There's a bomb on this sleigh," she said'

At the same moment he said, "The boxes are full of changelings."

They exchanged looks and said, "What?" simultaneously.

"I was trying to blow the sleigh up," Esther explained.

"With us on it?"

"I didn't know at the time. Changelings?"

"Yes. They're—" He pointed behind her. "Those."

Elves in hideous baby disguises rose up from the rear container carriages. Tired of being cooked alive by the encroaching flames, perhaps. Esther didn't know if their disguises had been hideous from the start or whether the fire had melted them. Either way, the dozens of creatures stalking towards them, crouching a little to avoid the tunnel roof, looked nothing like actual babies. Noses drooped. Eyeballs slid down cheeks.

Esther stared. "Are those ... *brown* baby elves?" She would have used some form of ethnically appropriate description, but there weren't many clues to latch onto.

"They're going to drop changelings all over the world," said Dave. "Got to blend in."

"But that's wildly racist," she said, appalled.

Dave made the kind of noise that would normally had ended with him pointing out yes, it was wildly racist, but the racism in this situation was perhaps a lesser issue than the greater elf-changeling-horror. Esther would have been forced to point out that racism needed challenging wherever it appeared, regardless of context. There was no time for such a conversation, and she was enraged.

Rage lent her a casual bravery, she raised her hand and with careful fingers (she didn't want to lose her fingers or her hand or her life) felt out for the next band of fairy lights they passed under. Her fingers snagged a row. There was enough grip in her hands and momentum in their passing for her to pull the wiring down. Pinging the lights from whatever nails and hooks held them in place, before the wire was ripped from her grasp.

The string of lights, swinging low, scythed along the train roof and through the approaching changelings. Several were ripped in half. Most were scooped up and hauled off the roof of the train and into the pursuing fireball.

"Man!" said Dave. "That was—"

"I'm sorry you had to see that. It's just—"

"Yeah, yeah. Racism. I get it. Now, you were mentioning a bomb."

"Wrapped up like a present. Tartan bow."

"And you made it?"

She heard the disbelief in his voice. "I followed the instructions!"

"Oh, right," he said. "We'd best find it then."

***

# 104

Guin crawled over container roofs towards the rear of the train. The noise around her, now including the whirling shrieking jet turbines, was deafening. If they survived this situation, she'd be able to play the "I'm sorry I didn't hear, I was deafened" card for several years to come.

Against this constant howl it was hard to tell, but she thought she heard booms and bangs from deeper within the hillside. Was that the train shaking, or the whole cave system?

The train burst out of the tunnel and into the storage cavern where she and Newton had been tied up and tried to escape on the miniature train. Guin hoped the train had been moved off the track or else this journey was going to end quickly and nastily.

She was distracted by the view across the cavern. From other tunnels gouts of exploding gas and fuel burst into the cavern, consuming stacked market stalls, piles of supplies and hundreds of hanging sausage links. Elves tried to flee the cataclysm but had no chance of outrunning the flames.

Her view of the destruction was whipped away from view as the sleigh re-entered a tunnel. The final tunnel before they were outside.

An elf, its hat scorched (the pom-pom still smouldering) charged at her over the container roof. She tried to rise to meet it, but there wasn't enough room for her to stand without braining herself on the ceiling. In this space, being short was an advantage.

The elf cackled, seeing her disadvantage and swung its knife. Guin fell onto her back. The elf came at her. She caught it in the belly with her feet and rolled onto her shoulders, lifting the elf up until it made contact with the ceiling. It fell away in a mushy mess.

There were some advantages to being taller.

***

Up ahead, reindeer stumbled and crashed against obstacles in the tunnel. Newton saw more than a couple of severed zomdeer legs go flying, but the herd kept going, hauling both sleigh and their fallen comrades along.

There was a change in the air buffeting Newton's face. He realized they were outside, fairy lights in the tunnel replaced by stars in a cold winter sky. He could see barely any distance ahead. There was the shape of trees, the slope of a hillside below him, and the suspicion the railway track still carrying the sleigh would run out in a matter of seconds.

"Up! Up!" he pleaded with the reindeer and shook the reins.

"Uppa! Uppa!" shouted Santa above him. "*Flúg mi hreindýrum! Flúg!*"

The reindeer responded better to his commands than to Newton's. He could feel the power flowing through the reins now: whatever magic powers Santa's beard provided. The leading edge of reindeer were no longer galloping through snow but curving up through the air, pushing through the upper branches of the trees above the town of Alvestowe.

\*\*\*

# 106

As the carriage beneath him rocked and lifted, Dave shouted out to Esther to hold on. She'd gone ahead to the next container to look for the bomb, while he searched this one. Boxes tumbled about around him. If the bomb's components were as delicate as Esther had claimed, he was surprised it hadn't gone off yet. Not that he was doubting her bomb-making skills, particularly if was following instructions. Especially if they were *authentic* instructions (and Dave felt that O-level Chemistry textbooks would be very authentic indeed).

A violent noise made him look back. The last two containers had not yet been lifted off the ground. Reaching the end of the railway line, they bounced and scraped along the forest floor, bucking and twisting and throwing parcels and awakened elf-changelings everywhere.

This sight alone should have been enough to arrest anyone's attention but Dave's was drawn further back to the tunnel and the hillside. Pillars of flame and exploding debris shot out of the tunnel mouth and from sinkholes all across the mountain. In the grey predawn, they were flashes of white and orange against the gloom. The boom of explosions was swiftly superseded by the sound of a cavern-riddled, snow-covered hillside collapsing in on itself. As ancient geological structures caved in, boulders were flung into the air, the whole forest shuddered and the thick layer of snow gave up its grip on the hillside and began to flow down towards the town.

"Avalanche!" he yelled.

***

Esther had to brace herself as the container she was crossing tilted upwards at a sharp angle.

They were flying! They were actually bloody flying!

It was exhilarating and terrifying in equal measure. She made a quiet mental note to appreciate being present at this ancient annual ritual when she had enough wherewithal and calm to appreciate such things.

Behind and below them, an avalanche of snow and rock swept over the town. The United Kingdom rarely had sufficiently high peaks or deep snowfall to make such things possible, but it appeared a catastrophic explosion underground was just the ticket to bring white death to rural England. In the low light, she saw the destruction of the town as silhouettes of black against white.

The avalanche swept around the church. Moments later, the tower spire tilted and fell. The wall of snow powered on into Alvestowe, tearing down alleys and streets, slicing through the brickwork and doors of houses which had stood for centuries. The marketplace, along with the nativity, the rides and the remaining stalls, was demolished in an instant. The cascade rolled on down the hill to the river gorge. Gone were the shops. Gone was Mrs Scruples' horrible hotel. Gone were the riverside barns and, she guessed, the remains of Dave's car. The old humpbacked bridge, the only route into the town, buckled under the snow and rock as the avalanche dashed itself against the far side of the shallow gorge.

Gone, all gone.

Esther felt a genuine sense of loss at the destruction of such a beautiful little town. The people – the humans – had either left at the close of the market or been turned into sausages long ago, but the death of the town itself was still a crying shame. And yet, she reminded herself, with the cave system gone and the town destroyed, the only elves left were the ones on this sleigh.

Ahead and flapping erratically was a blur of red and blue feathers. It was King Leopold of Belgium, Mrs Scruples' parrot. It flew in a desperate panic in a southerly direction, driven off into the winter morn.

"Sorry!" Esther yelled to it.

She thought she heard it squawk something back. It was indecipherable and probably too rude to repeat.

***

## 108

The reindeer's flightpath levelled out without much intervention from Newton. He was a terrible judge of distances but guessed they were at least a hundred metres above the ground. The landscape ahead of them, frosty fields cut through with winding roads, whipped by at speed. Either dawn had arrived without him realizing, or height had given them a sneak peek over the curvature of the earth. There was definitely light in the sky, and they were flying into the sunrise: east. South-east. Ish.

The reindeer, getting into their stride, were running hard and still accelerating.

If Father Christmas really did fly all around the world in one night then he would have to travel at several hundred miles an hour. Newton wouldn't want to be at the exposed front end if and when that happened.

Newton shouted back as loud as he could. "You all right back there? Mum? Guin?"

There was no reply. He hardly expected one. He'd have to go and look.

"Flying is always thirsty work," shouted Santa from above him. "Would anyone happen to have a cup of mead on them?"

Newton looked up, prepared to give another polite and apologetic "No" to the severed head. As he did, he saw two elves climbing down from their Santa-steering positions, finally aware there was an interloper on board.

"Ah," said Newton. "Now, can we just talk about this?"

"Friends! Friends!" called Santa. "Let's discuss this over a drink, eh?"

The nearest elf dropped on Newton. He grabbed it and the pair of them rolled in the foot well.

\*\*\*

# 109

The sleigh bucked in the air as it flew, the loosely-coupled containers rolling in a wave.

At the top of each arc, Guin had to hold on to something solid to avoid being lifted into the air by her own momentary weightlessness. She would have shouted at Newton to keep the thing steady, but she guessed she'd be no better at steering the thing than him.

They were racing over the English countryside, flying into the on-coming dawn. They zipped over a motorway and, for a few seconds, the countryside beneath them was replaced by the greys, red and greens of a still-sleeping town. Far ahead, electricity pylon towers marched across their path, frozen giants strung with heavy wires. Surely, Newton had spotted those?

One thing at a time, she told herself. Once she was happy her dad and Esther were on board she could go forward and give Newton all the advice he needed.

At the top of another wave, she clung to the fuel pipe on the side of the container. All the boxes and bags in the container beneath her lifted off the ground for a second. Her stomach flipped as gravity momentarily lost its hold on her. It was a disconcerting feeling. In her pocket, Tinfoil Tavistock gave a whoop of joy. This was both uncharacteristic and unhelpful. Guin suspected her brain was more than a little out of sorts.

Gravity resumed, Guin continued heading back along the sleigh. Blurred in the buffeting wind, she saw indistinct, moving shapes. That one did look like Esther. She looked like she was rummaging through the parcels. Whatever for? Was Guin's dad down there?

"I've found it!" came a wind-whipped shout from even further back.

"Dad!" yelled Guin.

Esther looked up. A moment later she pointed. As the sleigh's sinuous flightpath threw in another moment of weightlessness, Guin looked round.

Bacraut and the workshop elf, Gerd, had come up behind her.

"*Gríppa ha!*" snarled Bacraut, limping horribly.

Gerd leapt at Guin, knocking her over with her bulk. Guin came down heavily on the cardboard boxes.

"*Þú er veek gela,* ya daft apeth," grinned Gerd, drawing her knife. As Gerd pressed it again Guin's throat, Bacraut lurched forward and ripped the beard from Guin's chin.

"Ow!" said Guin, indignantly.

Bacraut pressed the beard to his own chin and straightened as though the beard would fix all his ills and injuries. He frowned, tried detaching and reattaching the beard. It was not having the desired effect.

"*Hva er þet crudl? Wull?*" he demanded.

"It's toy stuffing!" said Guin.

Bacraut threw the fake beard aside. It was gone with the wind. Guin tried to wriggle from under Gerd but the horrible elf had her pinned.

"*Égæt afá skeggi,*" said Bacraut.

"*Og hú?*" said Gerd.

Bacraut sneered disdainfully at Guin. "*Slautu ha! Kasta he aff hislei!*"

***

# 110

It must be the bomb, thought Dave, carefully levering out a box wrapped in red paper with a tartan bow. It was the odd one out among a sea of shiny Christmas boxes. Esther had wedged it in deeply, held in position by the surrounding boxes. Otherwise, if it was as Esther had described, it should have surely exploded by now.

Dave did not like bombs. He'd not encountered an honest-to-goodness bomb in real life, but he had attended enough hoax bomb calls to know the terrible heightened sensation of being close to capricious death. He'd also had training for what do if a bomb was discovered at the ambulance station or hospital. As he recalled, the role of the designated fire marshal was to stay with the bomb at all times and describe what it was doing until the police arrived. An unenviable job.

"Well, yes," said Dave as he lifted it free of the other boxes. "The bomb is a red paper box, officer."

He began to carefully climb up to the lip of the container, pushing the box ahead of him. If they were passing over open countryside or, better still, water he had every intention of tossing it overboard.

"It looks professionally constructed, officer. My girl Esther is a semi-pro parcel wrapper. Oh, the bomb? Just some chemicals she found in a lab." He tutted and rolled his eyes. "I know, women, eh? Always cooking something up."

His foot snagged. He shook it, but it wouldn't come free. He looked down.

A spindly arm had snaked out of a nearby box and grabbed him.

"Back to bed," he hissed at the changeling. "We're not there yet."

Another arm forced its way out of another box and clutched at his trousers. All around, boxes shifted and rocked. Sharp nails picked at and sliced through the ribbon holding box lids in place.

\*\*\*

# 111

Hearing Dave call that he'd found the bomb, Esther would have gone back to assist. Except Guin was having trouble with a couple of elves two carriages ahead. One was sitting on her with a blade in its hand. They were dangerously close to the edge, above the huge drum cylinder of a roaring turbine engine.

The other elf was determinedly making its way forward to the front of the sleigh. Esther's thoughts leapt to Newton. Of course, he'd be up at the front, with the reindeer. If they survived this experience, what were the odds of him asking her for a pet reindeer? What were the odds of her buying it for him? What were the odds of it then having its own Snapchat or Tumblr account or whatever?

Esther stumbled forward as quickly as she could.

Ninety percent of her brain was filled with worry and dread for the safety of her family. Ten percent was madly occupied with the wish Newton would just ask out that stable-girl Yolanda. Having a girlfriend must surely be cheaper and more fulfilling than owning a horse. Or a reindeer.

***

# 112

Newton was not a fighter, he didn't believe in fighting. So when he punched the elf in the face and threw it off the side of the sleigh, he shouted a heartfelt apology after it. The next elf dropped on him before he'd even got to his second "Sorry". It battered him with its tiny fists.

"Listen," said Newton, "we don't have to be enemies – *ow!* – We can just discuss our differences and find some common – *ow!* – don't *do* that!"

It was clearly in no mood to listen.

He hauled himself up and looked over the lip of the sleigh. The reindeer had been heading on a course that flew high over the electricity pylons ahead. They had drifted while Newton was distracted.

"We have to do some course corrections," Newton said to the elf. "Stop hitting me!"

"*Slautra alla menk!*" shouted the elf.

"I don't know what that means!" Newton yelled back, hauling on the reins to make the reindeer pull up. "Santa! Can't you steer this thing?"

"O-o-o-h, I appear to have lost all feeling in my hands," wailed Santa's head.

Well, yes, thought Newton. Santa's hands were just works of meat sculpture, constructed by a tribe of mad elves who had crash-landed here decades if not centuries ago. Why would they work?

"One might regain some sensibility if you happened to give me—"

"I don't have any mead!" shouted Newton and traded blows with the elf.

\*\*\*

# 113

Guin did not have the bodily strength to hold off Gerd for much longer.

The elf leaned down with all her weight, pressing the knife closer to Guin's throat. "*Þaðer syn sham*," spat Gerd. "*Þú haf madir góoð álf*, bugalugs."

"*Eg ne ekki álf*," Guin grunted. "It's hard enough being a girl!"

***

# 114

Dave was lacking hands. He had a bomb in one. He had an insulin syringe in the other.

He was successfully fighting off elf-babies (these were slightly less racist, olive-skinned babies, possibly destined for the Mediterranean or Latin American). He was successfully holding the bomb aloft in a gentle grip. What he was not doing was climbing out of the container.

It only took a drop of insulin to melt an elf but they were coming at him in an endless tide. The current waves were wading through the gloopy remains of their fallen comrades, clawing for him like nightmarish tar-babies.

"Will you just leave me the hell alone!" he yelled. "I'm currently trying to save your lives as well as mine!" The last statement rang kind of hollow, given the numbers of elves he was presently dispatching.

"Oh, screw this!" He stabbed a changeling, left the syringe embedded in its disintegrating face, and frantically made for the lip of the container. Desperation and an undeniable level of annoyance lent him the will to shake off pursuers and haul himself up.

He put the bomb down on the edge and spun himself to sit beside it. Below, the changelings clawed at each other in their desire to get to him. Further below, there were only fields and woodland, browns and greys. No human habitation in sight.

"You guys are just mental," he said. With as soft a toss as he could manage, he threw the bomb away.

The wind caught it. The sleigh buffeted. His aim was off. Whatever the cause, it did not sail directly away from the sleigh. Its path cut along the sleigh's side, close enough for a changeling, lifted up by its fellows like a cheerleader, to catch the bomb in flight.

Dave's maddened heart sank. "Idiots!" he hissed.

The bomb-catching elf dropped down and the others immediately fought him for possession of it. They were not doing it gently.

"To hell with you all!" snarled Dave and leapt for the next carriage.

\*\*\*

# 115

Moments before the sleigh abruptly sagged, Newton thought he heard a distant explosion. Fighting off the elf with one hand, he tried to haul on the reins with the other. Whatever had happened further back had caused the sleigh to drop a hundred crucial feet. They were going to slam straight into the electric cabling.

"Pylons!" Newton yelled.

The elf didn't understand or didn't care.

"Down, Blinky!" Newton cried. "Down, Sleipnir! Kicgut, Paugir, go under!"

"*Dunnið!*" shouted Santa.

The reindeer swooped, cutting between cables and ground, barely clearing the lowest wires. A metallic shriek and a crackle of electricity instantly told Newton they had not quite cleared the wire. Above him, Santa's giant body of slumped.

\*\*\*

# 116

The explosion took out the rearmost section of the sleigh. It also jolted Gerd's grip on Guin. The appearance of a tiny bearded head flying past, mournfully crying, "I was only thirsty," as it went was also a distraction.

Guin pushed at Gerd, managing to almost drag herself clear. But then the elf, tearing her eyes away from the sight of Santa's decapitated head, raised her knife high and stabbed hard at Guin's chest.

Gerd twisted the knife.

It hurt far less than Guin expected. The knife was embedded in the fairy folklore book under her shirt! Guin's surprise turned to violent anger. She punched Gerd in the side of the head and shoved her off. Gerd rolled off the side of the container, dragging Guin with her. As they tipped over the edge Guin's arm caught on something: a length of rubber tubing. Gerd dangled below her, hands gripping Guin's shoes. Gerd's own feet danced on the edge of the forward edge of the turbine engine. She tried to stand but there was little purchase in the howling gale.

Tinfoil Tavistock told Guin to hold onto the rubber tubing. Tavistock could be so obvious at times.

Wild-eyed, Gerd looked up at Guin. *"Takta mi upp!"*

"I did everything you asked!" Guin yelled back. "And you were horrible. Nothing but horrible."

*"Vi cudum ver vrendi!"* screamed Gerd and attempted a smile. "Friend-i!" It was a horrible rictus smile.

Guin shook her legs. Gerd slipped. Her foot dangled inside the edge of the turbine intake. It was enough to snag her. Gerd was whipped into the spinning rotors with a buzz and a crunch. A sudden plume of elf-blood and black smoke shot out of the rear.

"I've already got friends," said Guin.

*Damn right*, agreed Tavistock.

***

Driving a team of reindeer was very different to riding a horse, Newton decided. Particularly an articulated train of a sleigh that was mostly on fire with a lolling and rolling headless Santa sitting in the driving position. Newton gripped the reins and tried to keep the undead deer on a straight and steady course.

Something slammed into Newton from behind, shoving him into the foot well. "*Úr mí veg, hálfvit!*" shouted Bacraut.

The chief elf didn't look good. Newton guessed no one would if they'd been trouser-pressed, beaten, and forced to cross a bucking, burning sleigh to get to the reins. The elf had a limp and a half, a savage cut on his face and one of his arms bent in a way that couldn't be right.

"Hey, we're sorry about your sleigh—" Newton began.

The elf snorted and spat blood down his nose.

"You need a doctor," said Newton. "National elf service or something."

The elf ignored him and picked up the reins.

Bacraut wound the hair reins around his arm and looped them over his shoulder. The transformation was almost instantaneous. He straightened, even seemed to grow several inches. He looped the reins twice around his neck and down his other arm. The thick hairy ropes nearly swamped him, like that man made of tyres on old Michelin adverts. Bacraut wore it well. The power of Santa's hair gave him health and strength.

"*All hal góra skeggi,*" he said, with a grin.

***

# 118

Painfully, Guin climbed back up onto the container. To her surprise, hands gripped her shoulders and helped her up.

"Oh, God," said Esther. She went to hug her, and saw the knife sticking out of her chest. Guin wearily shook her head and, freeing the knife, pulled out the hardback book.

"Books save lives," she whispered.

Guin's dad stumbled forward and collided with them, sagging to his knees beside them. There were soot marks and a livid mark, like sunburn, on his cheek. His side was coated with a gloopy treacle mess: elf blood. He gripped her shoulder like he hadn't seen her for years.

"Are you all right, love?" he asked.

Guin thought about that. She had any number of scrapes and bruises. She'd pulled her arm. She'd knocked her head at one point and would probably have a bump. She had been close enough to a jet turbine to permanently damage her hearing.

"I'm fine, dad."

"You're sure?"

"Hundred percent."

The turbine next to them gave a loud bang and died. The sleigh bucked and tilted savagely. They hung onto each other.

"Newton's driving," said Guin.

"Then we need to get him and us off this thing," said Esther.

The sleigh settled in its new position. One turbine dead. The back half of the sleigh, along with the jet engines, was either on fire or missing entirely. A cascade of leaking fuel spewed a tail of fire that burned out before it reached the ground below.

"Come on," said Esther. She pushed herself to her feet and started to make her way forward. She nodded back at Guin and her dad. "I think someone needs help."

"I'm fine," Guin insisted.

Esther pointedly raised her eyebrows. Guin leaned in to her bloodied and charred dad and helped.

\*\*\*

Newton climbed into a sitting position in the shadow of the headless Santa as the beard-empowered Bacraut gloated.

Bacraut was giving Newton a big long speech about ... Newton had no idea. But Bacraut was clearly impassioned by it and Newton was too polite not to listen. There were lots of gestures, big encompassing ones. Maybe Bacraut was describing the exciting Christmas sleigh ride mission. Maybe he was bemoaning what had happened to the elves and was spinning him some sort of sob story. Maybe he was prophesizing an elf empire that would last for a thousand years. Newton didn't have a clue. Languages weren't his strong point. He wasn't predicted to get a passing grade in his GCSE French and he'd been learning that since he was eleven. He didn't have a chance with elvish.

He nodded politely as Bacraut ranted and raved. "Uh-huh. Uh-huh. Totally. Yeah?"

The speechifying was interrupted by a shout from above.

*"Newton!"*

His mum stood on the top of the lead sleigh, by the shoulders of the hideous, stinking giant Santa corpse. Her heart visibly caught in her throat at the sight of Newton alive.

"Quick! Up here!" she called.

Newton stood but Bacraut, with a powerful push that belied his elfin frame, shoved him back down into the foot well.

"Leave him alone!" yelled Esther.

"You don't have to do this," said Newton.

Bacraut sneered. *"Flúg!"* he cried. He rose up. Bacraut levitated, arms stretched, doing a slightly disturbing and possibly sacrilegious impression of Christ rising to heaven. Were the coils of beard rope around him glowing? All the way down from his body and arms to the teams of reindeer?

Newton felt a swelling in his own chest, which was a weird and unexpected feeling for certain. *"Flúg?"* he whispered.

***

# 120

Esther gaped in surprise at the creature hovering in front of her. She admitted she shouldn't have been surprised. If she was to draw up a list of things that had surprised her in the last twenty-four hours, a flying elf probably wouldn't make the top ten.

"You have to stop this," she shouted against the gale. "You can't do this."

Bacraut spat out some vile sentiment that required little translation.

"You've been hard done by," she nodded. "Cultural colonization. Your way of life under threat. I get it. Horrible appropriation of your indigenous ways. Like the elf on the shelf and the—"

"*Álfu á shelfu?*" he said.

"Elf on the shelf," Esther repeated.

"*—di ur shelfu? Wau?*"

"I don't know." She shrugged. "They're ugly horrible things. Not that your ways are ugly. I have nothing but the greatest respect for your people and—"

"Mum!" shouted Newton, in the unmistakable tone of a teenager who was embarrassed by their mum's wittering.

"Look, you've got to stop this crap," she said. "Doesn't matter what's happened. You can't replace all the children of the world with elves!"

"What?" said Newton.

"Operation Changeling," said Dave, coming up beside Esther with Guin under his arm, supporting him. "Let the boy go! Please!"

His words did not have the desired effect. The elf perceived Dave's pleas as an act of weakness. "*Þegi manð?*" grinned Bacraut. He floated down to Newton, blade outstretched.

"He's going to kill him!" said Guin.

Esther acted instinctively. To stop Bacraut getting to her boy, put something in the way. The Father Christmas corpse was already lolling forward and a shoulder barge sent the steaming, twenty-foot mass of Old Saint Nicholas tumbling forward. It slumped to its knees, then pitched forward over the front of the sleigh between Bacraut and Newton.

Its weight carried it through the front end of the sleigh, and shoulders first through the gap between the trains of galloping reindeer. Wood snapped. Pieces of leather whipped about and came free.

"What have you done?" whispered Dave.

"Are you criticizing a woman for taking the initiative?" Esther instantly retorted.

"Absolutely not," said Dave.

There was a lurch as the carriage shaft linking the sleigh to its animal-driven engine came apart. Newton, eyes staring wide at the gaping hole in the front end of the sleigh, scurried back and up to the seat that Santa had recently vacated, to his family.

\*\*\*

# 121

Like Bacraut, Guin found her attention drawn to the reindeer leading the sleigh. Scromdir and Bitber, wasn't it? The looped leather straps holding them together were now freed and the pair were drifting. Scromdir peeling left, Bitber up and to the right. Where those two led, others followed. The lines of reindeer were diverging, the links to the sleigh lost.

"*Ni! Ni! Samat!*" shouted Bacraut.

"If the reindeer aren't pulling this thing forward anymore—" said Guin, feeling a lightness within her as the sleigh began a rapid descent.

"Take hold of me," said Newton.

"No need to panic, dude," said Dave, hugging the lad.

"Take hold of me!" the boy shouted.

"*Flúga áfrass!*" Bacraut yelled at the reindeer. "*Flúga tigýrðar!*"

The reindeer weren't flying together. The two trains were heading off at forty five degrees to one another. Down the chain of paired zombie reindeer, they split off – Hlager and Gouper, Bultaða and Paugir, and all the others – until the final pair parted. With a wrenching of wood, the carriage shaft splintered.

It was only in that moment that Bacraut recognised the danger of wrapping himself in the reins. As the last reindeer went their separate ways and the two lines pulled in opposite directions, the thick reins tightened.

"*Ni!*" he shouted. His voice cut off in a gurgle as metres of rein went from coiled to rigid in an instant. He stretched. Coils sliced. The noose around his neck snapped taut. Guin's eyes involuntarily followed his forcibly ejected head as it literally popped off.

Both teams of reindeer shook as they violently pulled against each other and swooped to move in a vaguely unified direction, utterly separated. The sleigh, engineless, nosedived like a rollercoaster cresting the first drop.

The floor moved beneath them. Guin turned and grabbed her dad.

"I'm sorry," he whispered.

"Hold me!" yelled Newton. "Do it!"

Arms wrapped around chests, a family pressed in close together.

*"Flúg!"*

***

# 122

The sun rose. The twisted remains of several crushed containers and the awful cargo they had carried, burned fiercely against a hillside, given extra flame by whatever aviation fuel had still been on board. Crows startled out of their roosts by the explosive crash, circled in the air above. There was no movement around the crash site. Nothing living had crawled away.

To the far south, almost out of sight, dozens of reindeer ran on tirelessly through the sky.

"I wonder where they'll end up," said Guin.

"It's usually birds that fly south for the winter," said Newton.

Dave inspected himself and his family. They had landed softly in the snowy fields half a mile back from the sleigh crash. "How—?"

"We should be dead," agreed Esther.

Newton lifted up his jumper. A large quantity of bundled hair poked out. "I got it when I was fixing Blinky. I probably took more than I needed."

"You stuffed an old man's beard up your jumper?" said Guin.

"It's magical."

"Yeah. Still, it's a bit..." There didn't seem to be a word to cover it.

"It's been a weird night," nodded Esther.

Dave turned around. "I'm not sure I know where we are." He blew out his cheeks at a sudden thought. "The car."

"Underneath an avalanche," said Esther, patting his shoulder.

"You never liked cars anyway," Newton pointed out and then thought, "All our luggage!"

Esther pointed in what looked a likely direction to find a main road. "Not much of a Christmas is it, though?" she said.

"Dunno," said Newton. "Family trip gone horribly wrong. The worst possible accommodation. Flying creatures."

"People trying to kill them," added Guin.

"Sounds like the Christmas story to me."

"Kind of lacking the three wise men and some gifts," said Esther.

"The mead I bought!" said Dave. "Gone! Man! What I wouldn't give for a glass of—"

Newton put a hand over his mouth. "No, dude. Don't even say it." He looked at Guin. "You lost your toys."

Guin plucked Tinfoil Tavistock, the only survivor, from her pocket. "I'll make new ones. I've got loads of materials in my bedroom. I'll show you when we get to our house."

A look passed between Dave and Esther.

"You kids have surprised me," smiled Dave. "You've changed." They reached the brow of a hill. Below was a long grey line that might have been a country road.

"I'm thinking about going vegetarian," said Newton.

"That's not the change I meant, mate."

"Sausages." Newton pulled a face. "They've put me right off meat."

"Oh," said Esther, surprised but pleased. "No, I think Dave's right. You have changed."

"I'm sure it will wear off," said Guin, feeling the tops of her ears.

"Change for the better," Esther assured her.

A cool breeze blew in from behind them. The flying reindeer had vanished entirely into the yellow haze of dawn.

"Why do birds fly south for the winter?" asked Newton.

"I don't know," said Esther, recognising it as a joke. "Why do birds fly south for the winter?"

"It's too far to walk."

Guin groaned. There was a laugh buried in the groan. It was buried deep but it was there all the same.

Newton knew exactly what change his mum was talking about. The worry, the panic, the desperate need to please everyone...

He pulled the bundle of hair out from under his jumper. There was a lot of it but he made sure he gathered together all the remains of Santa's beard. He held it up until he could feel the breeze tugging at it. Then he let it go.

# The Authors

Heide lives in North Warwickshire with her husband and a fluctuating mix of offspring and animals.
Iain lives in South Birmingham with his wife and a fluctuating mix of offspring and animals.

They aren't sure how many novels they've written together since 2011 but it's a surprisingly large number.

Printed in Poland
by Amazon Fulfillment
Poland Sp. z o.o., Wrocław